From Behind the Curtain

A Novel by Sierra Kay

ISBN: 978-0-9848477-2-3

From Behind the Curtain

Sierra Kay

Copyright © 2013 The Vega Group

All rights reserved. Except for use in any review, the production or utilization of this work in whole or in part in any form by any electronic, mechanical or other means, now known or hereafter invented, including xerography, photocopying, recording, or in any information storage or retrieval system is forbidden without the written permission of the publisher, The Vega Group, 900 Polk Ave 1B, Dyer, IN 46311.

This is a work of fiction. Names, characters, businesses, places, events and incidents are either the products of the author's imagination or used in a fictitious manner. Any resemblance to actual persons, living or dead, or actual events is purely coincidental.

Cover and Interior Design by Art on the Loose, Chicago

This book is dedicated to Keith A., Keith P., and all believers in "what if" and dreams that extend beyond cubicle walls.

Thank you.

To Mama Watkin —
Thanks so much!
Enjoy!
Sierra Kay

Sierra Kay

6
From Behind the Curtain

CHAPTER 1

A not-so-distant door slammed.

"Dee? Dee?" her mother's raspy whisper came from the only bedroom in the cramped apartment.

Dee Bell walked in and saw her mother's eyes light up.

"Hey, Baby," Ilene said.

Dee was tired. So tired. But she couldn't help reacting to her mother's obvious joy. "Hey, Mom. Did you have a good day?"

"'Bout the same. The nurse came and your dad helped me out today. How about you? How was school?"

"It was good." The apartment was not big enough for Dee not to notice her dad, Nipsey, sitting in the kitchen sipping on a beer. Who knows how many he already had or even if he would have been any good if the inevitable had happened? Her mother had been on the downward slide for months. She had hung on longer than the doctors had anticipated, but both her mother and Dee knew Ilene was on borrowed time.

Dee and her mom lived in the projects in Chicago. Cheaper housing, yeah, but this building was scheduled to be torn down to make room for a mixed development community. All the people that lived here now wouldn't fit in the new development. *Where were they supposed to live if her mother lasted longer than their eviction date?*

Her father, who was not married to her mother, was pretty much shelter bound. He didn't really have an address. He stayed where he could, which was sometimes with Dee and her mom, sometimes with friends or at the shelter.

He always said he had big plans. He was going to be a musician. His friends had a band and wanted him to go on tour with them. His addiction held him back as surely as a leather tether to his ankle. Now they were playing places like the Chicago Theater and United Center; meanwhile Bootleg Bob in there didn't do shit.

Dee figured the closest he ever got to being a musician was teaching drumming to the bucket boys scrambling for their daily pennies on State Street, outside the United Center, on the sidewalk near the Cell after White Sox games, or wherever they could get a crowd.

Her mother had made it to Dee's sixteenth birthday. That was important. She had even managed to buy Dee a new television. A flat screen. Dee had no idea how her mother managed it since Dee had been responsible for the bills. She certainly hadn't gotten the money from the deadbeat in the kitchen. He had always been more of an ornament than a father. At least he was around more now. Whether or not he was sober didn't matter; all that mattered was her mother wasn't alone.

"Where are your books?" her mother asked frowning, straining to hold her head up.

"I dropped them by the door."

"Oh."

From Behind the Curtain

"Did you need something?"

Her mother laid her head back into the pillow and smiled again. "I was waiting for you to come home. We can watch *The Wiz* on your new television. Your dad can set it up in here. We haven't watched it in a while. I was sitting here thinking about it today. "

"Ah Mom, the DVD is scratched. I can run out and get another one."

The disappointment in Ilene's eyes broke Dee's heart. She had so little to look forward to that it made Dee feel doubly guilty about the fact that she sold her television. How could she tell her mother there wasn't any money? Her mother's disability check only went so far; and Dee hadn't wanted her mother to worry about things like choosing among electricity, food and medication. Her mother needed her pills. With them, she had made it this far. Without them, Dee feared what her mother's life would be like; that fear drove her on a daily basis.

When her mother succumbed to drug-induced sleep, Dee had been sneaking items out of the house. She sold the television, the DVD player, the art off the wall. There weren't that many things of any value. Then, Dee dropped out of school and started selling something else entirely. She still went to school every day. Her friends were her best clients. She only sold weed, though. Not the hard stuff. That would fuck a person up for real. Look at her dad.

"Oh no, no. You just got home. 'Sides, I got that online. It's not at the store anymore. That would be too much trouble." Her mother lay in the bed picking at the blanket.

The pain in Dee's heart was too much to bear. She just wanted to run away from all of this. She didn't want to worry about how the bills were going to be paid. That was a parent's job. No one should have to run a household at sixteen. But then again, no one should have to watch their parent give more and more of her pain over to medication. But it helped. Ilene was as comfortable as Dee could make her. She could concentrate on a conversation in between naps.

Dee waited every day for a miracle, but the doctors at the county hospital were certain her mother was terminal.

Dee walked over to her mom's bedside and stumbled on a pair of shoes in the middle of the floor. Nipsey must have left them there she thought as she put them in the clear box in the closet. Her mom liked shoes way too much to just leave them in the middle of the floor.

Every pair had a story, a memory. Her mom would always say, "You know I wore these black ones when I took your aunt to the airport. Girl, her plane was delayed and my dogs were barkin' but I did get a lot of compliments." Or, "I wore these when I left your father in Las Vegas. I strutted out of there on my stilettos with my head held high. I got a lot of second looks that day."

Every time her mother told the latter story, Dee thought her mother received second looks for a different reason. Dee's mother was truly beautiful. Even looking at her now you could tell. Dee's mom was always slender. She had slanted eyes courtesy of some distant Asian relative and the hazel eye color courtesy of the white woman he married. At five foot nine inches, everyone said that her mom could have been a model. She was pretty enough and tall enough, but it was really the personality that made her mom shine. She was always smiling and laughing. She truly brightened the whole room. According to Dee's friends, Nipsey wasn't bad to look at either.

Dee's mom had a hard time when they moved to the projects where being beautiful and happy means that you're lonely. No one wants to be around you, and no one wants their man to see you. Beauty means you have to watch your back. Someone is as likely to cut you as talk to you. Beautiful Ilene and Nipsey produced Dee. She inherited her beautiful face from her mother and her brick-house body from her dad.

When Dee started to develop, her mother was shocked. Ilene assumed Dee would take after her. But Dee's face went one way; her body, the other. Dee started getting stares from men old enough to know better when she was fourteen. Her mom asked her one time if she ever considered a career as a nun.

Dee just laughed. "I don't know about that. But trust me, they are not my type." Dee had plans. She knew her looks could pull her something beyond some bum on the street corner. She just needed the opportunity; but where she stood, opportunity was rare.

Fortunately, there was one neighbor, Big Rock—the neighborhood dealer/pimp/entrepreneur—who saved the lives of Dee and Ilene in the projects. Actually, he was the only one that called himself an entrepreneur and would sometimes just simply say that he worked in supply and demand. He extended his protection to Ilene after she became friends with his girlfriend. Then when they had babies at the same time; both the girls were protected as well.

Dee knelt down beside her mother's bed. "Cheer up, Mom."

"Oh, Baby. I'm fine. I just wanted to do something with you. Since I'm stuck in this bed, there isn't much we can do together and we used to love watching *The Wiz*. That's all. Tell me a story from school. How's your friend Rocky? I haven't heard about her in a while."

While they still had her father's protection, Dee's best friend, Rachel "Rocky" had been steering clear of Dee since Dee's mother had gotten really sick. It seemed all Dee did when they got together was cry. Guess Rocky got tired of that.

"Nothing much is happening at school." Dee tried to get her mother's thoughts off of school. "I know. How 'bout a verse of 'Slide some oil to me.'" Dee shrugged and pantomimed that dance of the Tin Man in her mother's favorite movie.

Dee dreamed of a career in music. She could sing, play the piano, and dance, but dreams like that don't last for girls like her from neighborhoods like hers. Most of them end up in the apartment in the next building across from their mother's with more kids than hope. So Dee had a new dream appropriate for her life. It started with a sugar and ended with a daddy.

"No, Baby. You know the song that I want you to sing."

"Come on, Mom. How about something upbeat? "

"That's upbeat to me. It's about strength. How to be strong. How to have courage. Life's a ghetto bitch. She'll just keep coming at you until you put her down for good. You gotta have courage to stand up to that."

Whatever. Dee didn't agree. She'd prefer a happy song, but it was the least she could do. She closed her eyes and began to sing "Be a Lion."

Dee lifted her head and belted out a rendition that would rival Diana Ross any day.

Her mother sighed, sank lower into the pillows, and closed her eyes.

Tears made tracks down her face, but Dee kept singing. By the time she reached the chorus, her mother was sleep.

Dee watched her for a minute. She noticed how her shallow breaths made her chest rise and fall. Dee often looked at her mother while she slept. It was like a little vigil with her. She wanted to be with her mother when she passed. God, just the thought made her stomach cramp. Dee lay down next to her mother, closed her eyes, and put a hand on her mother's chest. Her body was already set to wake if Ilene's breathing even so much as hitched. This was the only way she could really sleep nowadays. She closed her eyes and let the pillow silently collect more of her tears.

Dee woke up about an hour later, checked to make sure her mother was still breathing, and went into the kitchen. Her father was still there with a beer in his hand—as usual.

"You know you should be going to school." It was the same thing that he had been saying for the last month. The problem was he didn't say it with a check in his hand.

"Keep your voice down. I don't want her to wake up and hear you."

Dee opened the refrigerator door and took a beer out.

"What are you doing? You're too young to drink."

"Yeah, I'm also too young to watch my mother die." Dee gave her dad the look of a grown woman who had seen too much and done the rest.

"'Sides, how do you think the beer that you've been guzzling all day got in the refrigerator? Do you think Mom got up and went shopping? Listen, Pops. If I don't drink, you don't drink."

Her dad hung his head down and took a sip of his beer.

Dee cracked hers open and waited with him in silence for her mother to wake or die.

CHAPTER 2

Dee looked silently around Auntie M's house, also known as her new residence. Auntie M had swooped in as soon as Dee's father called about Ilene's … God, it was hard to say. Sometimes life just sucked.

The folks at the church they had attended faithfully before her mother had gotten sick had tried every single term they could find ever since her mom's passing, her transition, her homegoing, but Dee knew it was death—pure and simple. Final. Over. Painful. Every time she had to say the word death she'd start crying again. So she just started saying her mother was gone.

Dee had every intention of burying her mother right. She had money saved for that, but Aunt Maybelle had everything on lock. Maybelle Emma. That made Dee smile a little bit. Maybelle was the oldest name in the world and her auntie knew it. But in a family where Beulah Mays and Dorothy Jeans ruled, Maybelle counted herself lucky. Even Dee hadn't escaped the horrid family names, she was a Dorothy Jean. Her dad wanted Dee to have a family name and her mother loved *The Wiz*. No one dared to say Maybelle in front of her aunt. She was M or Auntie M to everyone.

Auntie M was Dee's paternal grandmother's sister and the matriarch of that side of the family. She wasn't going to let Dee get lost in the system or

Nipsey's downward spiral. Family takes care of family. So she brought Dee's mother's body back to Atlanta for burial.

Goodness knows Dee didn't have a recollection of everything since the day her mother's breath hitched. Dee opened her eyes to find her mother staring at her.

"Sing my song to me baby."

Dee began to sing. Her mother closed her eyes and then she was gone.

Dee called her name over and over, screaming for her to come back. She grabbed her mother's shoulders. "Mom, Mom! Please! God, please. Mom." Soon the screams turned to sobs.

Her father made it up from the couch and to the bedroom door. He grabbed Dee in his arms.

"Mom. Moooom! Please."

The months of illness had been torture, but nothing, nothing had prepared her for this. She thought she was so ready. She thought she had made peace. But the reality of never talking to her mother again was enough to knock her down. The pain was something she couldn't fathom. It hurt to breathe. Life. The ghetto bitch.

Nipsey gently led Dee out of the room with her steadily screaming, "Mom. Please. Mom." And then all strength left her body and she sank to the floor weeping.

Nipsey called her mother's doctor. Then he called Auntie M.

Auntie M flew up the same day. The first thing she asked about was the flat screen. Apparently, that's where Dee's mom had gotten the money. When Dee explained, Auntie M lit into Nipsey. All he did was shake his head and cry. Auntie M stopped suddenly, but you could tell by the tension in her face that she wasn't quite done. He was broken. What could you do at that point? At least, he didn't say anything when Auntie M told him that she wanted Dee.

So here Dee was in Atlanta with little more than her clothes. Almost everything of value in her house had already been sold off. She had her mother's engagement ring. The one her mother wore every day.

Nipsey had given it to Ilene when Dee was nine and they decided to go to Vegas to get married. But there was one problem—Nipsey still had a girlfriend. She kept calling to curse him out. Being the coward that he was, instead of putting his foot down, he tried to make amends with his girlfriend.

Ilene told Dee afterward that all she could envision was the four of them—she, Nipsey, Dee and the girlfriend, all trying to live together in projects. As Ilene said, "That was not happily ever after. That was a scenario for someone getting shot." She said she wasn't that crazy and took the next flight back.

Dee looked around the house. It was still so unreal. She wasn't supposed to be here. She was supposed to be in Chicago with ... with ... her mom. Yeah. There was nothing to keep her in Chicago. There was also nothing that had her yearning for Atlanta, but maybe there she could get away from all those sad eyes. Plus, Auntie M was a whirlwind. She wouldn't have taken, "No," for an answer. Dee hadn't even tried. She hadn't said much at all. It was easier to just go where she was led. And she was led to Atlanta ... with nothing.

Well almost nothing. Dee had her mother's shoes. Ilene and Dee wore the same size, and before the illness, her mother was addicted to shoes. She'd scour every Goodwill and second-hand store in the city and suburbs for shoes. She had dozens of pairs of nice, expensive shoes. Most of them were being shipped to Atlanta.

Dee brought one pair with her—the pair her mother bought for Dee's eighth-grade graduation. Those shoes had been brand spanking new from Marshall Field's department store. It was a 'snakeskin-ish' type shoe with red and black intermingled. In certain light, they sparkled. Ilene had bought Dee's graduation dress and plain black flat shoes from Field's to commemorate the day. Ilene had worn the same black pant suit that she wore to every special occasion but not the shoes. Ilene always said, you could get by in a "classic" outfit, but rundown shoes meant you were really poor. Being poor is bad enough without looking like it all the time.

Dee blew out a slow breath and hung her head. Had she started selling when she was younger, she could have bought her mother a new outfit.

CHAPTER 3

"Dee?" Auntie M brought her back from her reverie by gently shaking her. Auntie M didn't seem like she was ballin', but the emerald ring she always wore said otherwise. Even now, Dee could feel the weight of the ring on her shoulder. "Sweetie, go on and take your clothes upstairs. Yours is the first room right at the top of the stairs."

Dee trudged up the stairs carrying her duffel bag.

Auntie M watched Dee walk up the stairs. Her mind was churning. *What was she going to do with a teenager? What was she going to do with a teenager going through mourning? Why the hell hadn't Nipsey pulled himself together enough to come, too? How could he leave his only child?* Dee was safe with her. That was certain. Auntie M was used to getting in and out of most situations.

She didn't have a ton of lasting relationships, but she had a few special ones. There had been Pastor Clifton, but he had proceeded Dee's mother in transition. There was her best friend and next-door neighbor, Minnie Robinson, who was a bit flaky. Actually, that probably was the best thing about their friendship. They weren't in each other's faces all the time, but they had each other's back.

Dee was different. Dee needed her. And for Auntie M that was enough. She'd do the best she could to make up for her bootleg nephew.

Dee's room was larger than the one at her apartment. It was fully furnished and smelled lemony fresh. Fully clothed, Dee lay down on the crisp, new comforter and stared out of the open window. Her mother was gone. She cried herself to sleep.

Dee woke up to a dark, quiet house. The clock on the nightstand said it was midnight. The witching hour. She sat up and listened for the sounds of her old neighborhood. There was no one shouting in the streets, no loud music, no hustle, no bustle. This quiet was eerie, ominous. Walking to the hallway, she heard Auntie M prior to noticing the slightly cracked door of her room. *Lord. The lady snored like a bear.*

Making her way downstairs to the kitchen, she opened the refrigerator. Dinner must have been fried chicken. She grabbed a leg and went to sit on the back porch. As she settled down, a familiar scent wafted to her nostrils. She looked around and noticed a man on the neighbor's steps. Dee walked over, put her foot on the bottom step, and asked, "Hey! You ever heard of puff puff pass?"

The man's bloodshot eyes stared back at her. "Who are you? Thought that nosy M was the only person living in that house."

"I just moved in today. Lucky me. Fell asleep the minute I got here. This is nothing like Chicago. How do you stand it?"

He looked Dee up and down assessing her every curve. "I find a way."

Dee had seen that look before. "I'm jailbait."

The man's eyes twinkled. "Just how old is jailbait?"

Dee rolled her eyes and felt her nose flare. "Sixteen."

The man looked at Dee again. "For the record, you may be jailbait in Chicago, but you're just the right age for Atlanta. I'm not one of those little dick motherfuckers. All you have to do is grab it and I'm ready to go."

Dee continued chewing. She wasn't a virgin. She had gotten rid of that burden her freshman year in high school. But he hadn't been good … at all. She hadn't really done anything since then. A little kissing, a little fondling, but that was about it. She had just gotten to Atlanta. There was no way she was going to take this fool up on his offer. Just the nature of averages ensured that there had to be something better than him in Atlanta.

"Never mind. I'm good." Dee turned and waived her chicken leg.

As she entered Auntie M's yard, she heard faintly, "I'm Joe. And when you're ready, I'm good, too."

Great. This was just great. Is this what ATL had to offer? Dopeheads with bad pickup lines. She knew kindergarteners that had more game than Joe.

Dee finished her chicken leg and went back to her room, but she was wide awake. Her sleeping patterns had been erratic since her mother's death. Most nights she only got a few hours. Inevitably at some point in her dream, she found herself shocked awake thinking she had to check her mother's breathing. She went from that crashing shock to soul-wrenching disappointment when she realized that her mother was gone. She was alone.

Instead of going through that again tonight, she made her way downstairs to turn on the television. She turned the volume down so that Auntie M would stay sleep. Not that anything was likely to penetrate the noise Auntie M was making.

Dee watched some infomercials. She could really use that Bare Minerals makeup. She had broken out like crazy since the funeral. Her face was currently a connect-the-dots nightmare. She had also lost weight. She could give those struggling models a foolproof weight loss plan. Death. Watch someone they love die. Boom. A perfect size four.

She remembered early in her mother's illness, when sleep was hard for Ilene to come by, they used to stay up late and watch infomercials. Her favorite at the time had been the 'clip-in weave' — stick it in your head, close the clamps, and you were done. Ilene's all-time favorite was before Dee's time. "Baby, it was called the 'Flowbee.' It was basically a vacuum that sucked your hair through this attachment and cut it just like that," she'd say with a snap of her fingers. Ilene was easily amused.

Sometimes they would have a contest to see who could name the most machines that promised you flatter, sexier abs. Ilene had all the ones that started with 'Ab' down. Sometimes, though, Dee thought she cheated. It was hard. She thought her mother looked a bit stunned to find out that the 'Ab Rocker' was an actual product, but all she said was, "Told you so."

Dee fell asleep with memories of her mother dancing in her head and woke up with an ache in her heart. Auntie M was puttering in the kitchen. Dee groaned a bit as she sat up. That couch wasn't even close to comfortable.

Auntie M popped her head into the living room. "Glad you're awake. I'm making some sweet potato pancakes for breakfast. We'll get you registered for school tomorrow. You won't start until next week. Your dad got your records from your old school. Appears you missed quite a bit of school this past year, but that's understandable. Our public high school is pretty good. We'll have to get you some more clothes of course." Auntie M continued chattering along.

Dee tried to shut out the noise. It was irritating, like someone chewing with their mouth open. She excused herself and ran up the stairs to the bathroom. She used it and got into the shower. The steady, pounding hot water hid the salty tears that fell uncontrollably. Soon she was sobbing, biting back a scream. She sat down in the tub and let the water wash over her.

After a while, she turned off the water, regretting her breakdown.

Now Dee was sitting there with sunken eyes, skinny as hell, and messed-up hair. She slicked it back into a ponytail to let it dry. She considered going downstairs for pancakes, but she wasn't all that hungry and she didn't think she could tolerate chattering Auntie M. So she lay back down, wrapped in a towel.

A few minutes later, Auntie M showed up. "You have to eat," she said quietly.

"I'm not hungry."

"You still have to eat."

"I had some chicken last night."

"Yeah. I noticed the crumbs in the kitchen. Did you heat up some of the green beans and potatoes?"

"I wasn't that hungry."

"Here, start with this banana. A banana is easy. That's it for right now. Then, I'll leave you be."

Dee sat up and started to eat the banana, but her throat was almost too dry to swallow. She forced herself to, especially since Auntie M didn't look like she was going to budge until Dee finished the whole thing.

"Why did you help my mom buy the television? I heard about you over the years, but it wasn't like you were close with us or anything."

"Did Nipsey ever tell you that he used to live with me? He had a rough life. After his parents died, he moved in with my sister. He had already started drinking and using drugs. My sister kicked him out. He was a functioning addict for quite a while. I mean he didn't have much, but he made it. After my sister—your gram—died, he slid further.

"Your mother always helped me keep an eye out for him. Make sure he was OK. I hurt for her. Hurt for you. She had only asked me for something one other time—your eighth-grade graduation—and she didn't ask for much; just wanted to make it a little special for you. It didn't break me to help out.

From Behind the Curtain

So ...." Auntie M shrugged. She reached over, took the banana peel, and started to leave.

Dee thought for a minute and said, "I'm sorry that I sold it."

Auntie M turned and looked at her with a sad smile. "I'm sorry you had to."

CHAPTER 4

Dee had a busy week. Auntie M enrolled her in school and as usual she wasn't quick to make friends. Most girls took one look at her and turned up their noses. Of course, she had the mandatory friends, the ones her teachers made promise to show her around. But the most she got from them was directions to her next class. She already had a nemesis and she had only been in school for less than a week.

Her name was Evelyn Stone and she was a preacher's stepkid. She was unfailingly kind and polite to the teachers. Dee could tell all that bowing and scraping was fake. There wasn't a kid created that could be that sugary sweet *all* the time. Her smile never reached her eyes. It always looked as if she was calculating something. Those types could never be trusted—even for a little bit.

Dee watched Evelyn, just as Evelyn was obviously watching her. They didn't talk to each other, but Dee felt the tension. Every time Evelyn walked by, Dee's sensors went straight up. However, there was no one who could provide her with a bit of feedback on Miss Evelyn. Dee noticed most students outside of Evelyn's inner circle gave her a wide berth.

What was the deal? Did the girl carry a gun? Was she shanking people in the bathroom? What was it about this girl that had her running the school? Usually, girls with that much power were cute or cheerleaders or something. Evelyn wasn't even attractive.

Her hair was short in what looked like it was once a hairstyle. Today it was just a mass of 'could-have-been' half curls. She had a flat nose and a square face that reminded Dee of a bulldog. Her clothes were average, but a little tight. It wasn't the "I'm too cute" tight. It was the "I need one size larger" tight.

In addition to having teachers wound around her finger and apparently ruling the hallways, she also ruled the lunchroom. The only thing she didn't rule was the bathroom, and that might have been her next conquest.

Lunch was an interesting affair. About a week in, Evelyn straddled the empty seat on one side of Dee with three of her girls occupying seats on Dee's other side. Dee didn't have a posse at this school. All she had was a fast mouth and she knew that a fast mouth around here would only lead to a beat down. Dee started looking for weapons. She was not going down easy. Fuck that. She'd at least show them what it meant to mess with the Chi.

Evelyn swiped her finger along the icing of Dee's chocolate cake and proceeded to lick it off. "So you're the new girl."

Dee's nose flared. "Yes."

"And your name . . .," Evelyn turned to her friends for comic effect, "is Dorothy."

Everyone except Dee started cracking up.

"Yes." Dee crafted her face in an innocent expression. "What do they call you? Evileen?"

Evelyn squinted. "Cute. But my name is Evelyn. I'm the welcoming committee around here. I only have one rule. Don't piss me off. Follow that and everything will be fine."

Dee started playing with her Coke bottle. It was plastic, but it was still full. In a pinch, this would have to do. Evelyn got up from the table kind of awkwardly and proceeded to dump the rest of Dee's cake in her lap.

Dee jumped up. "What the hell?"

This of course caught the attention of the lunch monitor teacher.

Evelyn's act began. "I'm so sorry. I'm so sorry. Here, take my napkins. Maybe you can get that cleaned off in the bathroom. I hope I didn't ruin your outfit." She threw Dee her thousand-watt smile and sauntered off with her gaggle giggling behind her.

Dee went to the bathroom, but there was no saving the outfit. Now she walked around all day with a brown splotch on the front of her shirt. To which Evelyn didn't try to resist saying in passing, "You really are full of shit aren't you?" Again her gaggle giggled and proceeded to class.

Tuesday didn't get any better. This time she was tripped on her way down the hall and did a home base slide into the lockers. When she turned, she saw the same gaggle start laughing. *So this is how they were going to play it.* Dee didn't believe in getting mad. She believed firmly in getting even.

She'd bide her time, get the lay of the land. When the time was right, she'd start with Queen Evelyn and work her way through the posse. The only way to take down an empire was to start at the top. She knew she had to start with the strongest link if she wanted to make an impact. If she could turn her around, the others would fall in line.

Dee got up, dusted herself off, and smiled at the girls. Her smile was met with smirks and sneers. She turned and flounced down the hall.

The boys were a different issue. They were buzzing around her like bees to nectar. No matter how low key she was, they were hawking. No matter what was on the front of her shirt, they were hawking. Dee was tired and didn't have the energy to deal with all this drama. She got through school the best she could, went home, and slept.

On Saturday, she planned to spend the whole day under the covers. She didn't have to watch her back down the halls, didn't have to ignore tired pick-up lines, didn't have to stay alert during lunch lest she miss some prank. There was just blessed quiet and time—time for her to reflect, time to miss her mom and, amazingly, her deadbeat dad. There was no point in getting up and dressed. She had no place she wanted to be. Dee's only plans were to find a place for all of the shoes that had arrived earlier in the week and go through her photo album.

As Dee snuggled into the covers, Auntie M came into the bedroom absently playing with the emerald ring on her right ring finger. "Baby, you can't spend all day in bed."

"Why not? It's Saturday."

"I know. We shop on Saturday and spend Sunday in church."

Dee was no stranger to church, but she didn't feel the need to go every week. That was excessive. She had planned on stretching out those lessons; that way she didn't get repeated sermons year after year. There would always be something new and interesting.

Dee peeked out from the covers. "Are you one of those go-to-church-all-day-every-Sunday people?"

Auntie M laughed. "No, but I am one of those give-God-his-due people. Sunday service is only about two hours."

Dee sighed. "I guess I can do that."

Auntie M mocked her. "'I guess I can do that.' Thanks for blessing God with your presence. Now let's get crackin' or we'll be late."

Dee reluctantly got out of bed, showered, and dressed.

Auntie M was bouncing up and down as Dee came into the kitchen for breakfast. *For an old lady, she sure has a lot of energy.* Dee asked Auntie M what was up, but Auntie M just smiled.

Next thing Dee knew, they were pulling up to a salon and day spa. Dee smiled. Auntie M gushed. She gushed a lot for an old bird. "We are getting the whole show. Massages, manicures, pedicures, facials. We might even get a little trim for your hair. It'll be great. Come on."

Dee let herself be whisked away with Auntie M's enthusiasm, but she couldn't match her gush. *Hell, Auntie M had to have been a cheerleader in a former life.* Sometimes she turned on the perky and all of a sudden the whole sucky world was all rainbows and four-leaf clovers. Dee was just along for the ride hoping for the best.

Dee entered the spa and looked around. *This was definitely some television shit.* The walls were too cool light blue. Something like sky blue, but not really. The chrome against the blue was sophisticated. The wall had these sand colored waves on it. Dee felt like she should take off her shoes just to step in the door. Hell, she was surprised they didn't have those hospital booties sitting around somewhere. The only time Dee had actually been to a … OK … she had never actually been to a spa. She had been to a salon, but since her hair was naturally wavy, the most she had to do was wash it and put it up in a ponytail. If she wanted it straight, she'd blow it dry.

Dee's eyes started to tear up. She took a deep, shaky breath, and exhaled. She gave Auntie M a smile that she hoped was strong, but had the feeling it was as broken as she was feeling.

Auntie M looked at her a bit concerned.

"Sorry. Some memories are …" Dee paused looking for the right word to describe the pain that squeezed her heart twenty-four hours a day. There weren't any words. So Dee shrugged and said, "This is an amazing place. Do you come here often?"

Auntie M was still looking at Dee a bit warily. "Not as often as I used to or would like. Good thing is that this is owned by the pastor's wife. As church members, we get a discount on all services that they offer."

Auntie M was told that they would be taken back in a few minutes.

Dee and Auntie M sat on the cream sofas. Dee looked around at the paintings. The black and white photos didn't really warrant the scrutiny that she gave them, but she got up and took a closer look anyway. Dee walked around the small room, taking in the potpourri on the tables. She noticed the water with lemon slices and glasses on the counter. She thought about having a sip, but she wasn't really thirsty. It would just be something to do.

She sat back down on the sofa and began to leaf through a magazine. Most of them were yoga magazines. *Really?* Dee had heard of yoga, but she didn't know anyone in her neighborhood that did it. She definitely didn't know anyone that would have gotten a magazine about it.

She guessed that it was one of those 'rich folks' things. She continued to flip through the magazine. She could just about touch her toes; and if she practiced for a while, she'd be able to do a split. She could not twist herself into the poses in that magazine. *Was that even natural?*

Dee was on edge and decided to walk around again. She told Auntie M that she'd be right back. She started walking down the hallway and noticed an office door open. She peeked in and to her surprise, there was Joe. *What the hell?* Joe did not look like the type that frequented spas.

He glanced up and his eyes opened wide in surprise. Someone out of Dee's line of sight asked him what was wrong. He said something about forgetting to do something. That was Dee's cue to leave. She could always ask dear Joe what the hell he was doing in a day spa later.

Dee walked back down the hallway and looked into an empty room. *This was a pretty good hustle. If you start small with just massages, you should be able to break even. You only need a table, some water, a few lotions, and music. One couldn't get more basic than that. Right? You could set up a few rooms at first and move on up.*

This place had to have been open for a while because there were a lot of people around. If Dee had been a different type of person, she could have lost herself in the atmosphere, but Dee was never good at relaxing at that level.

Sierra Kay

She really needed to be busy, to keep active. She had a problem staying in one place too long, which is why she found herself wandering around the day spa.

It was weird to see Joe there. Maybe he worked there. He had to keep up his habit some way. A job at a spa was as good as any. He didn't seem to be the 'uber driven' type. Of course, she had only seen him the time he was smoking the good stuff on his porch. She wondered if he was the one giving the massages.

Dee came back and noticed Auntie M sitting down. Her leg was jiggling up and down. She had a far-off, worried look in her eye.

"What's wrong, Auntie M?"

Auntie M looked at Dee for a minute with her head slanted to the side before shaking it. "Nothing, dear."

"You look kind of wound up, a bit tight there, Auntie."

"Hmm. Did you go to church in Chicago?"

"Yeah. We used to go more often when I was in the choir."

"You were in the choir? We have a great choir at my church. Maybe you can sing again. What are you?"

"I'm a soprano."

Auntie M was more or less bouncing up and down in her seat with excitement. "Do you think you'll want to sing at the church?"

Dee gave Auntie M the saddest smile. "You know I used to sing to my mother, especially when she was sick. She'd ask me to sing one song or another. I don't know if ... I just."

Auntie M looked horrified. "Of course. Of course. If you want, when you are ready of course."

"It's no big deal." Dee picked up the yoga magazine again and began to flip pages. She felt raw all the time. She didn't know what to do or what to say. She didn't have time for this mopey, life-is-hard shit. She had to get her mind right. She needed to take the edge off. However, you never buy your own supply. That's why Dee never really smoked a lot of weed. But it wouldn't hurt to start trying. It might help numb the pain. Dee was all about that. The only problem would be Dee would owe Joe a favor, but she figured she could keep him in line. She'd kept better men than him at arm's length. She'd learned at the feet of the master.

She remembered the time Rocky's dad had hit on Ilene. Dee wasn't supposed to be back at home; if there was sunlight, you were out.

Dee wanted to sneak her new CD over to Rocky's to listen, even though her mom really didn't like her to take stuff to other people's houses. She always said that's how things ended up lost or broken. Dee had meant to take the CD on her way out, but completely forgot. She was very quiet when she went in to retrieve the CD from the table by the door. She saw Rocky's dad sitting at the kitchen table like he paid the rent.

Ilene didn't see her come in, but Rocky's dad did. He gave her an assessing look. Then turned and continued to rub on her mom's arm, giving her the full court press. "Ilene, I don't know why you keep saying no. You know you want it."

Ilene stopped, smiled, and caressed his cheek. "You have both a wife and a girlfriend. I'm good."

"You know this situation can change at any moment." He waved his arm around like their one-bedroom apartment was the epitome of style and grandeur. If that's all he was providing, it was no wonder her mother wasn't letting him 'hit' that. Ilene stopped. "I know. That's why I'm glad we're such good friends with Rocky and her mom. If a change happens in our situation, they'll be impacted too. You know, since we're friends and all. Anything you open on us will definitely flow that way."

"Do you really believe that Rocky would stand by while Dee got beat up? She'd have to jump in. We're lucky to have them."

"No, sweetie. You're lucky to have me."

Ilene smiled serenely. "That too, but it's just not meant to be. Your girlfriend and I are best friends. And our daughters are best friends. It's just not the right time for us."

Big Rock got up and moved further into the kitchen out of Dee's view.

Dee knew that she should let her mother know she was there, but at the same time she was immensely curious about how all this would play out. Ever since Dee was born, Ilene and Nipsey went back and forth with their relationship, but now that he hadn't been around for a few months, others were moving in. This wasn't unheard of, but Dee thought her mother was immune. Even though her father was a sad, sad man, Dee always thought her parents were meant to be together.

Dee continued to hear Big Rock's deep timber. "So why don't we make this thing work?"

Shit. If Ilene gave in, there would be all types of hell to pay. The battles between the wife and the girlfriend were already legendary. Rumor was there were others, but her mom … her mom would get tongues wagging for sure. The wife and the girlfriend would not take it too kindly either, especially the girlfriend, Rocky's mom. There was a hidden code that friends don't betray friends like that. It is the ultimate betrayal and there is no turning back.

Dee heard her mother's light, amused response. "Right. So now you want another female telling you what to do? The way your current women go at it, I'm surprised you'd want to add anyone else to the mix."

"I want you."

"No, you want to fuck me. Two different things. Now you know me well enough to know, I'm a one-man woman. Hell, I'm still messing with Nipsey, and he's the one that gave me HIV."

There was a long, pregnant pause. "No, Ilene. Not you. Please. It can't be true."

Dee stood there thinking, *"What the hell?"*

"I thought you knew. I thought everyone had guessed. You know I've been back and forth to the doctors lately. All the tests that I have to take. All of the medication. I thought everyone had guessed that was what's wrong. I haven't told Dee yet. It's hard to think that both of her parents are going to leave her one day.

"And we're leaving her with nothing. She's going to be alone." There was a break in Ilene's voice. "You know how hard it can be for her. I just hope she's OK. I just hope I haven't inadvertently passed something on to her."

Big Rock quickly hightailed it back to a chair at the table. "I'll make sure she's always taken care of. You don't have a thing to worry about."

Although it was impossible at that distance, Dee swore she saw sweat dripping down from his brow.

Ilene touched Big Rock's cheek again. This time he drew back just a bit. Dee's mother pulled her hand back. "I'm sorry. I didn't think. I'll keep my hands to myself."

"No. It's fine. I just … "

Dee grabbed the CD and snuck out. By the time she reached Rocky's floor she was trembling and could barely catch her breath. She leaned against the wall and let out a huge laugh. She laughed until she got a stitch in her side and laughed some more. She walked to Rocky's door and knocked.

When Rocky saw and heard her she wanted in on the joke, but Dee couldn't tell her. She just made up some story and kept the truth to herself. She didn't know how Rocky would take the news that her father had pushed up on Dee's mom. Her mother wasn't HIV positive. People lived with HIV every day. Ilene was dying of cancer. It was cruel. Not even remotely politically correct, but there was no doubt it was effective. She just ensured that Big Rock stayed away from her now, and Dee, even after she was gone. Ilene was ice cold.

CHAPTER 5

At the spa, Dee ended up getting the works including a new hairstyle. Auntie M also bought her a couple of outfits. Auntie M was unimpressed with the clothes that Dee had packed. She didn't think there was anything in there appropriate for church. Dee's church in Chicago was more of a come-as-you-are type of place.

Although the Atlanta church didn't require parishioners to dress up, everyone did, according to Auntie M. People might come in jeans, but they would be so uncomfortably underdressed that they never made that mistake again. Auntie M even went so far as to wear a hat. Not just any hat, but a 'church hat,' which was the basis for deciding what outfit to wear on a given Sunday.

Dee stuck with the basics. She wanted a simple, timeless black pantsuit, but Auntie M wanted something different. They compromised on a pair of high-waisted, wide-legged black pants with a black-and-white, ruffled-front shirt. Dee was thinking longevity. Auntie M was thinking if it went out of style just buy a new pair of pants. Auntie M wanted to buy her shoes too, but Dee reminded Auntie M that she already had her mom's shoes.

On Sunday, Dee woke up early. She hadn't been in church since the funeral. That was just a quick one-hour service. Since they dressed up, Dee wanted to make sure her hair was tight. For Dee, that took a while. She fought with, bargained with, and bribed her hair to act right. Sometimes it did and other times it didn't. So Dee was helliglad that Auntie M got her hair done. All Dee had to do was convince her hair that it was all right to lay flat.

She heard Auntie M making noise in the kitchen. Usually before Dee and her mom went to church, the only thing they had time for was a quick croissant sandwich at Dunkin' Donuts, but Auntie M was pulling bacon and eggs out of the refrigerator and making toast.

"Is it Christmas?"

Auntie M laughed. "No, I just had a reason to cook is all. I can't have your stomach growling in the middle of service."

Dee sat down at the table. The kitchen was just about the size of her apartment in Chicago. It had a four-person table and chairs in front of a huge floor-to-ceiling bay window looking out on a small backyard and what looked like a small forest in the back. The appliances were stainless steel and the countertop was some fancy material with marble swirls of tan, brown, and shades in between. It opened up on a family room with a big tan couch, a huge television, and a fireplace. A real fireplace that looked like it had been used.

Dee hadn't really needed a robe at home. The most she'd wear was a big T-shirt. However, Auntie M seemed startled when Dee came out of the bedroom in only a T-shirt and panties. *They were both women. What was the big deal?*

Apparently, it was a big deal to Auntie M because when they went shopping, Dee wound up with a robe—not a cute sexy satin robe like Dee wanted. They had this short number with a lace inset in the back. Auntie M looked Dee up and down and explained, "I don't know how to put this delicately so I'm just going to say it. With your, um, proportions, you can bend over and all of a sudden it's a peep show and I don't need to see all of that.

From Behind the Curtain

So let's find you something a bit less … or better yet, a bit more appropriate."

At least Dee got to wear red, but it was long and cotton. Auntie M tried for a pretty pastel. She came with pink, blue, yellow. Dee wasn't five anymore. She needed a color with some pow, some excitement. And she bought her slippers, "Wouldn't want her feet to get a chill," Auntie M told her. They were in Atlanta. She was from Chicago. *What was this 'feet chill' business?* She wore gym shoes to school even in the winter, which meant her feet did more than catch a little chill. Most days they were almost frozen clear through. But Auntie M was nice and she was buying, so Dee was wearing the robe and the slippers.

Auntie M placed the plate on the table. She figured out the clue to getting Dee to eat. Guilt. It was starting to work. If Dee knew she slaved over a hot stove for her, she was more likely to try to eat.

Auntie M had never cooked like this before Dee came. She was a social person. She could usually find someone that wanted to get something to eat. Even though she was older, she had quite a few gentleman friends. Auntie M had decided long ago that just because she hadn't gotten married didn't mean she had to be a nun. There were also a lot of gentlemen that just wanted to enjoy a nice meal with a nice woman.

Some women couldn't just enjoy a man's company. Auntie M didn't have a problem with that. A gentleman appreciated a woman that could converse without counting the steps to the altar.

Now, Auntie M was focusing on Dee. That meant cooking at home.

Dee snatched a piece of hot bacon off the top of the plate. Perfectly crispy. Heaven. How Auntie M managed to have hot toast, eggs, and bacon right out of the pan ready at the same time was a mystery to Dee.

On the rare occasion that they had cooked breakfast at her house, something was always cold and burned. Usually, it was the toast that didn't make it. Not that toast was difficult; their toaster often didn't pop the toast up automatically. They were a toast-scraping household.

Based on the fried chicken, this was the house of a foodie. Dee had heard about such places, where people made pancakes on griddles instead of in frying pans. These places didn't just have mixers, they had food processors. Dee's house had a spoon, bowl, knife, and cutting board. That's how they got things done.

As they sat down to eat, Dee took a close look at Auntie M. She was old, but you could see hints of beauty. Her eyes had the slightest tilt up at the outer corners that gave her a more exotic look. Her skin was blue-black, but her smile was something to behold. It lit up everything around her. Even at the funeral she dealt with everyone with an ease, a grace. She was all formal without being stuck up.

Dee hadn't seen her smile much lately, probably because she had just taken custody of someone else's kid.

Auntie M looked up. "What?" She immediately grabbed for her napkin.

Dee looked down and mumbled, "Nothing."

They continued to eat in silence with nothing but forks and plates breaking the silence. It made Dee self-conscious, like she needed to read a book on how to eat or something. With Auntie M being so proper and all, she wasn't sure she was stacking up, but Auntie M did extend the invitation. Dee was family and her family was going to be taken care of.

It was strange. Dee expected that from her mom, but this was her dad's side of the family. She just assumed they were like him. It was sort of nice to have some extended family. She was still a bit leery. Her father had taught her there was always another shoe that could fall.

Dee swallowed. "Tell me about your church."

"Oh. OK." Immediately, Auntie M lit up. "Well, we're a large church. You know what they call a megachurch. It was started by Pastor Clifton. We started in a storefront. I still remember bringing chairs from home that first year. There was always something that required fixing. It took us eight years before we could move out of that church. I remember the second church we built ourselves. Problem was, we had just about grown out of it by the time we got enough money in the building fund to finish it. Of course, part of it was us. The church was doing so well that we kept adding things on that of course extended the timeline. Pastor Clifton had bought the land surrounding it. So years later, it was a new building fund. It only took us four years to buy, plan and build the new church. We moved into our present location. Pastor Clifton was a blessed man for sure."

"Was? What happened to him?"

Auntie M took a deep breath and leaned back in her chair. She looked out the window over the trees. She waited a minute before continuing. "They found Pastor Clifton dead in his office. The news called it an apparent overdose. Everyone who knew him knew that he didn't touch the stuff. He was working to regain the neighborhood." Auntie M's voice shook and her hand balled into a fist.

"Well, they dragged his name through the mud. All those years. All those people he helped. And he's known for 'OD-ing.' It's a lie. And a shame."

Dee looked closely at her aunt. Her lips were pressed tightly together. Her whole body was rigid. Apparently, this was something that she hadn't quite let go. Dee wanted to ask more questions. It wasn't totally unheard of for someone to overdose. It happened every day.

"Maybe it got to be too much for him. You know. He wouldn't be the first person that needed a little break from everything."

Auntie M continued to look at the trees. Her body stiffened even more. "He. Did. Not. Do. Drugs. You didn't know him. That wasn't him. When I say no drugs, I mean no drugs. He was clean. And good."

Auntie M pushed herself away from the table and stood up. She stretched a bit and then kept looking outside a bit more. Dee followed her gaze.

There was Joe in the backyard. Smoking—and it wasn't a cigarette. Auntie M's nose flared. "That one; a shame—and at that age, too. He's at least twenty-three if he's a day. Born with the sense God gave a mongoose."

"Come on. We're going to be late. Late means having to sit in the overflow church and you don't feel the power in the overflow church. Just put your plate in the sink."

Dee put her plate in the sink and ran as fast as she could in the fuzzy slippers to get ready. She threw on her slacks and top, and in fifteen minutes found herself waiting for Auntie M.

A few minutes later she heard a slight noise at the top of the step. She watched Auntie M make an entrance in her own home, posing at the top of the stairs in an elegant purple hat that dipped a bit over her right eye. She wore a suit, but nothing like her mother's basic black suit.

Auntie M came down the stairs in a lavender two-piece suit. The suit was trimmed in a sheer scalloped material with rhinestones that sparkled when they caught the light. The skirt was long with a pleat in the back with an inset of the sheer material. It looked like Auntie M was ready to go to a formal wedding or something. *What kind of church was this anyway?* Dee did a wolf whistle.

Auntie M threw her head back and laughed. "Where did you learn how to do that?"

"You pick up odd habits in the hood."

"So I take it you like?"

"That dress is fire. I feel like we need to go back shopping again."

Auntie M laughed again. "I'm always up for a shopping trip, but that's not necessary. The young people dress down a bit. You'll be fine. I have a reputation to uphold. I used to be a member of the board. So I come sharp every week. I always figure that if I could dress up for a job, I could surely dress up for God."

From Behind the Curtain

Dee was blown away. Auntie M's outfit was hella tight—and the shoes! Thank goodness, Dee had worn the red heels because her aunt's lavender leather peep toes would have put her to shame. And her feet looked good. Or at least the big toe did.

Auntie M looked at Dee critically. "Now let's put some lip gloss on you. You need a little something. And what's going on with your hair? Sit down." Auntie M took off her heels and hustled up the stairs. She came back with a little bottle, poured some in her hand, and in a minute Dee's hair went from straw to soft hair with a bit of sheen. And it wasn't greasy. She didn't know about Auntie M's miracle tonic, but she was going to have to get some.

Dee turned her head to the left and then the right. She backed up to get a better look at her outfit. Even with lip gloss instead of lipstick, she looked a bit older. Plus Dee had never dressed like this. She preferred baggy clothes to these tight-fitting garments.

Auntie M laughed. "Now, I look kind of old," waving at her wrinkled face. "You look just right. Come on." Auntie M put her heels back on and hustled Dee out of the house.

As Auntie M and Dee pulled into the parking lot, they were met with uniformed crossing guards directing traffic and showing people where to park. Fortunately, they found parking pretty close to the front door. Looking to the back of the parking lot, Dee noticed two buses. "Auntie M, who do you all bus in?"

Auntie M looked up. "Oh, those are for the parishioners that end up in the far lot. They don't have to walk. The bus drives them up to the door."

Dee looked back at the waiting chariots. *Damn, that's hot.* As they entered the church, Dee noticed a placard by the door. 'Welcome to the God Is Love Church, Xavier D. Love, Pastor.'

"Auntie." Dee just pointed at the sign. "Really?"

Her aunt paused for a second as if she just realized the sign was there.

The hauntingly sad look came back into her eyes. Then she continued to hustle Dee into the door. "The church name was the name chosen by Pastor Clifton. He wanted something simple."

Dee looked really closely at her aunt. There was something about the whole Pastor Clifton thing that was odd. Dee frowned as she focused. Her aunt always looked sad when she talked about him. It was appropriate for her to look sad after losing a friend, but there was always something else to cause her aunt's eyes to shift away. That was it. She never looked at Dee when she talked about Pastor Clifton. Dee nodded to herself. That was it.

Dee and her aunt turned a corner, and Dee stopped dead in her tracks. This was a big-ass church. Cursing in church was wrong, Dee knew, *but damn. It was more like an upscale theater than a church. Did they sell out through Ticketmaster?*

As they entered, she noticed the ushers guiding people to their seats. Some parishioners spoke to Auntie M and gave Dee the once over couched in a polite nod. The nod was done with the head, but most people's eyes remained on her after the nod was over.

Dee returned the nods with a head hitch.

The other ladies in the church looked like their clothes came straight from someone's runway right on over to the church. That was the only way to explain not only the 'flyness' of their outfits, but the lack of duplication. Dee noticed a few people who apparently didn't get the memo. They did look a bit uncomfortable.

She noticed a group of boys from her high school in the corner. A couple of them stared blatantly. This outfit was a far cry from what she wore to school. She had learned the baggier the better in her old school.

It wasn't as if she never dressed up. Please, her mother was a shoe horse. She had known how to walk in three-inch heels by the eighth grade. Dee could tell they were interested. She was well aware of what she was working with.

Dee rubbed her head with her hand making sure her hair was in place. She gave them the same nod she had been getting. However, none of them were worth her time. They didn't do anything about her issues in school. No reason for them to jump on the bandwagon now.

Dee continued to look around, taking in the size of the pulpit. She noticed a large projector screen and three microphones on three different sides of the stage.

In the front center row, she saw Evelyn who was definitely mean-mugging her. Evelyn was wearing a simple dress. Well, a simply bad dress that didn't accentuate anything. It actually looked as if someone stuffed her in it like a chorizo sausage. Dee knew she looked good. Even more important, she looked better than Evelyn.

Evelyn continued to stare, and Dee continued to stare back until she felt eyes on her. It wasn't Evelyn. It was coming from somewhere else. Dee turned and noticed the most amazing man staring at her. He was waiting a bit off of the stage. He was divine. *Thank you, God.* He had a cinnamon brown complexion, dark hair. He had to be about six feet tall. She began to tingle at his look.

Dee broke the look. He was grown. That wasn't cool. It couldn't have been more than a few seconds; but even as they moved into their aisle, she felt him. She snuck another look after they sat down.

By that time, Evelyn had stopped mean-mugging and started whispering to her friends and smirking in Dee's direction. Dee just sat up tall and tried to sneak a peek back at the stage. The man was talking to a musician. Even so, Dee felt something in her gut that she had never felt before. She touched her stomach in shock. Her hands shook just a little bit. It was the faintest of tremors, but Dee knew there was something going on with her.

Needing a distraction, she asked her aunt, "So how did Xavier D. Love become the pastor of the God Is Love Church? That seems a bit crazy."

"After Pastor Clifton had his homegoing, the church had a variety of guest speakers with varying degrees of success. Some were just boring. Others were really bad. There was one that stood in to do a eulogy for one of our most honored members. This lady was here when we started the church. She had gone on a pilgrimage and passed on during the trip back. Everyone was so stunned and hurt. Now this preacher talked to the family, said he was comfortable doing it. He got up there and did the worst job ever. Didn't even remember Jasmine's name. It was sad. The family was hot. It was a slap in the face for everything she had done for us. People talk about that to this day.

"Another speaker had his own agenda. Let me tell you. Everyone was crying and wiping their eyes. The choir had just finished a fantastic song. The spirit was strong. Next thing you know, he started talking something about Beyoncé and one of those other famous singers. It didn't make any sense. He was all over the place. There is absolutely no way Beyoncé should ever make her way into a eulogy. It wasn't her cousin, no aunt. Nothing. It just made no sense. Again, the family complained and he was not invited back.

"So you can see we were in dire straits. Attendance was way down. We had started a letter-writing campaign trying to get someone else. We didn't have high expectations. But we did have some expectations. Then we heard that Pastor Love had married Sister Stone and moved into the area and was looking for a new church. We weren't expecting anything like this."

Sister Stone. Evelyn's mother. That would explain her presence up front; and if she has all of this behind her, it would also explain her queen of the world complex. Of course, there is always a threat to the crown.

"Pastor Love can stir up anyone. He's a natural. I guess that's why he was sent to us. Believe me our PR person got significant mileage out of the God Is Love Church being led by Xavier Love. It is too crazy. But he's been good to the church. He's been really good to the neighborhood."

The church continued to fill up. Ushers asked people to slide in so all of the extra seats were in the aisle. The balcony began to fill up. After about twenty minutes, they announced all other parishioners would be located in the overflow church. When the music began, softly at first, people began to head to their seats. As the music got louder, the chatter of the parishioners began to cease. Then the choir stood in unison and rang out the sweetest sound. Dee turned around. She guessed it was time for the service to begin.

The music was the sweetest testimony, stirring something deep inside. It made one remember the darkness and believe in the light. It touched Dee.

As she looked around, she noticed many parishioners had their hands in the air testifying. Some raised both arms and had their heads back hoping for deliverance from their pain. Dee thought she was witnessing a miracle, a well-planned and well-thought-out miracle. Dee was way too jaded by seeing some of the inner workings of a church to truly believe all that she saw, but this was damn impressive.

Dee didn't want to be bitter. She wanted to believe as strongly as the next person. And then, the piéce de résistance. Cinnaman stepped to the front. His voice. It wasn't Boys II Men deep, but it was heartfelt. It was as if every burden, ever felt by anyone in the room had descended on one man and weighed so heavily that he couldn't take one more step. Then the burden began to crack. There was light. Then there was hope and then salvation. All in one song. All in one voice. All in one man.

Dee was mesmerized. Her aunt began rocking to the beat of the music. Dee felt compelled to sing along. Her aunt turned to her and smiled.

Dee was mesmerized, which was OK because everyone else was also looking at him. She followed his every note, his every gesture. Even though he was looking out into the crowd, she felt he was singing to her directly. Her soul stirred.

After the song, Cinnaman went to the pulpit. "Did you feel that? God is definitely in the house tonight." Energy flowed off him in waves. Every word was accompanied by a hand gesture or a bounce or something. "To the members of this church, it's good to see you again. To those who are contemplating joining, friends or guests," he turned and looked straight at Dee and stopped all motion, "Welcome home, beloved." He looked over the audience and when he said, "I am Pastor Xavier Love," Dee's stomach dropped straight through the floor.

CHAPTER 6

Joe was sitting on his back porch again. It had been about two weeks since that sweet girl moved in next door. He knew that first night the honey was cute. Nah, honey was fine. Even then, when she walking around in that T-shirt and shorts, her hair unwashed, waving that chicken drumstick, he knew she was hot. But when he saw them leaving for church, that girl was fire.
It should be illegal for teenage girls to be built like that. He closed his eyes and pictured her in his head. He pretended that smile that she had thrown to her aunt before getting in the car was for him. Hell, in the two weeks since she moved in, his day dreams had her doing more than smiling. Shit. His night dreams had her doing more than smiling.

    He smiled to himself. He'd risk jail to hit that. Just the night before, he had a dream that woke him up sweating in a very good way and it was in color. They were in a room with a king-size bed. She walked in wearing three-inch heels, short shorts, and nothing else. She walked forward and with one hand pushed him back until his legs hit the bed. She continued pushing until he fell on top of the bed. She never said a word. Her smile. Well, that was enough. The dance she did, man. He was shocked awake when she bent all the way from the waist and looked at him through her legs. He had tried to go back to sleep, tried desperately to get the dream back, but it was gone.

The memory haunted him the rest of the night. So much so, today he was willing to do something he rarely did. He got off his ass and went to church. He made his way into the church and stood in back. That was better than going to the overflow church. Those tired heifers were always hawking him. Joe had slipped through the church doors just as the music was starting. If nothing else, these people were punctual. They didn't play.

The old bitches were clucking their tongues at him and telling each other that his poor mother must be so ashamed. You'd think that good Christians would know to keep their opinions to themselves. He wondered what they said in the Bible about gossiping about people behind their backs. Joe was sure that was frowned upon just like some of his extracurricular activities. The only difference was they did their dirt under big church hats.

Didn't matter; he wasn't there for them. He was there for her. He watched her expression as she took it all in. He could tell she was a little bit overwhelmed. *Who wouldn't be? That is a huge-ass church.* When he saw it being built, he wondered who the hell was going to come there. His contacts had the neighborhood lowdown. They were trafficking a lot of shit through the hood.

Then Pastor Clifton had to stick his big neck into the operation. People didn't take too kindly to the fact that he decided to "clean up the neighborhood." He was shut down pretty quickly. Now everyone kept their game on the down low. They were still selling, but the operation was more organized now. It was mostly just crack and heron.

The place was like a roach motel. "Roaches get in, but they don't get out." It was the same here. Parishioners could get in, but they weren't getting out unless there was a fire. They had security at the door. It was supposedly to keep people out, but honestly they didn't encourage people to get up during any part of the service. He figured it was because they couldn't miss an offering and there were a few of those every Sunday.

From Behind the Curtain

As Joe stood there watching Dee, he noticed she was watching someone else. He should have known she would have noticed *him*. She wasn't the only one either. It was like he cast a spell on all of them—young and old, hot and cold. *Bitches treat him like the second coming. Shit.*

Joe had read the Bible. Not recently, but he had read it. He knew for certain that there wasn't any mention of Jesus coming back as a gold-diggin' motherfucker. Everyone knew he married that woman for her money. No matter how much they cooed at each other in public. They'd sit around holding hands, laughing at inside jokes. He knew 'game' when he saw it. He'd been running it too long not to recognize it. He had game of his own that he kept under lock and key. But if *he* wanted to pretend that he was the one that was going to deliver the flock from whatever ailed them, Joe didn't have a problem with that. As long as he left Joe alone, everything was good.

Later that evening, Joe leaned back against the porch steps and lit his joint. His mom was cool peoples. When he had caught a case, she came to court for his trial. She didn't make big beans about it. Now that he was on probation, he stayed with her.

It was better if he had someone who had his back watching his comings and goings. He didn't want to give the man another reason to lock him up. He had his business to handle and he couldn't do that in jail. Not that his mother knew the particulars of his business. She's cool people, but she would not appreciate at all the stuff he was into.

After that first case, he got a lot smarter. Now he kept his business tight and hidden—and he had a cover story. He got that job at the spa. It was a good gig. He mostly swept up stuff, kept the place nice and neat. He showed up on time and didn't cause any trouble. He even got tips from the women; some gave him more than tips. He got more snatch working at that place than ever before.

Matter of fact, he started working out just because of that place. The first time he pushed up on this female he didn't get anywhere. Then he learned you need a hook. His boy told him, "Bees yearn for honey." It's either honey or money. He couldn't go around flashing his money. That's how he had caught a case in the first place—trying to impress some female. Now he just put on his T-shirt and let his muscles do the rest. Those high-rent hoes loved to come down to his level. Actually, they loved to come all the way down to their knees.

What they didn't know is that he was piling his stacks high as hell. One day, Joe would be the man. Joe would be the one that made the ladies wet with his bank account. He took another puff and blew the smoke in the air. Yeah, they'd be giving him that eye. He'd have his pick then—even the high-end jailbait next door. She'd come around when he started clocking major dollars.

He closed his eyes and enjoyed the one joint he allowed himself a day. His mom was asleep. She didn't know about this particular habit. She was probably already praying for his immortal soul. She might give him the boot for real if she found out about this. But weed leveled him out in a way that nothing else did. It opened his mind. That's how he was able to concoct his plan.

Joe heard her before he saw her and smiled. "You know. I think even Little Red Riding Hood wanted to be bit by the Big Bad Wolf. Coming over for your nibble?" Joe opened his eyes.

Dee sat down next to him on the steps and wrapped her hands around her knees. Tonight she was wearing a big puffy robe with slippers. Her hair was wrapped in a scarf. This homely look should have turned him off, but he just imagined what was underneath that robe and he started getting heavy.

Dee rolled her eyes. "Are you for real? Do you get any play?"

Joe looked her in the eye. "Oh, I get plenty."

"Good. Then you don't need me. Are you in the mood to share tonight?"

Joe looked her over again and contemplated whether he wanted to hold out. He could be patient when he needed to be. So he silently held out the joint to Dee.

She took it and inhaled. She let it settle into her chest before blowing it out. She took a few more puffs before handing it back. She started rubbing her hands together.

Hell, he had to give it one more try. "I got something you can rub."

She merely gave him a look and turned her head to look out on the forest.

"So what brings you out here, princess? Well, you're obviously not too much of a princess. You took the weed like a pro. Maybe I underestimated you. What are you anyway?"

Dee smirked and with a horrible accent quoted a line from one of her favorite movies.

"Ah, so you've seen A League of Extraordinary Gentlemen."

Dee turned and gave him a real smile.

Joe almost sucked in his breath. *Really, why didn't they make them like this when he was in school?*

"Yeah, I love the League of Extraordinary Gentlemen, Van Helsing, X-Men. All that."

"OK. Halle Berry as Storm. Good or bad?"

"Are you kidding? They needed Iman or something. Storm was an African Queen. When Halle Berry ran out of the room while the old dude liquidated, I almost threw my popcorn at the screen."

Joe nodded. "So what's your story anyway? Why are you sitting here on a school night puffing on the chiba?"

Dee picked at invisible lint on her robe. "No story. I'm from the Chi. My mom left and now I'm living with my aunt."

"Where's your dad?" Joe asked as he blew another puff.

Sierra Kay

"Chicago. He's still there. But he can barely take care of himself."

"And you're back here because … ?"

"I smelled a good reason to come out in the middle of the night," Dee said with a smile.

"Ah, your aunt wouldn't like this."

Dee shrugged. "Yeah, but she doesn't know what I'm going through on a daily basis. School's a bitch. That Evelyn Stone is a straight bitch."

"Evelyn? That's an easy nut to crack. Tell you what. I give you ammo against her and you do something for me."

"I'm not fucking you, man."

"I promise. It won't be anything sexual. I want you to come to me willingly. I'll show what an older man can do for you." Dee rolled her eyes. Joe continued. "It'll just be a favor. "

Dee looked skeptical. Joe could see Dee thinking. The wheels were obviously turning. "What you got?"

Joe smiled and handed her the rest of the joint. He was done for the night.

CHAPTER 7

Dee chose her outfit very carefully on Monday morning. She was engaged in war, and armor was very important. She was no longer the girl content to lounge around in baggy clothes hoping to stay below the radar. She wasn't the girl who was afraid to keep her hair down in case someone decided to put gum in it or worse chop it clear off. She was no longer the girl who was being teased and abused in school.

She was a new Dee. New Dee didn't fear school. New Dee wore her long hair curled beguilingly around her shoulders. She wore clothes that fit, but Auntie M and Dee agreed that she didn't want to show cleavage. It just seemed inappropriate for a teenage girl to have the girls hanging all out. Instead, Dee was wearing a light sweater in a nice springy green. The sweater accented her breasts without putting them on display.

Dee had gone through the pros and cons of communicating the information she now had in her possession. On one hand, Evelyn deserved it so badly. On the other hand, Dee felt triumphant that she was the one to deliver the news. Still Dee didn't know how Evelyn would react. She'd either back the fuck off or she'd make Dee's life even more of a living hell.

Dee's life was already a living hell so she felt comfortable giving

Evelyn the chance to back the fuck up. On one hand, no one deserved to be publically humiliated. On the other hand, it was Evelyn. She was always on her high horse dictating how others should be, putting people down. It would be different if she was all that. But she wasn't. She was average at best. Average face, average body, average everything.

As Dee pulled the brush through her hair, she contemplated taking the high road, but not for long. Evelyn deserved every humiliating moment considering all the moments she gave the other students as often as she possibly could. The only problem was, Dee normally didn't do this. She kept under the radar. She didn't cause any trouble. But this time it might just be the most appropriate thing she could do to stop the madness. There was no way Dee was going through the school year as the sad transfer student. *Fuck that. Time to even the playing field.*

Dee shimmied into a new pair of jeans. Then she sorted through her mom's shoes until she found the right pair. Dee preferred gym shoes to heels, but wearing heels was in the blood. Looking at the heels in her hand, she decided to downgrade just a bit. No one was wearing stiletto heels. And if it was on and poppin' she couldn't mess around with such a narrow heel. They were good for clocking a bitch, bad for running from a posse. Instead she chose a pair of brown wedges. It would give her height and stability at the same time.

Dee took a look at herself in the mirror. Thanks to Auntie M's stylist, her hair was together. Thanks to Mother Nature she was taller than most of the girls in her class, with the possible exception of the volleyball and basketball teams. She turned the other way to make sure everything was tight. She grabbed her bag and a jacket and went downstairs.

Auntie M was in the kitchen. She smiled and nodded her approval. "That's much better than all those baggy clothes. I don't care if they're in or not. They aren't attractive at all.

Auntie M was doing her morning ritual of fixing breakfast. While Dee wasn't all that hungry, it would have been rude to not even have a bit of the cheese grits that her aunt was ladling on a plate next to turkey bacon. Dee tried to eat at least some of the food. However, she didn't have the stomach to clear the plate like she usually did. She pleaded nerves over a test she had to take.

Auntie M hustled up to give Dee her customary ride. As they traveled to school, Auntie M started her normal morning chatter, explaining to Dee what her day was going to look like. Auntie M seemed downright chipper.

Dee was feeling a little reticent. *What if this didn't work and Evelyn turned everyone against her?* Granted, it wasn't as if Dee had any friends anyway. She had enemies and people that didn't give a care about her. *What if it just turned into a school of enemies? That wouldn't be any fun at all.* Dee had turned this over and over in her mind. *It had to be done. There was no other way.* Well, maybe it didn't have to be as bad as Dee had originally planned.

Dee started to figure out a Plan B. It was possible to get the benefit of the secret without telling the actual secret. But Dee kept going back to the fact that Evelyn deserved to go down. It was Dee's natural human right to take her down. It was written in the constitution or something. Evelyn's harassment was not protected. Those were fighting words, and Dee was gearing herself up for the battle that was to come. That was the only thing she remembered from her eighth grade constitution test: fighting words and the right to bear arms.

Auntie M's chatter was a constant in the background. Occasionally, Dee would grunt as if she was really paying attention. Actually, she switched up between grunts, 'umms,' and 'oh really.' At one point, Auntie M had apparently said something to Dee. The silence shocked Dee back to the present. "I'm sorry. Did you say something?"

Auntie M laughed. "You must be really worried about the test. I wanted to know if you needed a ride home after school."

Dee smiled. "I definitely will. This is the first time in a long time that my footwear consisted of something other than a rubber tread. I don't know if I'll be walking out of the school door or crawling. It would be nice if I knew there was a ride waiting for me."

Sierra Kay

Auntie M beamed at Dee. It seemed Auntie M really enjoyed giving Dee rides. *Whatever wet her whistle.*

They made it to school with time to spare. Auntie M generally made her way around traffic with inches to spare. The first day or so Dee held on tight to the 'oh-shit bar' in the car. Now Dee barely registered Auntie M's driving. Of course, other drivers definitely noticed. There was constant honking and swearing. What did they expect from an itty bitty woman rocking an Escalade? She actually used a donut to see over the steering wheel.

It must have been nerve-wracking to see that big honking vehicle bearing down on you and at the last minute veering off to another lane. Dee would have shit in her pants. Auntie M drove with a solid dedication. She loved speed. Apparently, she also loved to scare people within an inch of their lives. But that was just Auntie M.

Dee got out of the car and walked into the school. A couple of people snickered. Last week she would have cowered, but today she merely waved at the rude girls. This time the girls waved back in apparent shock. Dee walked past the giggling gaggle with her head held high. One of them tried to trip her, but Dee avoided the motion and kept going.

Today was different. She tried to use the old hood rules of fitting in. That didn't work. So now she was content to stand out. She knew she looked tight. She needed to be up for the confrontation.

She guessed clothes did make the man, or in her case, the woman, because few people gave her the crazy looks she had been receiving the past couple of weeks. Matter of fact, a couple of guys did a double take. She made it to her locker all right except for that one incident. She walked with attitude and started turning her combination. She felt the air change before she noticed Evelyn coming up behind her.

"Oh, did your grandma buy you new clothes?"

Dee turned and looked at Evelyn. "Yup. New clothes. New bras. I thought about going with water bras, but decided against it. One. I don't need them. Two. Someone could accidently prick one and cause it to leak. Could you imagine? Leaking all over the place. How embarrassing would that be?"

There was a pause. It was one of those moments when you didn't know if you were safe or someone was going to break out a shank and cut you. She noticed Evelyn's eyes narrowing with awareness and temper after the veiled threat. Dee would have taken the chance and come out swinging. But Dee had nothing to lose.

Apparently, Evelyn wasn't in the same position; she just continued to stare. Her crew started to look confused. No one moved. Suddenly, Evelyn spat, "No one cares what kind of bra you got you freak. No one cares about you at all. You're just a piece of ghetto trash. And I'm way too good to be bothered with the likes of you."

Giving Dee her most evil smile, Evelyn turned and flounced away. Her giggling gaggle looked confused and then rushed to catch up with her. Dee smiled and turned back to her locker. Evelyn was already her enemy. All she had done was even the playing field a bit. She would have to watch her back. They had gone from checkers to chess. Now, she had to fortify her position. It seemed as if Joe was the best way to do that. She should be worried how he got the down low on Evelyn, but if she guessed right, he was into young girls and Evelyn was into older men. If that's what got them off, fine.

She'd use him to fortify her position. But in the meantime, she could really use some friends. She knew she was in grave danger of being late for her first period class and that teacher was a witch of the first order. That heifer needed her pipes cleaned fast. As Dee hustled to class, she felt less like an outcast than she had in the three weeks since she had started school.

CHAPTER 8

Joe looked over at Dee sitting on the passenger side of his truck. Dee was a 'ride or die' chick. The kind you need at your side. She didn't flinch when he lit up. More often than not, she'd get her drag in as well. Not only that, but the last time they were on the back porch, she grabbed his beer out of his hand and tossed it back. That shit was hot as hell. The look of the bottle neck against her lips made him hard instantly. But he was no closer to closing the deal on that than he was at the beginning.

They laughed and joked, but she never looked at him. She never even gave him the same attention that she gave that pulpit-pounding Pastor Love. Like that limp-dicked bastard had anything on Joe. He was being led around by the dick by his wife. Joe laughed to himself. She probably kept his dick in her purse and only gave it back to allow him to pee. Joe couldn't imagine kicking it with an older woman. He liked his woman young. Tender. Like Dee.

Dee needed something to do with her spare time. So Joe offered to hook her up with a job at the spa. That's where they were going now. He just had to make one quick stop.

"Hey, I need to make this quick run. I'll be back in a few." Joe started to open his door when he heard.

"No, no, no, no. What the hell is that? Is that a crack house?"

Joe turned and looked at the dilapidated building where hypes crawled in and out like mice getting a good whiff of cheese. "Yeah. I'll be back."

"I don't sit outside of crack houses."

"Girl, what are you talking about? You used to slang. Why are you acting brand new?"

"Yeah, I used to slang, but I didn't slang crack and I was smart enough not to be seen near the crack house."

"Girl, we've got this thing on lock. There are lookouts and technology and shit to monitor what's going on."

"Yeah, while that's all good, I know for a fact that the police always know what's going on in a crack house. They know who is going in and who is coming out. They know where it is and how long it's been there. I refuse to be associated with a crack house. Take me to the spa. Take me home. Take me somewhere. I'm not staying here."

"Well, shit. How did you get your stash then?"

"My stash came to me."

"Look at that. The pampered princess of the puff, puff, pass. Well, it's not like that for me. I need to get my stuff."

"Drop me off first at the spa and I'll get a ride home. Then you can come back for your stuff."

"Dude, the cops not going to bother you here. They wouldn't dare. You're with me."

"Yeah right. Aren't you the one that caught a case? There ain't no one to bail me out, remember? My mom's dead. Take me home."

"Girl, I didn't know you were chicken shit."

"I didn't know you were stupid as hell."

"My stuff is tight. Getting caught cures you of all that sloppy mess real fast."

"Hmm. I don't need any lessons on how to get caught. Take me home."

Joe leaned forward, took the keys out of the ignition, leaned back, gave Dee a good look and asked very softly, "Where you gonna go to little girl?"

Dee looked even more determined, but didn't say a word.

"Hmm. I have the key to the car. This isn't a neighborhood where you want to get out of the car," Joe said as he gently brushed Dee's arm with his free hand.

She didn't recoil or scream. Her eyes were still blazing, but her body was firm.

He gave her a half smile. "What do I get for taking you home?" He noticed her eyes narrowing just a bit. She was a hard shell all right. He was enjoying this little game. He looked her up and down. She had sent every signal in the world that she didn't want any piece of him. That intrigued him. She still came over at night dressed in whatever was available. If nothing else told him stay away, it would have been those outfits.

Today, she was wearing jeans, a T-shirt, and a short leather jacket. Her hair was in a high pony tail, and all he wanted to do was wrap it around his hands as he pulled her in for a kiss. *Those lips. They were dick-sucking lips if he had ever seen any.* That full pout of hers gave him shivers. Age didn't matter. But he had only one rule; he didn't force any woman into his bed. He could tell by the way she looked at him that she was trying to figure him out. He smiled, and her eyes narrowed a bit more.

He went back to rubbing her arm. "The question still stands. What do I get?" Joe raised his eyebrows with the question.

Dee tilted her head a bit to the left, but kept her eyes on him.

"Self-fulfillment."

Joe wanted to laugh out loud, but just smirked.

Dee pressed her back against the door.

"That's not enough. If I recall, you still owe me a favor. We just upped it to two." Joe turned on the ignition and turned the car around to head back to the house.

"What about the job?"

"Tomorrow is soon enough."

"I might be busy tomorrow."

"Might is the operative word here. I'll pick you up tomorrow."

Joe's mind was turning as he drove back to her house. He let her out and watched her walk to the door. *Damn, she was hot.* He'd have to figure out a way to change her mind about him. Ride-or-die chicks were often swayed by money, but Dee didn't figure to be the type to be with a guy just to get a few extra ends. He was sure it helped, but this girl had ghetto class.

She sort of reminded him of his friend, Stacy Wallace. Through grammar school, it was he, Stacy, and Tim Strong holding it down. High school changed them a lot. Well, not high school maybe, but everything that happened through those years. He missed his friends. Somewhere between getting popped and now, they'd grown a bit distanced. Girls like Stacy didn't come around too often.

Stacy started out as the biggest tomboy there was. When she hit high school, it was all over. She grew up fast, grew up and grew out. Her mother split when she was sixteen. That tore her up in a way that Joe hadn't seen before or since. She started as innocent Stacy. She learned fast how fragile innocence was.

Pastor Clifton tried to put her with a family, but she wasn't the type to depend on other people. And the church wives were a bit leery of inviting a high school girl that was not a relation into their home. They were saved and/or sanctified. They weren't crazy.

So she said fuck it and started with a sugar daddy. When he split, she had enough to get a fake ID and started to strip. Pastor Clifton tried to get her into a different occupation. He even tried to get the owner to fire her, but Sizzle was hot like her name. Even though a bit of her innocence left her eyes, her intelligence never wavered.

Pastor Clifton didn't give up. He kept trying to save Stacy. She sat him down one day and told him. "The biggest frustration of your job is that you are going to learn that you can't save everyone. God gave us free will. With that free will, we will make decisions that you may not like or approve of. Don't judge me. Just know it was my decision to make. My soul is fine. Remember Jesus died for everyone's sins, including mine."

That started another tangent that Stacy listened to, amused. She loved Pastor Clifton. He was like a very fit grandfather. He was sort of balding. He had a full head of hair in back and on the sides, but the top of his head was a bit sparse. His eyes crinkled when he smiled, which was most of the time. Pastor Clifton also tried to get all the young people at the gym into a fitness regimen. He said it was one thing to be old. It was another to look old. He would challenge the guys in the parish to push-up contests. If he could do more than they could, he would insist that they go to the neighborhood gym. Stacy always got a kick out of that.

Stacy also loved pushing Pastor Clifton's buttons. Sometimes she just threw out statements that she knew he couldn't let go. She'd listen intently with a twinkling eye. Most people avoided the long lectures. Stacy couldn't resist poking the bear. She used to say, "The only way you know people are telling the truth is when you challenge them to go off script. Plus, it's fun. Pastor Clifton always throws up his hands to the heavens for Divine intervention then says, 'God help us all' before launching into his tirade. Love it."

Pastor Clifton didn't give up and one day Stacy said, "Pastor Clifton,

I can't keep being counseled by you if it means you are going to try to change me with every meeting. I know I have a choice. I realize I have a choice. I got it. I know that God wants more for me. Got that too. For right now, this is where I am. This is who I am. I know you will never agree. But if you can't accept that, I can't … "

Pastor Clifton stopped after that. He still welcomed Stacy into his church, but he no longer tried to get her to leave the club. He basically told her when she was ready, he'd help her. That was that.

Dee, like Stacy, lived by a certain code. Hell, even he lived by a certain code. He didn't try to get anyone addicted, but if they were already addicted, he would sell to them. If they lost their house, didn't pay their bills, ended up on the street, that was their problem. He wasn't a social worker. He was a business man. Business was always good.

All he had to do was wear that honey, Dee, down. She'd eventually come to her senses and see what he had. In the meantime, he had plenty to keep him busy. One was blowing up his phone a lot lately. She was pissed, of course, that he told Dee one of her secrets. But she'd get over it. He'd done worse to her. She wanted what he had and because of that, she kept coming back. She was a dog in heat, a possessive dog in heat at that. She wouldn't like the fact that he was hanging with Dee. She'd do anything to keep her shit tight. He liked that in her. It worked out well for him. Looking at his text messages, it was almost time to call her back. Almost. She wasn't begging yet. He loved it when she begged.

Dee walked into the house and shivered. She didn't know what Joe was going to ask of her, but these favors were starting to pile up and she couldn't get a read on Joe. It was odd. She was so good at reading people's intentions. She thought he'd be easier to control, but he was no flighty motherfucker. He meant business, and she might be writing checks her ass couldn't cash.

Lost in her thoughts, she didn't notice Auntie M by the window.

"Dee?"

Dee looked up startled. Auntie M was pissed—seriously pissed.

"Hey, Auntie M."

"Why are you riding around with Joe?"

"You weren't home. He was going to take me to the spa to get a job."

"I didn't know you knew him that well. Hell, I didn't know you knew him at all."

"We're just neighbors helping each other out."

"Don't. He's bad news. I'll drive you to the spa. I'll help you fill out the application. Stay away from him."

"But he's the neighbor. How am I supposed to stay away from him?"

"Find a way." With that Auntie M turned on her heel and left the room. Dee followed her with her eyes. She made a face at Auntie M's retreating form, then folded her arms to contemplate her aunt's request.

Auntie M went up to her bedroom and paced taking deep breaths. She didn't lose her temper often, but when she did, it took a while to cool it down again. That little girl better realize. She tried to grab on to the edges of the logic that usually ruled her decision-making, but it was hard. At the low end, Joe was a drug dealer; at the high end, he wasn't too bright. That wasn't a good combination.

And there were rumors about him and Evelyn. They were discreet rumors, but M's source was trustworthy. M had a hard time picturing Evelyn with anyone. M wasn't prudish enough to believe all high school girls were virgins, but even Joe could do better than Evelyn. However, Dee wasn't his come up. M would be damned before she'd let that go down. Now she was cursing in her head—true indication that the deep breaths weren't working. M hoped Dee was smarter than to fool around with Joe. That would be a bad decision to put it mildly.

Dee was still thinking. Normally, dumping someone like Joe wouldn't be a problem; she'd welcome the opportunity. He didn't have much going for him. He thought he was the shit. Truth was his shit was all types of sloppy. Who the hell walks up the front steps of a crack house, unless they're of course a crack head? Then it didn't matter what entrance you used.

But Joe proved to be useful with the Evelyn situation. She was sure he hit that. That was the only way to have that intimate information about her. That meant that he didn't mind younger women. That alone should have raised Dee's antennas, but if it kept Evelyn in her place and rides for Dee, she'd hang out a bit longer. There was another issue. Joe was the only friend she had in the neighborhood. Who else did she have to hang out with? Even after the crazy stunt he pulled today, she didn't have much of a choice.

She would need to make sure Auntie M never saw them together again. Apparently, Auntie M thought he was no damn good. She was partially right. He wasn't the type of guy you bring to Sunday dinner. Hell, she wouldn't even bring him to Monday or Tuesday dinner. Truth of the matter, she wouldn't fill up a bowl with kibble and sit it outside of the door for Joe. Auntie M had a valid point, but time would tell with Joe.

In the meantime, she needed to get to the spa job to get a little pocket change. She didn't want to dip into her savings, and she didn't feel the need to slang anymore. Anyway, there was already one dealer in the neighborhood; they didn't appear to need any more.

She'd just keep an eye out for any additional opportunities to make money. Until then, she'd get a job at the spa. It couldn't be that hard—as long as they didn't need someone to clean up. That place was a bit too meticulous, and Dee knew she didn't have what it took to keep the spa straight. She could do reception, though. That seemed easy enough.

She went to Auntie M's room and sat down on her bed. Auntie M followed her with her eyes as she walked across the floor and sat down in a chair in the corner.

Auntie M didn't say a word.

Damn she must still be hot about Joe. Dee cleared her throat. "I'm sorry, Auntie M. I didn't realize it was that big a deal. He seemed nice enough, and he was a neighbor so I thought it would be OK. I'm good at taking care of myself."

"Hmm."

"I'll stay away from him as much as possible. We might be working together at the spa. Outside of that, I don't need to see him."

Auntie M looked at her so long without saying a word that Dee began to squirm. *Damn it. Dee would be working at the spa.* She could tell her to get a different job, but that seemed like overkill. Trust. Right? Auntie M had lived long enough to know you can trust most people as far as you can see them. However, Dee was family, and technically she hadn't done anything.

After a minute, Auntie started talking. "People talk. You can only take a portion of what people say as the truth, but no one says anything nice about him so I worry a bit more. I'm not saying you're not a good young lady. I just know that boy damn near has three sixes somewhere on his body."

Dee's eyes began to twinkle as she regarded her aunt. "Oooh, Auntie M, have you been looking?"

Auntie M gave Dee a droll look. "Why, he's so skinny you can see his ribs through his T-shirt. What am I going to look for? If my men are going to go away, I prefer a tropical destination and not jail. Goodness knows, that's where that boy is heading again. I just don't want you to get caught up in anything. Besides, that boy is too old to hang out with a high schooler. Nothing good can come of that. Trust me."

"OK, Auntie M. Since Joe got distracted with errands for his mother or something, I asked him to take me home before we got to the spa."

Auntie M seemed to be contemplating something. Finally, she just asked Dee to get her stuff together and off they went.

As they drove through the streets, Dee was shocked at the neighborhoods that they had to pass through to get to the spa. She hadn't paid close attention the first time. Now she listened to Auntie M ramble on about who lived where and a nice gossipy tidbit about each. Dee noticed they had passed through about three towns before hitting the spa. She asked Auntie M about that.

"Girl, there seems to be a new suburb every few blocks out here. It's not like Chicago where things are spread out a bit more. In Chicago, you can drive for an hour and still be in the city. Here, if you drive for an hour, you have passed about ten cities."

Dee smiled at Auntie M. She was glad that the tension that existed when they first entered the car had left. She was not really a confrontational person and Auntie M provided the roof over Dee's head. Not only had she opened her home, but she stocked Dee's closet. Dee didn't want to piss off her fairy godmother.

As they drove up to the spa, Dee noticed Joe's car in the parking lot. She squinted. His ass could have come directly here instead of stopping. She'd have to find a way to pay him back for that inconvenience. Dee and Auntie M got out of the car, walked inside the building, and up to the reception area. As Dee filled out the application, she noticed Joe walk out from the back and smirk. She wanted to flip him the bird, but she couldn't very well do that in front of Auntie M. So she just ignored him.

Auntie M struck up a conversation with the receptionist, who was apparently a member of the church. According to the receptionist, almost everyone who worked at the day spa was a member of the church. They definitely got preferential treatment when it came to open positions. With Auntie M being one of the original members, Dee's application automatically went to the top of the list. Dee liked the way they spread the love.

Dee refused the tour the receptionist offered. She could always get a tour if she got the job, and she didn't want to run into Joe again.

As Auntie M wrapped up her conversation with the receptionist, Dee felt a prickle at the back of her neck. She turned to see what was behind her. She didn't notice anyone, but the door to the back area where spa services were performed was swinging a bit. *That damn Joe was eyeballing her again.*

PHANTOM

Wow. She did look like Ilene. There were rumors, of course. It had been years since anyone had seen Ilene, but just to look at her progeny brought all the memories back. However, she was different. Ilene shone from the inside out. Dee, she smoldered. She didn't radiate happiness the way Ilene did. This one was more Nipsey, more cerebral. Ilene made men want to smile. Dee made men want. That was even more powerful.

All she was doing was filling out a simple application and even with that simple task, she was turning heads. It wasn't obvious. Well, for some it wasn't obvious. It was more subtle shifts, changes in energy. A few were blatantly staring.

Looking objectively, it was more than a gorgeous face. It was also the body. The slim legs leading to narrow hips attached to a full ass. It was almost worth dropping something in front of her to see her pick it up, to see how they would react.

The resolute position of her shoulders said she needed to be in charge. Others would spend a lifetime trying to control her. Oh, there'd be a job open all right. Of course there'd be a job open; a little schedule shift and someone was bound to quit. That was too easy. The long list of applicants would be ignored.

Aunt M wouldn't have a clue about what to do with someone like Dee. She'd want to mother her. You didn't mother that. You harnessed that power and used it for the greater good.

One didn't get in this position by passing up opportunities. One leveraged every opportunity that came their way. This one would be tricky. This one wouldn't take kindly to strings, strings would be pulled anyway. How could they not? She was too unique to be left to her own devices. She deserved to be part of an empire.

CHAPTER 10

Dee laid down in her bed lulled into a sense of tranquility by Auntie M's incessant snoring. Dee had gotten used to the sound. It let her know that everything was as it should be in a world that was definitely off kilter. She rolled over trying to remember the last time she had heard from her father. Granted, she hadn't expected any long, flowing, sappy letters, but she at least thought he would check on her. She should try to get a cell phone from Auntie M. Her budget hadn't stretched that far in Chicago. There she could only afford luxuries like gas and electricity.

Of course, a real father would have gotten in touch with her by now whether, or not she had a cell phone. Auntie had a cell phone and a landline. It was archaic to say the least. She said that if the world went from sugar to shit, at least she wouldn't have to worry whether her phone was working.

Dee tried to explain if the world went from sugar to shit, they would have a whole lot of other problems. Auntie ignored her. At least at the minimum, there would be a phone. Everyone might be dead. Zombies might be roaming the earth. The water might be undrinkable and the food might be inedible, but you'd be able to call someone on M's phone. Whatever.

M never answered her home phone. She always used her cell. So what was the point of having a landline if she never used it?

Dee settled a bit deeper into the pillows and imagined her dad tried to call on the landline and could not get through. Even though he was bootlegged, this was crazy even for him. He usually checked in at least once a week. It had been a month since they had heard from him. He had disappeared before, but this was almost unheard of. She had to remember to check with Auntie in the morning. She might know where he was. He was surely checking in with the one holding the purse strings.

Dee turned her head toward the window. What would happen if he decided he didn't need any money and he was just going to roll out solo without a care in the world? Nipsey wasn't much of a dad, but he was all Dee had. She wanted him to call.

Unfortunately, she didn't have a way to reach out to him. Dee didn't know how long she was going to wait before she sounded the MIA horn. Actually, it was more like a former hype call tree. It was the one she activated whenever she really needed to get a hold of Nipsey. She'd call some current or former hype who would get her call and then pass her message on. As a last resort, she could always call Big Rock. He knew where the mice traveled in her hood. Nipsey wouldn't be that much of a problem.

Dee closed her eyes and relaxed, anticipating sleep. Somewhere in between asleep and awake, he appeared. Reverend Love. She saw him in her imagination as he had been in the pulpit on Sunday. That voice. The way he sang. The emotion he put into every single chord. She seriously considered joining the choir after his performance.

Dee squirmed with an uncomfortable feeling, restlessness. This was great. She was hung up on a grown-ass man. And this wasn't like a random guy; he was the reverend. But then again, she wasn't the only one hawking. She had felt his eyes on her too. They had connected. She felt him somewhere deep, which is odd because they hadn't actually met.

Reverend Love had this older, taller Trey Songz/Bow Wow thing going on. When he ducked his head, closed his eyes and smiled, the whole female congregation got wet. No doubt even those old gray-haired ushers felt a little juicy. He was an adorable type of fine. It made him approachable and it made Dee want to be a member of the church, but that wasn't enough. It was going to make the week long as hell.

Dee understood now why the congregation was so large. Females were regulars. Wherever females were, males followed. She might come in contact with the good reverend at the spa; but that was owned by Evelyn's mother, and any woman who raised a girl that evil was to be avoided.

Dee contemplated joining the choir, but she definitely wouldn't get anywhere with church busybodies always in her business. In Dee's experience, people involved in the church were very concerned with everyone's soul.

Dee didn't know how she was going to get some alone time with the good reverend, but that was definitely on her list of things to do. She wanted to see what it felt like to be near him, up close. She needed to know if she would still feel the tingling sensation that she felt now.

A bit antsy now, she threw her covers off and sat up. She walked over to the window and peered in her neighbor's yard. There was good old dependable Joe, probably smoking and drinking. She wondered how he could keep this late-night schedule if he had to get up in the morning and get to the spa. Sometimes even Dee couldn't hang with him. She had school in the morning and no one was going to get in between her and a good "A."

One night he invited Dee to do more than just smoke the weed. He was looking for a new distributor, and he thought Dee fit the bill. However, Dee wasn't about to set up shop in a new neighborhood. She didn't want to catch a case. Joe didn't get it. He saw dollar signs before he saw anything else.

Dee didn't sell weed before because that was her profession of choice. It wasn't like she told her school counselor she wanted to be a dealer when she grew up. She didn't ask for Rocky's dad to attend career day. Slanging was her profession out of necessity—and she didn't go into it blindly. Rocky's dad had her back. Dee knew that if she had to start from scratch, her situation would have been very different. Joe hadn't figured out his issues. There was no way he was going to help someone else if needed.

You didn't grow up in the hood and not understand the rules of the game. The truth was Dee wasn't hard enough to be a full-time dealer, even in a small market. Dee thought it was just good sense. All the money in the world meant nothing if you were dead or in jail. Just like she skipped tours of the crack house, she didn't think she should be trying to build up a clientele. It wasn't like she could hang out on the edge of the subdivision. Joe was going have to find a different patsy. Dee was not the one. She was going legit. She had a little stash for emergencies. The rest would come from a real job, one with a W-2. If Uncle Sam didn't know you were working, all you were really doing was working your way to jail.

She guessed her real fear of jail was the stint that Nipsey had done. When he got out, he was worse off than when he entered. He had lost weight and looked haggard and beaten down. It was a while before he got back to normal. Apparently, he had gotten in a fight the first night there. He did the unthinkable; he lost the fight. That meant he had to fight more often than not.

To this day, Nipsey doesn't talk about his experiences in jail. He just described it as a place you don't want to go. The haunted look in his eye reached Dee. Every time he spoke of it, he would grab a beer or go for something stronger. That was enough to tell Dee she never wanted to do anything to get there. That's why she was so thankful to Auntie M for taking her in. That also meant she had to be on her Ps and Qs. She didn't want Joe to mess up her good thing.

She considered joining him in his nightly chill, but decided against it. It would do her good to start to distance herself. She walked back over and lay down in bed with vision of the delectable Reverend Love dancing in her head.

CHAPTER 11

A couple of weeks later, Dee received a message from Auntie M. She had an interview at the spa. Auntie M picked her up from school.

Things had been going well for Dee overall. Nipsey had finally resurfaced. At the beginning of the month he contacted Auntie M for cash. When Dee talked to him, he didn't sound good at all, but he was alive. She asked if he wanted to come to Atlanta. She was sure Auntie M didn't mind, but he declined. She even went as far as to remind him that Ilene was buried near Atlanta and they would be able to visit her grave. He still declined. He didn't want to leave all of his people, the ones that kept him hooked on that stuff. Dee didn't say anything. She was just relieved to know that he was OK.

School had started improving. In a striking coincidence, there were quite a few people that hated Evelyn. It gave them common ground and that meant Dee was making new friends. It was like their own resistance movement. At first they didn't know about Dee. She looked like she could be stuck up, but once they got to know her they realized that they had a lot in common.

It wasn't just their universal dislike of Evelyn, they also loved music.

They would spend hours arguing over whether Lil Wayne was actually cute. There was one girl who swore that he was 'it' … even with tattoos on his face. Dee didn't get it. She gave them that he had swagger, but that was all. One insightful crew member reminded her that sometimes swagger was enough. That was definitely true.

Even some of the guys were coming around; some of them hung out with her crew. There were intermingled boyfriend/girlfriend pairings within the groups. One guy was doing a straight full-court press on Dee. He was OK looking, but to talk to him, he was the shit. Dee wasn't really into him, but she wasn't opposed to letting him pay for a meal or the show every now and again.

She was actually having more fun than she had in Chicago. At home, she had to take care of everything. Here, she was a bit freer than she had been in years. The only hitch in the works was the times when she wanted to share something with her mom. She'd lie in bed and contemplate the day thinking she'd have to tell her mom about one tidbit or another in the morning and her heart would ache. Sometimes she even cried herself to sleep. Sometimes life still sucked, but overall she was pleased with how things were going. She had laughed more in the past couple of months than she had during the past two years. Sometimes she surprised herself with her happiness.

Now Auntie M was speeding to the spa to get them there in time for her interview. She had decided to wear her mother's Charles David black heels for good luck. They were a simple timeless shoe; the leather was butter soft. That's why her mother rarely wore them. She didn't want to scratch the leather. How can you show off your cool shoes if they just stayed in your closet? Her mother dusted them twice a month and made sure to Lysol them so they wouldn't funk up the small apartment.

While she was at it, she 'Lysoled' Dee's shoes. She would say she knew they had to be funky. She would call it getting ahead of the funk. "We don't want anyone walking through our front door and the funk in our house knocking them right back out the door before you even get a chance to say a good hello."

Dee looked out of the window. Her mother made up a whole bunch of crazy sayings to fit the situation. She would say, "Ma'Dear always said … " Ma'Dear had passed when Dee was about ten. Dee had stayed there for a few summers. Ma'Dear cooked and cleaned a lot, but she didn't make one pithy comment. Dee confronted her mother when she returned home. Her mother merely said, "You spent two summers with her. I spent a lifetime."

Dee felt her eyes welling up. That often happened when she thought of her mom. Even now, she saw Auntie M glancing at her through the corner of her eye. Sometimes in the middle of the day all of a sudden she would have to wipe tears from her eyes. She pretended that it was her allergies acting up. She'd blame it on a perfume or cologne, but it was just memories.

Auntie M pulled up in front of the day spa with five minutes to spare. They gathered their materials and hustled through the door. Auntie M sat in a chair by the door while Dee was shown to the back office. There sat the first lady.

Mrs. Reverend Love had her long, thick, black hair down. She was brick house for sure. She had the boobs and a very narrow waist. Then she stood and Dee's mouth dropped. This bitch was about six foot three, and her paw enveloped Dee's hand when they shook.

Dee got a crick in her neck from having to snap her neck up to look at the woman's face. She was glad when they were able to sit down and were a bit more eye to eye. It was hard to concentrate on the interview when Dee was busy looking for an Adam's apple. Mrs. Love was a more affected female. Her mannerisms seemed unnatural.

Dee stumbled through the first five minutes. Her inner dialogue got in the way of her outer dialogue. Eventually, she hit her stride and answered the appropriate questions. Since she didn't really have an employment history and she was new to the area, she could basically make up anything that she wanted. As she was breezing through the rest of the questions, she threw Dee for a loop.

"So tell me, do you get along well with others?"

"Oh yes, I consider myself a team player. I try to treat everyone with the same consideration that I would want."

"That's not what I hear."

Dee was shocked. *What could she have possibly heard?*

"I told my daughter that I was interviewing you and asked her opinion. She seemed to believe you have behavioral issues. She said you were a loner and didn't get along with other students at your school. I'd like to hear your side."

The response Dee wanted to give was that she would knock Evelyn out, but she was starting new. That meant not threatening her potential boss's daughter. She wracked her brain to find an answer that didn't include violence.

"Well, when I first came to the school, it was a difficult time for me. My mother had just passed and I was quieter than I normally would be. Some people took that as standoffish, but the truth was, I was in mourning." She saw Mrs. Love's face start to soften a bit.

"That's why I really want this job. I want to focus on something else."

"I heard about your mother and I'm very sorry. I understand how that would be difficult for you."

Dee wanted to shout that her broken-down daughter didn't make it easier. At least now she understood why Evelyn felt the need to wear the water bras. If she was flatter than a pancake and her mother was guiding airplanes with her boobs, she might look into some enhancements too. Shit, that lady could balance a plate on her boobs. It was like a little shelf. It was incredible.

"Well, Dee, I believe in giving everyone a fair chance. I think you will be a good addition to our team."

Dee wanted to jump up.

"All new employees are subject to a three-month probationary period before they are considered permanent employees. Someone will call you with your schedule. Welcome to our family."

Mrs. Love stood with Dee. They shook again – hand to paw. Dee walked out of the office. As she approached Auntie M, she gave her the thumbs-up sign.

Auntie M jumped up, clapped, and enveloped Dee in a hug. "Let's celebrate by getting you a cell phone. I'll get the phone and you can pick up the bill with your check. This is so exciting. Is this your first job? Did you work back home?" Auntie M kept firing questions at Dee, who did her best to answer within the confines of not telling her about activities better kept under wraps.

As Auntie M linked arms with Dee, they walked toward the car. She saw something out of the corner of her eye. Joe was talking to Mrs. Love. He lifted his water bottle to her in congratulations. Dee turned around and headed out with her aunt.

PHANTOM

This was almost too easy. She only worked two evenings a week and then all day on Saturday. The day spa was closed on Sunday and Monday. They wanted the staff to make time for church.

Frankly, three days a week was more than enough exposure to learn exactly how to insert oneself between Dee and Auntie M. Gaining trust would take time to be sure. However, anything that was worth it required effort. Dee felt the connection. She didn't even know what it meant. In that way, she was a little girl in need of molding. That's why she turned. Subconsciously, she knew that something was going to be different.

Dee was still fresh from Ilene's death. She depended on Aunt M. Now wasn't the time. Or it could be the perfect time. Dee was trying to find her place. She was trying to navigate the changes in her life. She was trying to survive. One either had that survival instinct or didn't. If it was never tested, one never knew when push came to shove what would happen. Would one fold or fight?

Dee was clearly fighting. There was no doubt that shadows crept into her eyes, but only those that watched her closely knew that ghosts were chasing this girl. This was the time when one would insert themselves into the life of a weaker girl. The stronger ones built up walls that would need to be navigated. Dee was a wall builder. She laughed. Sometimes she even flirted. She never connected. She wasn't trying to make those connections. It was best to stay on the perimeter, watching, gaining trust. Allowing others to navigate toward her, yearn for her. Dee's power would be her effect on others. For that to work, patience was paramount. Sometimes the thought of what could be was overpowering and it was hard to be patient. However, it was necessary.

It took nine months to prepare a person for this world. There was no time limit on Dee's rebirth. However, it couldn't wait forever. Dee would need to be trained. That took time. However, her rebirth would be special. It would energize an entire community. And before it was over, the power that would come with it would be monumental. No one would be able to touch her. It was better without Ilene or Nipsey holding her back. Dee would be free. She would soar.

CHAPTER 13

It was Joe's turn to open the spa. Most days he hated the early shift. It was hell getting up this early for anything other than sex; he didn't mind that at all. Today, though, he had peeped at the schedule. It was Dee's first day. He already knew which 'hard legs' were going to be a problem. Some of these fuckers could barely keep their cock shut down for the average girls. Dee was going to be a distraction for sure.

Joe would get them in line as soon as he could. He wouldn't have them pushing up on her like that. He heard a car pull up and turned. Auntie M was dropping off Dee. He smiled and nodded at M. The look she gave him was ... well shit if she could have shot him dead she would have. He smiled a bit wider, and she looked more pissed off.

Dee said something to her and got out of the car.

Damn, it didn't make any sense for someone to fill out a T-shirt like that. The spa name stretched across her chest. Once again, Joe's reaction to Dee was involuntary. He was way past the age where he had to act on every urge. Joe turned off the alarm system. He held the door open for Dee and began to flip on the lights.

Dee's legs were encased in the traditional jeans worn by the staff. Well, not exactly traditional. Her jeans molded every... single ... curve. No mom jeans for her. They were also required to wear black shoes. Dee's shoes were not the athletic type worn by most or even the ugly Crocs® that all the women were wearing now. No, she stepped in heels. *Have mercy.*

He leaned against the counter and eyeballed her a bit before speaking. "You've been kinda MIA lately. What's going on?"

"For some reason, Auntie M doesn't like you." Dee laughed. "Go figure. That makes it hard to get away."

"She sleeps. See if you can fit a midnight chat back in your schedule."

The door opened and Grace entered. Grace considered herself a manager, even though she didn't have the title or responsibilities. Grace was amusing. What she didn't realize was that if she was going to do all the extra manager work, they had no reason to promote her.

Grace gave Dee a once-over. Joe already knew this wasn't going to bode well. Grace didn't like competition. She wouldn't even consider the fact that Dee was so far above her league that competition wasn't even possible. Plus, Grace was old as hell. Well, she was in her thirties, but she was always hanging around the young guys. She'd buy them food and they'd all go to the show together. Joe never went. Grace had pushed up on him when he first started. She was alright, but not nearly as fly as she thought she was. If Grace thought about it, she would have realized that if she was that fly, she wouldn't always be paying for everything.

Joe introduced Grace to Dee, making sure she understood the girl was in high school. *No way one can hate on a teenager. Wait, knowing Grace she would hate her anyway, but maybe she'd keep it to herself.*

Other employees began to filter in and a clap came from the back. Ahh. Someone snuck in the back door. Wonder how long he had been there. Reverend Love appeared from the office. Interesting. Reverend Love often came to the spa. However, he never came out in the front unless the First Lady was around. He said that she had another appointment and introduced himself to Dee.

Joe noticed her look and the reverend's. Someone less observant would have missed the extra hand squeeze or the look in their eyes. Someone less interested would have missed the catch in Dee's breath or the unusual shy duck of the head. Someone less intrigued wouldn't have noticed how she edged to the back of the crowd. Someone who didn't know how observant she was wouldn't think twice about the fact that the reverend had her undivided attention. Someone that didn't know the reverend as well wouldn't have figured out that he missed several points that he should have communicated to the staff, and how he never looked at Dee again after that first handshake. This was getting interesting.

For the first time in her life, Dee was developing a tick in her eye. She was proud of herself for managing to catch herself before she lost control, but anyone could see by the clinch of her fist what it was costing her.

Grace pretended to help Dee, but only gave her half an assignment and waited until Dee fucked up to tell her the rest. Grace was driving Dee crazy. This lady had issues. Dee and Grace went into the storeroom one time and one of the guys started flirting. Dee wasn't interested, but Grace seemed to get hella pissed after that.

Was she for real? She had a good ten years on both of the guys. Whatever. Grace also took the time to tell Dee that generally no one wore heels around the spa. Dee pinned Grace down with some pointed questions and realized there wasn't a rule against heels. It was just no one wore them. Dee was trying to collect a check. She didn't have time for the madness.

Behind the closed office door, Joe leaned back, closed his eyes, and brought up visions of Dee in that T-shirt. He had kept tabs on her during the day to make sure that the guys didn't lose themselves. However, Dee seemed to shoot down everyone with a smile. If not, it would have created a difficult situation. The First Lady didn't play that way. She would have found a way to get rid of Dee. She liked her shop working as smooth as clockwork. He was surprised she hired Dee at all considering what Evelyn had been saying about her. The First Lady must have seen something in her.

Thank goodness, she hadn't seen Dee today. That coke bottle body made what seemed like a simple outfit look like something straight out of *Playboy*. It didn't help that Dee tied the T-shirt in a knot at the base of her back. Not only did that mean it was tight against the delectable breasts, but when she bent over you could see the small of her back.

Heaven help him, the girl had a tattoo. He almost lost it. He wanted to walk right over there and tell her to take that knot out, but at the same time he was intrigued. One time during the day, she had flipped her hair and saw him staring at her. He merely nodded and he saw the speculation in her eyes. This was their workplace. He'd have to be a bit more conscious of that fact. For now, when no one was around, he could imagine what the twat was like. *Nothing wrong with that.*

Chapter 14

A month after Dee started at the spa, Auntie M asked, "Dee, how would you feel if we had another roommate?"

Dee looked up at Auntie M. Maybe Auntie had gotten her groove back. It was always a possibility. So Dee bit.

With a little twinkle in her eye, Dee looked at Auntie out of the side of her eye. "Someone been creeping while I'm at work? It's fine of course, but I would have thought that I would have seen at least evidence of this mystery gentleman."

Auntie M popped Dee on the back of her head. "Be serious." Then she came around and sat next to Dee.

Dee stopped eating and looked in Auntie M's eyes.

"Remember a few weeks ago when you asked me about Nipsey? I kind of put you off a bit."

"I thought you didn't know where he was. I thought he was lost in Chicago." Dee squinted as realization set in. "You knew?"

Auntie M ducked her head. "Yeah, I just couldn't say until now. He's been back in rehab. Your mother … well, her death tore him up. You know. So he kind of hit rock bottom really fast. Honestly, I didn't know what was going on until a few weeks ago. I swear you have a sixth sense. A day after I found out, you asked, and I had already promised."

Dee sat back in her chair and started playing with her fork. "So he's been in jail—again."

"No, no. This time he went to rehab. Voluntarily. He's almost finished with his thirty-day program. He wants to stay here. He doesn't have anyplace else to go. I know that you and Nipsey don't always get along, and I don't think you ever lived with him before those last months with your mom. I just wanted to make sure you were OK with this."

"The question is why are you OK with it? I mean he's an addict. Why would you want him living here?"

"Well, the easy answer is I'm a sucker. But the real reason is I don't have a lot. I have this house and some friends, but at the end of most days, I'm alone. You have no idea what's it's like to be alone—truly alone. You talk to people, but they aren't really invested in you. They care, but they have other priorities. Lonely isn't a good word. My life is pretty full, but sometimes I just feel hopeless. It's been so wonderful having you here. It'll be great having your father here as well. But only if you're OK with it."

"If he was so low, how did he end up in rehab? I don't get it, and thirty days at that. He never committed that long before."

Auntie M smiled. "I asked the same question. Apparently, his friend, Big Rock, saved his life. Nipsey was binging. Big time. He was wandering the streets. Big Rock saw him. Nipsey tried to hustle Big Rock for something, and Rock took him home.

"As Nipsey was coming down, they had a frank conversation. He asked Nipsey about you. Nipsey just knew you were with me. Rock apparently had a lot of choice words for him, and he threw Nipsey in a car and drove him down here and put him in rehab. I don't think he gave Nipsey much choice.

"Apparently, Nipsey had also been running a tab with some people that didn't take kindly to someone owing them money. Rock cleared the debt on the condition that Nipsey got clean. Nipsey told me he remembered Rock saying, 'She lost her mother and never really knew her father. You left her with a relative, for what? She's the best of you and Ilene. Plus, Lil Rocky will kick my ass if I don't look after her best friend. That means getting you straightened out and down there with your daughter.'"

Dee looked up from her plate. "I didn't know Big Rock had it in him."

"Your father didn't either. He tried to check out once. The staff called Big Rock. I don't know what happened, but he hasn't tried it since. So what do you say?"

Dee looked out of the window and contemplated. Living with Nipsey full time was no joke. Dee remembered what it was like. She didn't think he had been clean and sober at any point in her life. She didn't know Nipsey with his shit together. He sometimes went off of drugs, but never alcohol. He was a drunk of the first order. He wouldn't, couldn't live without a drink. Auntie M's house was damn near dry. She had a few bottles of wine, but that was about it. *What if he came and got back on that shit and left again?* She didn't know how she'd make it through that. She was starting over. She didn't want Nipsey fucking it up. But somewhere she realized that she did miss him.

She remembered the night when she couldn't sleep, how she lay awake hoping that he was OK. How her first thoughts were of him when she woke. She missed him and worried about him. She wanted him to be alright. *But does that mean he has to live with us?*

He brought a whole bunch of issues with him. That's why it didn't work the first time he lived with Auntie M. But her thoughts went back to her mother. Her mother who, regardless of everything that she was going through, worried about Nipsey, kept tabs on Nipsey, took care of him. At the end, her mother would want him taken care of. Regardless of whether she supported this move or not, that fact made her decision for her.

"I'm good. He can stay."

Auntie M beamed. "Great. He'll be here next week. "

"Hmm. I have to get to school."

A few days later at the spa, the First Lady was on a rampage. All Joe could do was sigh and keep his head low. He had no intention of fucking up the gig he needed to fill out the terms of his probation. The First Lady didn't like anything anyone at the day spa did. It made it difficult to say the least.

Everyone was on edge including the sweet Dee. She spent most of the day looking like a deer in the headlights. Her uniform was wrong. It had been wrong all along. That knot in the back was not approved—unless you asked every guy in a ten-mile radius. Then there was a resounding thumbs-up.

She seemed to be a bit nervous around him lately. There was something under the shell of her confidence. He found it ... endearing. No endearing was the wrong word. Maybe sexy. No. Enticing was a better word. He had to be very careful though. The First Lady was sharp. She didn't miss much. He thought her issues were due to the attention being heaped on Dee. She was used to commanding all eyes when she entered the room, if only because she was the most statuesque woman in the room. She commanded it, demanded it.

Dee didn't demand it. But she noticed it. It was interesting to watch her turn on, especially when she needed something. That smile, those poses. One stylist "accidently" knocked over a can of spray as she walked by. She bent to pick it up, bent from the waist. She flipped her hair over her shoulder and saw the stylist blatantly staring at her ass. She got up, smiled, and handed him the spray can with one brow raised. "Is there anything else I can help you with?"

Until that day, he would have sworn the stylist was gay. *What did he know?* But it was interesting that she didn't seem to have all of that bravado all of the time. He wondered why she lost it around him. True she smiled and sometimes he'd even get a wave, but she also made sure she kept her distance, which on days like this was a great idea. He walked to the back office. He had work to do.

Dee turned to the day spa door slightly swinging. *Weird.* She walked to the door and peered in, but only saw the ample bosomy Mrs. Love. She was willing to bet those weren't real, but what was she to do. Feel them up? She went back to her work at the desk. She nodded to Grace, who worked the front desk with her. Grace didn't like her much. Every time she flirted a bit with Gary, the stylist, Grace got a little bit more pissed off.

Dee smiled. It was funny really. Gary was twice their age if not more. She heard the scuttle "overextended." Translation: Broke. She didn't do old and broke. There was no point. But he was cute, and he was obviously into her. So she gave him a good view of what he would never have. One day she was playing with her hair and noticed him staring at her. So she returned his stare and dared him with her eyes. She saw him adjust his package soon after.

Joe had been pretty quiet since she started working there. She still sat with him on the back porch every now and again. She'd have to tell him Nipsey was coming. Those late-night conversations would have to end completely. Nipsey was a light sleeper, had ears like a freaking cat. Not only that, but he wandered in the middle of the night. She'd miss those chats. Sometimes she just felt like being somewhere else. Joe's back porch was as good a place as any.

Occasionally she felt his eyes on her, but for the most part, she stayed professional. According to him, he was still stockpiling money for his "Big Escape." *Whatever.* Some of that stockpiled money should go to a new place. *What is the statute of limitations on living at your momma's house? There has to be one.* Joe clearly had exceeded it by years. She wondered if he was still sleeping in the same twin bed he had as a kid.

He still tried to push up on her sometimes, but those occasions had lessened over time. He hit on her more out of habit than interest. However, sometimes he got that look in his eye or he'd rub her leg in a way that was very not friend-like. Usually, she just joked and knocked his hand away.

That's why she had never entered his mother's house. No need to truly test his boundaries. He was a man after all. She had no intention of giving in to him. She still felt as she did in the beginning. She could do better. She didn't have proof that he was sleeping with Evelyn, but that would explain how he knew more about what was going on in the church than anyone else. That would make him both a freak and a statutory rapist. But now that she thought about it, what was the first thing he told her when they met? *The legal age in Atlanta was sixteen. So he wasn't a statutory rapist, but he was still a freak, kicking it with high school girls. He should have higher standards. He should get a woman that at least has a job, if not an apartment. This living off momma shit had to be getting old. How did he get any play like that?*

It would be different if he was on that rough shit, but he only smoked a little weed every now and then. He should be able to get a better job than at the spa. It wasn't like he was the owner there. He was a worker bee. He probably made more than Dee, but that wasn't really saying much. Even her father, every now and again, managed to find his own spot. It might not have lasted long, but he is a hard-core hype. Or at least he was. Now he is a reformed addict. *We'll see.* Dee didn't believe too much in the reformed act, but she'd find out soon enough.

Chapter 15

Dee was holed up in her room. She had been there almost all day. All the bowing and scraping was straight grating on her nerves. When Nipsey walked through the door, he was all contrite. Always apologizing for each and everything he did. Auntie M was treating him like he was made of glass. Between the two of them, Dee was close to slitting her wrists. She was not the walk-on-eggshells type. The tension in the air was stressing her out and pissing her off.

So she gave up and started hibernating in her room. It was a rare Saturday when she didn't have to work. She had been putting in major hours at the day spa ever since Nipsey came home a week ago. They pretty much had started circling each other the minute he walked through the door.

He kept trying to talk to her. He would ask about work and school as if he was a real father. But a real father didn't crack brews open with his daughter. A real father actually laid down some rules. *Nipsey was ... he was ... shit. Besides a sperm donor, who the fuck knew?* That's what made both of them wary. Dee didn't have time or patience for another one of his rehab efforts. Nipsey obviously didn't know what to do with his teenage daughter.

Dee remembered the look in his eye when she opened the door to him. He actually took a couple of steps back as if he had seen a ghost. Dee snorted and then called her aunt to the door. She heard Nipsey mumbling as she walked away, "She looks just like her. I didn't realize."

It's amazing the things sober people noticed. Dee had favored her mother her whole life. Nipsey just started noticing. As Rick James once said, "Cocaine's a hell of a drug."

Dee sighed. She'd really like to leave her room, but the bumbling efforts of her father actually trying to be a father was too much to bear. She had completed her homework. Dee walked over to the window and looked out. She weighed her options. It might be possible to make it over to the porch overhang and work her way to the ground. If she made it to the overhang, it should be easy enough to make it to the railing and then she'd be home free. *But wait. Was she really that much of a punk that she was willing to risk life and limb just to avoid talking to her father? That really was a bitch move.*

Dee yanked the bedroom door open and walked to the kitchen. She was looking in the refrigerator for a snack when Nipsey walked in. She didn't bother to acknowledge his presence. She went on evaluating the contents of the refrigerator. She really didn't know what she wanted so she kept moving food to the side.

Nipsey joked. "Hey, what are you trying to do, air condition the kitchen with the refrigerator?"

Dee turned and looked over her shoulder, rolled her eyes, and continued to look for food.

Nipsey shuffled further into the kitchen. "Yeah. That's what um my mother used to tell me when I held the refrigerator open. So. Well you know. Umm. So you didn't have to work today, huh?"

Dee sighed, closed the door on the fridge, leaned against it, and began to assess Nipsey. His body looked like hell. He was maybe a buck o' five soaking wet. He was shuffling from one foot to another under her scrutiny.

Then Auntie M walked in. She looked from Nipsey to Dee and rolled her eyes. The chill in the room had nothing to do with the refrigerator door having been open earlier. She had tried to let the situation work itself out. By proximity alone, one would think they would have addressed at least one issue. Dee was a tough cookie. On one hand, M admired that. She was not one to be messed with. On the other hand, the camaraderie she had with Dee had disappeared. Dee had shut down—all the way down. This couldn't go on. It was time for intervention.

Auntie M stated simply, "It's not that you didn't know he was coming to live here. So stop playing your dad and answer his question. The sooner you learn how to talk to him, the sooner you will be able to stop hiding out at work and in your room."

Dee tilted her head to the side and continued to scrutinize Nipsey. She was contemplating whether she was going to answer him.

Auntie M tried cajoling. The next step would be forcing. Dee was a stubborn one. "Dee. Come on. Give him a chance."

Dee turned to Auntie M. "A chance to do what, exactly? A chance to start using drugs again? A chance to disappear? A chance to clean out your house, even though you are the only person that has stuck by him all of these years? What chance am I supposed to give Nipsey?"

Nipsey's head was still down. He was still shuffling from one foot to another.

Dee was about to roll her eyes again.

Auntie M gave her the don't-go-there-with-me look.

Dee checked the attitude … for Auntie M.

"Give him a chance to be different. Give him a chance to recover."

Dee looked at her father. "Is that what you're doing, Nipsey? Are you recovering? Or are you itching for your next fix? Which way are your shuffling feet going? Huh, Nipsey."

"Dee, in my house we are cordial."

"I just asked a question. I was only exploring his feelings. Isn't that what they did in rehab? Explore his feelings? So how do you feel Nipsey? Do you feel like taking a hit?"

Nipsey stopped shuffling. "Stop. OK, Dee. Just stop. I know that I've tried this before. I know it hasn't worked. I know you don't believe I'll stay clean. I know. I get it. I know you're pissed at me. How can I not know you're pissed at me? Disgust oozes out of your pores every time you see me."

"Well then—"

Nipsey stopped shuffling and balled his fists up at his side. "Shut up for a second Dee. Damn. Let me get a word in."

Dee looked shocked. Nipsey had never dared to challenge her.

"Take a breath and a break. Like it or not, I'm your father. I won't say that 'I brought you into this world and I'll take you out.' Even though there are times when that sounds like a good fucking idea. I know more than anyone that it was your mother that raised you. It was your mother that made sure food was on the table. It was your mother that made sure you were taken care of.

"And I know better than anyone that it was you that made sure she had her medication. It was you who made her eyes light up just by coming into the room. It was you that made sure she was never lonely even during those last few months. I know the sacrifices you had to make to make sure that was happening. You think Big Rock didn't come to me when you started slanging?

"He intentionally made sure you made just enough to live off of and not enough to get you caught up in the game. Fucking look at you. Old-ass motherfuckers were panting for you, and it was Big Rock that made sure you were protected every step of the way.

"I know how it feels to have to look someone you love in the eye and they snarl back with their eyes full of contempt. I know damn well I deserve every sarcastic thought that swirls in your head and every bitchy ass word that falls out of your mouth.

"I know. I know. I fucking know.

"But I'm trying. So I'm going to need you to back the fuck off and let me try. And I promise you one thing. If this shit doesn't work, if I can't keep myself clean this time, I will walk away from you and never bother you again. You deserve better. Your mother deserved better. It's too late for her. I can't make it up to her. But it's not too late for you. So I'm trying again. Every day I'm trying again. Every day I wake up at the beginning and hope to make it to the end clean and sober.

"So I don't need you telling me every minute of every day with every look and every word what a fuckup I am. I get it. But every day I'm going to try to not fuck up. So I'm going to need you to step off and let me try. If you can't do that, I'll go upstairs, pack my shit, and forget this address."

This time Nipsey didn't shuffle off. He stomped off.

Dee and Auntie M looked at each other.

Auntie M spoke first. "You were slanging?"

All of that and all she heard was that Dee was dealing.

"You do what you need to do to survive."

"Some people work at McDonalds."

Dee laughed. "Yeah, some people do."

"And now?" Auntie M crossed her arms.

"Now I work at a spa."

"That all?"

"Yeah, that's all."

Auntie M nodded toward the empty doorway. "Well what do you think?"

Dee thought for a minute. "Well, damn, that was new."

"How so?"

"He's never been the confrontational type. Normally, he would have just cracked open a beer or something."

"Can you give him that chance he's asking for?"

"I can't erase history. It is what it is. I will try to keep my comments to myself and bide my time for you because I know you want your family around you. And like it or not, he's family. He's the reason I have you and I didn't end up on the street. At this point, that's all I can offer. I'll wait and see. You can tell him I'm OK with him staying."

"Why don't you tell him?"

"Because I don't believe in happily ever after. Disney deals in hope. I deal in reality." Dee started to walk away and then stopped. She turned with flat, determined eyes. "For the record, I don't care who he is, if he fucks this up in any way, if he dares to hurt you again, he's going to wish he would have walked out of that door today and never looked back."

Dee walked out the front door slamming it shut. She took two deep breaths and then opened it again, mumbled sorry to Auntie M, and closed the door more quietly. She sat down on the back porch and looked over the yard. She tried to relax, but it wasn't working. Her leg continued to shake. She needed to work off this tension.

PHANTOM

Seeing Dee at the day spa was different than seeing her in full temper stomping down the street. The spa clientele had shifted since Dee started. There had never been many male clients, but now apparently, there was a run on manicures and pedicures for men. It was definitely good for business. It kept the First Lady happy. Even when the First lady was out of sorts, she wasn't stupid enough not to take that new money.

People moved left and right out of Dee's way as she kept walking, her eyes glazed by temper. M was too soft to harness that.

I knew exactly what to do with that fire. All that is required is opportunity. That is in short supply. Though there is plenty of evidence to the contrary, I could be patient if I wanted to be. It is so rarely needed. No one is important enough to warrant that consideration.

However, anyone could look at Dee and see that she wasn't your average 'chicken-head.' She had something that even she didn't know. She played at it. She toyed with it. She flirted with it. She didn't know yet the danger of fucking with the wrong motherfucker. If she had learned that lesson, she'd be a bit more careful about whom she bent over in front of.

Dee was fearless, fearless and uneducated about the true nature of life. Oh sure, she'd be unstoppable. That did cause some hesitation. There was a danger in showing her true potential. She could turn. However, never one to turn away from a challenge, if Dee strayed too far out of line, she'd be dealt with as many before her had. However, she'd be different. She'd be special. She'd fulfill every promise. She's meant to be here. Her timing is impeccable.

CHAPTER 17

Joe watched Dee stomp off. His gaze was so intent that he didn't realize until it was too late that Reverend Love was coming down the street. Joe quickly rushed up his walkway and started into his house. Reverend Love stopped him.

"Hi there, Joe."

"Reverend."

Reverend Love walked up the porch and leaned against the railing. "I haven't seen you at service for a while."

Joe stared at Reverend Love and wondered why in the hell he was hanging out in this neighborhood and where he left his car. "Well Reverend, I figure that being at the spa so much has put me in touch with the most anointed of the congregation, so I was covered."

The reverend smiled. "How about first Sunday? We're putting together a special program. I'm sure you'll enjoy it. I'll see you on Sunday."

"My schedule—"

"I'm sorry. Maybe I was mistaken. I thought I was a reference for your probation officer. Isn't he that guy that calls me to make sure you turn up for work?" The reverend smiled.

Joe stared at the reverend. "Oh look. My schedule just opened up."

"Good, good. Nothing better than spending time with your church family. It will uplift you. I promise."

With that Reverend Love turned around and went to the house next door. He smiled and waved at Joe who was watching him. Reverend Love was met at the door by Dee's dad. They talked a bit at the door and then the reverend went into the house.

It piqued Joe's interest. What was so important that the reverend had to show up in person? *Interesting. It could be Dee.* Almost every male he knew was trying to get an introduction. Apparently, Reverend Love was no exception.

The reverend talked with Nipsey for a few minutes, handed him a pamphlet, invited him to church on first Sunday and even offered him a job at the spa. When Nipsey turned that down, the reverend offered him a job as his personal assistant before he went on his way.

After he left, Nipsey sat down on the edge of his bed in his small room squished between Auntie M's front bedroom and Dee's back one. The room had a tiny closet, so it counted as a bedroom. As rooms go, it was fine. He was just feeling a bit claustrophobic, especially after his encounter with Dee that morning.

Auntie M had given him a thumbs-up. So he could stay, but he didn't hear it directly from Dee. He knew Dee didn't trust a word that came out of his mouth. He couldn't really blame her; so many of his words had been lies. The way Dee looked at him sometimes made him feel like he wasn't a man. She treated him like more of a joke than a father. He wasn't sure how to get past that. Right now, he had to concentrate on getting through each and every day. But something inside of him wanted Dee on his side, in his cheering section.

Dee was on the sidelines watching, always watching. He swore that girl didn't miss a thing.

He remembered the day after he came home, he woke up early to cook breakfast for Dee. He fixed bacon, eggs, hash browns, and pancakes. Out of all of that food, there had to be something she liked.

She came down the stairs and called out to Auntie M. When she saw him in the doorway, she stopped in her tracks and leaned against the door jamb, her eyes full of unconcealed contempt. He made the first move.

"I thought we could have breakfast before you went off to school."

"Hmm. What made you think that?"

"It's early enough. Auntie M said you two generally eat breakfast together."

"Yeah, well that's with Auntie M."

"Well you have to eat. There's so much food here."

"That's where you're wrong. I don't have to eat. Nice try though. Cute even. Did you read a self-help book on connecting with your teenage daughter?" Just then Dee's stomach let out a loud growl.

He had smiled. "See, even your body is thinking that you should have something to eat."

"Well, my body is going to have to get used to disappointment. The rest of me is." With that, Dee turned and walked away.

He really wanted a drink, a smoke or something to settle his nerves. But even as he was thinking that, the reverend had rung the doorbell and invited him to come to church.

How he knew about Nipsey was a mystery.

He decided that it was probably Auntie M. She was definitely involved in the church. She had always been involved one way or another in church. The funny thing is she didn't have any allegiance to any denomination. She just loved church. When she was younger, she had changed denominations every few years. However the God Is Love Church was different. She had been there for a number of years. Nipsey guessed it was God's work. He was the lowest he had been in a long time when the reverend paid him a visit. It was like a miracle, like God was saying, "You better not. I got this."

Even more puzzling was the job offer at the spa since Nipsey knew that was where Dee was hiding out. Nipsey figured he'd already invaded Dee's new home. He didn't want to push his luck.

But as the reverend's personal assistant, Nipsey's schedule would be a bit more flexible; he would only be running errands for the reverend. The reverend would even provide him with a car. On one hand, Nipsey was extremely grateful. He needed to be able to contribute something to Auntie M's house. Even though Auntie M probably figured as long as he was broke, he couldn't backslide. But he couldn't continue to let other people take care of his responsibilities. One, he was running out of people. Two, Dee was his daughter. He needed to step up.

This offer from the reverend was almost too good to be true. The only catch was that he couldn't tell anyone about the position. Apparently, the reverend had to be very careful about showing favoritism to any one parishioner. He said that the parish had a few rental properties close by and there was a caretaker's car. Nipsey could use that when he needed to make his runs.

Nipsey wasn't completely comfortable with all this undercover shit. He was going to have to keep some tight documentation. This may be a little thing for the reverend, but for Nipsey it was big. He was staying all the way on this side of the law. He'd have to check into what that meant as far as taxes and everything. It would be his luck to be caught up owing the government $5. They always came after their money.

If it was church business, maybe the reverend could eventually put him on the church payroll. That would really help when he went to get a real full-time job. He knew how hard it was to find work when you had no real skills, no real experience, and a sporadic work history. It was damn near impossible.

He had learned that the hard way over the years. Every time he'd get clean and go look for work, they'd reject him with every excuse in the book. "Oh that job just got filled," they'd tell him even though the sign was still in the window. Or if he opened his heart and told them the truth, they couldn't wait to get him out of there. There was no winning for an ex-addict. Motherfuckers wanted you to be perfect. Life wasn't fucking perfect. Some bitch-ass, pimply-faced teenager would have just as much reason to rob a store as he did, but no—they wanted the teen. It really pissed him off that people didn't want to give him a chance. Maybe that one chance would have been the one that would have gotten him straight. They didn't know.

Nipsey got up and started pacing, and that wasn't good. When he got irritable, he got anxious. He retreated to his bed and closed his eyes. It was a process he learned at the halfway house. There he had learned to be still. He had learned to live in the moment. He guessed some people called it meditation. But he couldn't get into that chanting shit. Really. Sometimes he would go to the garden at the halfway house and feel like he had been transported into the Tina Turner movie. He swore that's where some of those people got their chants. If he heard one, 'nam myo ho renge kyo,' he'd heard them all. Pussy-ass fakers.

He preferred music. He would sit and sing a song in his head that meant something to him or his situation. His favorite right now was Donnie McClurkin's "Stand."

For him, that worked. When his cravings were their strongest, he wouldn't talk, he wouldn't walk anywhere, he wouldn't go anywhere; he would just find a place, sit, and sing in his head. He would just stand.

Some people in his support group said they needed to work their way through it. They needed to be distracted. Not him, he already knew what he lost because of his drug use. He knew what his life had cost him. He only had to remember the daughter that looked so much like her mother and he knew how much he had lost. He needed to face his life and give his craving to someone else. After the first verse was over, he'd go to the second verse.

He would know that if he could make it through a minute, he could make it through two. He could make it through five. He could just make it through. So he did. He would slowly start moving again. He would do whatever needed to be done, understanding that he could get through the next minute. That minute was a gift. So now sitting in this claustrophobic bedroom, he just sat still and made it through the minute.

He had never been much of a churchgoer. Sundays had been for recovering from whatever he had gotten into Saturday night. But the fact that he continued to wake up every day was a testament to the power of God. He had friends that he partied with who went to sleep right next to him and didn't wake up again. The fact that he kept waking up confirmed his belief in a higher power. He didn't shout about it or speak in tongues about it or get the Holy Ghost about it. It was just a part of him. He believed. It was that simple.

He knew Dee was pissed. She had always had a hell of a temper. He had always tried to stay out of her way. They preferred it that way. But to be a father, the father she undoubtedly needed, he was going to have to get in her way more often. Today went pretty well—considering. But he doubted she would give him much leeway. He just hoped he could earn another chance.

When she was younger, she had once asked him why he lied so much. He had told her sometimes to be nice and not hurt people's feelings, you had to tell them what they wanted to hear.

Fortunately, her mother came busting into the room and set Dee straight. She told her she should always tell the truth. She said sometimes the truth hurts, but lies catch up and hurt more. No matter how hard, the truth was always better.

"But dad lies all the time," Dee had said.

"Then we have to work harder to help him find the truth," her mother had replied.

Dee started giving Nipsey the eye after that conversation. Sometimes she would bust him out on his lies. Other times she would just look at him like he was the fuckin' scum of the earth. Either way, she could give less than a rat's ass about her father.

He remembered one time he was supposed to take her to the show for her thirteenth birthday. He didn't remember what he had been doing. He could guess, but he didn't have any details. She had lit into him the next day. Her mother just threw up her hands.

Dee told her father that day, "There must be a special room in hell for lying daddies. You'll have to sleep on a bed of nails for eternity. My only hope is that you'll slowly sink into the nails. Wait I have two hopes. The second one is that someone can tell me that I was right." Nice.

He was getting agitated again. He cleared his head and concentrated on the lyrics. He started at the beginning.

His hands stopped shaking. He took some deep breaths and centered himself.

***

Dee stopped walking when she reached the park. She plopped down on the grass. She couldn't believe that she still hadn't managed to shake Nipsey. He was like poison. God help her, if she ever got serious about a guy, he would have to be able to stand on his own two feet. No freeloading. No mother's basement. No "Can I get a loan?" No lying with every second word. He would have to be a man.

Dee looked at the other side of the park where there was a slide and jungle gym. She saw mothers playing with their children. Mothers. She wished she could lie up under her mom and ask her what to do about Nipsey. Her mother always gave such good advice. She would have known what to do.

Since Nipsey had just admitted that he had no role in her upbringing, what good was he? Hell, Big Rock had more of a role than he did. She closed her eyes and remembered her mom. Soon she was singing "Believe in Yourself" softly.

Dee smiled. Something in her heart grew a bit. The weight was temporarily lifted. She was softly singing to herself when a shadow fell over her. She opened her eyes with a start. It was either an angel or a man. If it was an angel, it had better have the decency to provide her winning lottery numbers.

As she adjusted her gaze, she heard, "I'm sorry to disturb you. That really wasn't my intention. I saw you here and heard a bit of your singing. Did you ever think about trying out for the church choir?"

It was Reverend Love. As delectable as he looked on the pulpit, he was truly even more fascinating this close. He was wearing a pair of high-end jeans. Even she could tell quality jeans when she saw them. If he really kept his stuff tight, they would be Kenneth Cole to match the T-shirt he was wearing. That smile. She started to get that feeling lower in her stomach again.

"You know who I am?"

Reverend Love laughed. "I have to admit I don't know every member of the congregation, but since you also work at the spa, it makes my job easier."

He sat down next to Dee. "You know sometimes it's difficult. Someone will come up to me at the store or something and they clearly know me. I have never been great with names." He turned and looked at Dee and with a voice as smooth as a soft caress. "Faces, faces I know."

Dee shuddered.

Reverend Love looked concerned. "Are you OK? Feeling a chill?"

She was not feeling any chill. She was feeling heat. Rising up, engulfing her. "No, I'm fine."

"I'm sorry I just interrupted your singing, sat down, and started a conversation without asking permission." Again, he looked straight in her eyes as he asked, "Dee, do you mind?"

There was something about him. He didn't touch her, yet she was warm. He was a respectable distance, yet she felt his caress. He was asking about the church choir in the same tone others had suggested something just as recreational, but far more horizontal. They were sitting in a public park, and all she wanted to do was crawl over on her hands and knees and see if his lips were as soft as they looked.

"No, I don't mind at all. I used to sing in the church choir, but I kind of got out of it. Your choir is really good."

"Thanks. They work hard at it. I would love to say that I have something to do with it, but I don't even get to weigh in on the song selection."

"But I saw you singing."

"Guilty, but that's a rare occurrence. Unfortunately, our main soloists were out that day. So I stepped in. Not a big deal."

"Your voice is tremendous."

"So is yours. You should use it for singing for the church instead of … what was that … show tunes."

Dee plucked at the grass and ignored the statement. "Hmm. Do you live around here?"

Reverend Love shrugged. "Close, but no. I was just over at your house inviting Nipsey to church. The word spread that you had another member in your house and he had a hard time. We have some support groups at the church that can help him."

"Do you always make house calls?"

"With a congregation as large as ours? No, I would never get home."

"What makes Nipsey special?"

Reverend Love squinted. "Do you always call your father by his first name?"

Dee shrugged. "Well since he's a father pretty much in name only, so, yes."

"Maybe I'll invite him to the parental support group as well."

Dee snorted. "It's a bit late for that."

"Ahh, you're never too young or too old to need a little help." Reverend Love stood up. "Think about the choir. I think you would be the perfect addition."

"You know, between school and work I may be tapped out right now."

Reverend Love looked down at her. "Some things are worth making time for." He held out his hand and helped her up. "Don't rule it out. Now I have to run. It's a bit of a walk home, but walking helps me clear my head, keeps me in shape." He let go of her hand to pat his flat stomach.

He smiled a bit again and walked away singing the second verse. He turned and winked at her as he continued to make his way out of the park.

Dee started back to the house. *God. There was something ...* she couldn't think of the right word to describe the reverend. He was engaging, but more than that. It was like she was the only person around when he spoke. She felt that at church surrounded by thousands. She felt that today. She hugged herself and turned back in the direction that the reverend had walked. She laughed a bit. He was the total package. He was like ... she couldn't even think. He definitely had the T.I. swag. It was his eyes. That was it. His words were one thing, but his eyes said more.

CHAPTER 18

The spa had an eerie feel on Sundays. This was the second Sunday that Nipsey had met Reverend Love at the spa. He usually got the week's assignments this way. It was always really dark with the exception of the back office.

The reverend rushed in and sat down. "Sorry about that. Early morning service was phenomenal. Our first Sunday program is really going well. So here's your check for last week and the list of duties for this week."

The list included a number of things to fix at one of the rental properties. "You know, I'm not this handy."

"Well do what you can. For the rest of it, I will bring in professionals."

"You know, it would be better if I could tell my aunt that I'm working for you. I don't want her to worry."

The reverend smiled. "You can tell her, but I wouldn't recommend anyone else. Your Auntie M seems like the type that can keep a secret. Just don't want it to appear as if I'm playing favorites in the congregation. You know? She's been such a pillar in the church community. After Pastor Clifton's homegoing, she continued to support the church. That shows loyalty. Loyalty should be rewarded. Now I think we should head over to the church. I would hate to be late for my own service."

Something about this whole setup smelled fishy to Nipsey. Only illegal activities occurred in closed businesses. They could as easily meet in the church. No one would disturb them if he set up a meeting with the good reverend. But no, the reverend insisted that they meet at the spa.

Joe always showed up, too, but he didn't get any assignments. He rarely even talked. He wasn't a bodyguard. He was just there. He would just appear and disappear with no real purpose. *Why was his presence required? Maybe he had to open the spa, but the reverend would have keys to his own business, right?*

Reverend Love jumped into his car and headed back to the church.

Nipsey walked slowly over to the church while Joe leaned against the building smoking a cigarette. Nipsey figured he would be along soon enough. He knew Auntie M and Dee saved him a seat, but he didn't want to be too late. He realized last week that the ushers didn't take too kindly to seat saving or latecomers in the main sanctuary.

Nipsey made it to the church with a little time to spare. The overflow lot buses hadn't started running yet. He walked in the front door and paused at the head of the aisle where Auntie M usually sat. He looked for the row they were in and noticed a few high school boys poking each other and pointing. Following their gaze, he saw Dee. If he knew how to shoot a gun, he'd own twelve just to keep that girl safe. It was different in the city.

Big Rock kept a close eye on her. Shoot, Big Rock had threatened more than one too-eager punk ass. There was a rumor that he had shot off someone's foot for spouting off in great detail about what he wanted to do to Dee.

Nipsey knew for sure there was one guy that not only talked about Dee, but also mentioned Rocky in his drunken delusions. Rumor had it that guy accidently overdosed. It was odd because the guy was just known for having a beer or two. No medicinal wine. No medicinal herbs. No one had ever heard of him doing anything harder. After that though, there wasn't any crazy talk about either of the girls.

But Big Rock wasn't here to keep an eye on Dee. It was left to Nipsey; he didn't have a network or a gun. He hustled up to sit down next to Dee and started mean mugging any hard legs he saw eyeing her. *Maybe he could start working out. He could stand to bulk up a bit because, honestly, even his mean look wasn't enough to scare most people.* He had always been more of a lover than a fighter. He rarely got his hands dirty. He preferred to use his mind. However, as Dee continued to get older, he didn't know if his mind would be enough. He should probably, at the very least, get a big bat. At least now he could afford that bat.

He felt the check in his pocket. He was going to give the whole check to Auntie M. That way she knew the money was on the up and up. She could just give him a budget and he would stick to it.

Odd as their meetings were, Nipsey was grateful for the reverend for giving him a job. The ability to pay his way was a good start. Maybe when he got on his feet, he could find a small place for Dee and him. Not that she would move in with him. She still didn't quite trust him. He would work on that. Who would have thought even thirty days ago that they would be attending church together?

Her words cut pretty deep, but at least she didn't pick up scissors or a knife. She blamed him for a lot. She blamed him for their lack of money, their lack of insurance. She hated every time her mother tried to trust him and hated him even more every time he let the family down. One day her barely concealed anger would turn into tolerance and tolerance would turn into like and like would turn into love. He wasn't sure exactly how many years that would take. She'd probably be about fifty by then.

Even now, he could feel the disdain rolling off of her in waves. It made his back tense up; but once again she hadn't cut him, so it was a start. The choir began to sing, and he directed his attention up to the front.

Dee rocked a bit listening to the music. It was a tight choir. She had heard choirs that had way too many sopranos and ended up sounding like a field of howling cats. This choir was kicking out a *Preacher's Wife*-worthy rendition of "Joy to the World." The congregation was up and clapping. Nipsey looked uncomfortable, like he wanted to bolt any minute. He was wearing the suit he wore when they buried Dee's mother. Dee figured that was the only one that he owned.

Dee leaned over to whisper to Nipsey. "What happened to you being more spiritual than anything else?"

"Well, I figured that with what I'm trying to accomplish, I'll take any help I can get. Plus, I'm not anti-religion. I'm just not pro-religion—at least not organized religion."

Dee harrumphed, unconvinced.

Now that they were at church, she decided to forget about Nipsey and concentrate on her Cinnaman. He was sitting listening to the choir. *What a waste.* That man could blow, but he gave all the singing to the choir. With a voice like his, he should be front and center every service.

The man was damn near a genius. The crowd stayed with him. He didn't lose them once. They cried when he told one story, they rejoiced at another. When his voice lowered, everyone leaned in to listen. He held the whole audience in the palm of his hand. He controlled their every emotion with his words, with his tone, with his message, with his smile. He wound them into a frenzy and then settled them into the rapture. That was more than skill. There was naturalness to Reverend Love. This was truly his calling.

Dee smiled. This man was more than she ever thought she would find. She reminded herself that he was married to a woman who could take her down with complete ease; he also had a psycho stepdaughter. She would do well to remember that.

However, there were times when it was really difficult. There was a time when her mind played tricks on her. She imagined his laugh. She imagined his conversation. She imagined his touch. Those times she couldn't care less that he was a reverend. She wanted the man. She wanted the man with the smile. However, even as she daydreamed, she was acutely aware that if she shifted her gaze a bit to the left, his wife would intrude on the dream. The woman who had every right to sit on the stage with that little arrogant smile—the First Lady of Love.

CHAPTER 19

Nipsey groaned and rolled over. His head. *What the hell happened to his head?* It was like it was full of cotton or something. He knew he went to church yesterday. There was the service and singing. He enjoyed dinner with Dee and Auntie M. Although Dee was less than polite, she had managed to clamp down a bit on the open hostility. Progress. Then he went to bed. As Nipsey opened his eyes, he realized something was different. He turned slowly. Wait. This was not his bedroom. *What the hell?* His groan became more external than internal.

He was trying to think. He woke up this morning. He remembered that he had come to the house to paint. Yeah. He had stopped at the hardware store and stopped by the house to paint. There was a girl. As he struggled to sit up, he noticed there was still a girl sleeping next to him. *Shit. What? Why was the girl sleeping in the bed? In this room? Without clothing?* Nipsey realized she mirrored him. They were both naked. He let out a loud, "Shit."

Naked and hard. He didn't understand. *What the hell?* Obviously, he had sex. The sheets reeked of it. *But why? Why would he do that?* The girl next to him wasn't all that. She was a bit larger than he liked. He hadn't been celibate over the years, but he never had done this except when he was drinking or high. He was supposed to be painting. He had come here to paint. Nipsey lay back down. His movement caused his bedmate to squirm. She reached over and touched him.

"Wow, how could you possibly have anything left?"

"What happened? I don't remember … "

"I don't know how you couldn't remember that. Damn!" She stretched and winced a bit. "I'm going to remember this for a while. Who knew you were packing all of that?"

"I'm sorry. Are you OK?"

She smiled confidently. "Sure Nipsey. I'm fine."

"Were we drinking?"

"No, sweetie. It's illegal to ply me with alcohol."

Nipsey closed his eyes again. He wanted to retreat, but he couldn't. He had a girl that he obviously had sex with in his bed and he didn't remember, and obviously she wasn't old enough to drink. "How old are you?"

She laughed. "Isn't it a little late to ask about my age? Try asking that before the first kiss. Or before the first fuck. Obviously, you didn't care then, why should you care now?"

Nipsey took a deep breath and exhaled slowly.

"OK, you sexy beast," she looked at her watch. "Wow, I'm mega late. I have to go. But since you seem to have a huge gap in your memory, let me fill in a few pertinent details." She sat up and straddled him.

Nipsey tossed her off. "What are you doing? I'm not trying to have sex with strangers."

She tossed her head back. "It's a little late for that lover." She rose up on all fours and kissed him on the cheek. "My name is Evelyn. I go to school with Dee. And you, sexy beast, are one hell of a lay. We will have to do this again."

"Wait, what do you mean you're a friend of Dee's? That's high school. Do you know how old I am? Do you have any clue what you just did?" Nipsey grabbed Evelyn's arm.

Evelyn's smile turned downright chilly. "Really, we're turning this into a domestic. The police would love to get a load of this."

Nipsey dropped her arm. "I don't understand."

"Calm down. It's not like you popped my cherry or something. I saw you around church. You are a fine one. Even for an old man, you're a fine one."

"But I'm old enough to be your father."

Evelyn hopped up and started putting on her clothes. "But you're not. You're a fine ass man who happens to be Dee's dad. I don't see the problem."

"You're a child."

"Not the way we were fucking, I'm not. Trust me when I say, a child doesn't do the things that we did."

"OK. OK. Let me think. Condoms. Did we use condoms?"

"That we did. But only because, with your history, I wasn't sure what was swimming around with your sperm."

"Oh my god. Oh my god." Nipsey jumped up and went to the trash can in the corner and proceeded to puke until only dry heaves were left.

Evelyn watched. "You might want to clean this place up before you leave. Trust me. You wouldn't want word of this getting around. Fucking the poor, impressionable preacher's daughter. That truly isn't a good look."

"What? Who?"

"Oh yeah. Evelyn Stone. My mother is the first lady of the Church of

Love. I'm sure you're already acquainted with Reverend Love, my stepfather. That's how you got here in the first place, right?"

Evelyn finished dressing and strutted out of the door.

Nipsey got up and started getting the house back together. He put the sheets in the washer and got rid of the condoms. He took out the garbage and started painting.

He had to paint. That's why he was here. Someone might wonder if he never got any paint on the wall. So, he painted. The more he painted the more frustrated he got. *What the hell? Where had she come from? Why couldn't he remember?*

He went over all the moments. He walked into the house. She was at the house when he came in the front door. Cleaning. She was there cleaning. She asked him if he wanted something to drink. They only had Coke. He remembered laughing and feeling funny, but not drunk funny. He didn't remember anything after that. He drank the Coke. *What was in the Coke?*

What the hell was going on here? What was he going to tell Dee? She definitely wouldn't believe he had been drugged. She would think he was drunk. Auntie M would kick him out. He was trying. *Why had this happened to him?* He didn't get it.

"She won't tell, you know."

Nipsey almost had a heart attack. He whipped around to see Joe.

"What the hell are you doing here?"

"That girl can keep a secret like no one's business. You would never know she's seventeen."

Nipsey gave up and slid down the wall in a defeated heap. "Tell me."

Joe leaned against the door frame.

"The first time I had her it was similar to your experience. Didn't remember a thing. Over time, I got used to it. Sometimes even enjoyed it. The girl does have a mouth like a vacuum. She was born to suck dick. It's her specialty. She never gets tired. She likes you. She'll be back."

"I don't want to fuck a high school girl. What kind of sick shit is this?"

Joe walked over to the television and took the plastic off and then slid in a DVD. Nipsey was treated to a view of him with Evelyn, clearly a willing participant.

"You no longer have a choice. The difference between our two experiences is she was underage for me. I was facing statutory rape charges. For you, it's only a reputation thing."

"Why?"

Joe looked over and cocked one eyebrow up. "Does it matter?"

Nipsey roared and jumped across the room. He managed to get his hands around Joe's neck and started choking him.

Joe overpowered him and pushed him back across the room. "I'm sorry man. This sucks. I know. Trust me. But it's not bad as you think. Just paint. Go home. No one will ever know."

"What do you want from me?"

Joe smiled. "Amazingly nothing. Not one thing."

"Then why?"

"I don't know. Funny things happen around here all the time. We used to say, 'What the fuck.' Now it's like, 'Hmmm, that's interesting.' It's almost routine now."

"Why? Why isn't anyone asking questions?"

Joe shrugged. "That's probably the oddest part. No one is asking questions. That makes people lose their curiosity. The minute the busiest of the busy bodies started saying, 'Hmmm.' everyone else stopped questioning, too. Someone has all this on lock."

"Who is that someone?"

"No one has ever asked that question. Everyone is afraid of knowing the answer. You know your daughter will never forgive you for this if she ever finds out. Finish your painting. Go home."

"Wait. Reverend Love. He gave me the keys. Why would a reverend pimp his daughter? How could he do that? I don't understand. The DVD. You have to give me the DVD."

Joe shrugged and took the DVD out and tossed it to Nipsey.

"It's not that easy. Unfortunately, that's just a copy. There's always a master. I could give you five of those and it wouldn't matter."

"Why?"

"Leverage. Nothing will ever be simple again. You don't own your life anymore. You are more like renting to own. You could go to the police of course, but you had sex with Evelyn. They won't believe a word coming out of your mouth. You never know when someone is watching or listening. Anything out of pocket could result in this being released."

"But wait. You said it wasn't statutory rape. You said she was old enough."

"No, it isn't. You're lucky that this isn't a prison offense. However, you are just out of rehab and fucking a girl your daughter's age. No, you won't go to jail, but public opinion is a bitch. Can you risk it? Can you risk Dee's reaction? Can you? Just go along like you have been. I'm pretty sure your trip was just an insurance policy against future acts. If someone wanted to put you to work, I would know that already. Really. No one has to know."

"How can I trust that?"

"You just do until you can't anymore." Joe turned to leave. He looked back. "I really am sorry, you know. I hate doing this to people that truly don't deserve it. You didn't deserve this."

"Did you? When it happened to you? Did you deserve it?"

Joe gave a half smile. "Well, there are those who would say I deserve whatever it is I get." Joe shrugged. "Who am I to argue?" With that, Joe walked out of the house.

Nipsey howled and punched the wall. Then he wept. He was so thirsty.

CHAPTER 20

Dee and Auntie M were sitting around the kitchen table.

"Really, Auntie M? I understand the whole eating as a family thing. I do, but he isn't here. He hasn't called and I'm hungry. He could be at a bar somewhere."

Auntie M's eyes snapped, crackled, and popped.

"Alright. He could be out with friends—or working. You said he had a job right? He could be there."

"You're right. I should probably spring for a cell phone for him, but he was so excited about being able to pay his own way I wanted to let him. However, his last check was enough for one of the prepaid phones. You know the pay-as-you go kind. Maybe I'll suggest that to him."

"Good idea. Now can we eat?"

Auntie M stood up and looked out of the window again. "Fine, we can eat."

Dee jumped up and started fixing plates before Auntie M changed her mind. Auntie M was a stickler for tradition and family. She went out of her way to ensure certain things were done a certain way. If possible, dinner was a family affair. They sat at the table together. Short of starving, there was no way for Dee to avoid this.

She had tried to wait it out and then go down later. One night she went down and Auntie M was in the kitchen. She highly recommended that Dee make herself available for dinner when everyone else was eating. Dee started eating at the table with everyone else, but it was clearly under duress. Given the option, she always chose to eat without Nipsey. He ruined her appetite. Unfortunately, it was rarely an option.

Just as Dee started to fix her plate the key was in the lock. *Son of a bitch. He was back.* Dee put her plate back on the table. She knew they were going to wait for Nipsey to get to the table. Nipsey walked in with more paint on his shirt than he could have possible gotten on any wall. It was an odd pattern. It was almost like he kept leaning against wet paint. She could have done better than that.

"Sorry I'm late. You all can go ahead and eat without me."

Auntie M looked at him closely. "Come sit with us anyway."

Nipsey's eyes shifted a bit, but he came to the table and sat. Dee immediately finished serving herself. She blessed the table and started digging in. Nipsey didn't say anything. Something was definitely off. He always made an attempt at conversation, but today was nothing. Auntie M looked puzzled as well, but she wasn't saying anything.

"Did you have a drink today?"

Nipsey turned to Dee. "I told you that I wouldn't do that again and I meant it."

"Well something is wrong and you're stressing Auntie M out so you might as well tell us what's going on?"

Sierra Kay

"There's nothing wrong."

Dee snorted. "As if. Come on, spill it. The faster you come clean, the faster you can pack."

Nipsey glared at Dee. "I have not broken any rules of this house. I'm not going. So you can stop the party I know you are planning in your head. Something at work didn't go the way I thought it would. It just threw me a bit. That's all."

"Looking at your shirt, I would say nothing at your job went the way you thought it was going to today." Dee laughed and took another bite.

Nipsey took a deep breath and turned to Auntie M. "May I be excused? I'd like to get cleaned up."

Auntie M nodded. "Are you OK?"

Nipsey smiled. "Of course."

As he was getting up to leave, Auntie M put her hand on his sleeve. "You know we were just talking about you getting one of those Wal-Mart phones so that if you are late again you can call."

"That's a good idea. I'll do that tomorrow. I may need some more money this week. If you can give me another $50 from the check, I can pick it up tomorrow."

"You sure you don't want me to pick it up for you?"

"You too? I can pick up a damn phone. I'm not drinking. I'm not using drugs. I'm just having a bad day. I'm allowed."

Auntie M looked a bit concerned. Nipsey was on edge. Anyone could see he wasn't settled. This was a different edge than she had seen before. He wasn't drunk. It wasn't hard to tell when Nipsey had been drinking. He was alert and jittery. *What could go wrong with paint?* By the look of his clothes, a whole hell of a lot. Auntie M hoped it was just paint. Anything else would ruin this family she was trying to bring together. She'd let it slide for now. She told Nipsey. "Of course dear, go get cleaned up."

Dee just rolled her eyes.

Nipsey wanted to say something to her, but he let it go. He went to his room to shower and change.

A couple of hours later Auntie M came up to his room. "You do still have a job, don't you?"

"Yeah. I still have a job."

"You want to talk about it."

"How well do you know Reverend Love?"

"That's an odd question."

"Well, he's my boss, but I rarely see him. I mean, he doesn't seem to check my work at the site. I was just wondering what kind of man I'm working for."

"Did you mess up that bad?"

Nipsey shook his head. "No, nothing like that."

Auntie M shrugged, but she was still studying Nipsey. Something was off, but she didn't know if she was going to get it out of him. "Well, I don't know him really well. Nothing personal anyway. He's married and has a stepdaughter. Outside of that, not too much."

"Do you know where he came from before he came here?"

Auntie M's radar went up. She'd let Nipsey go down this path for a while. However, she may need to reel him in. Having issues with his boss was bad business. She jumped up, went downstairs, and came back up again with a piece of paper.

"I was part of the selection committee. I have his resume right here.

Here are the references he used. They all check out. Nothing much here, but if you just want some general information, this seems to be as good a place as any to start. I just know he has brought a lot to the congregation."

"Any church rumors about him? Usually the parishioners know stuff before the police."

Auntie M smiled and then laughed. "Police? Do you think he's stealing money from the church? Are you sure you're going to be OK?"

Nipsey reached over and hugged Auntie M a bit desperately. "Yeah, I'm good. Scout's honor. Let me just have my bad day. I'll be better tomorrow."

Auntie M nodded and left the room.

Nipsey lay down and looked up at the ceiling. He needed a plan. He got up and looked at the resume. It seemed Reverend Love didn't have significant church experience when he came to the Church of Love. He did work at a couple of other smaller congregations.

Nipsey knew from having been fired from a number of jobs that they would just as easily give a good recommendation as a bad. Most of the time, **they figured as long as he wasn't their problem; then good luck to the next** employer. He wondered about the truth of these earlier places of employment. He knew he wouldn't get anything over the phone. He planned on visiting these churches to see what they were about.

He didn't have a car, but the good reverend did offer the rental wheels. He looked at the churches. These would at least be overnight trips. He needed some leverage of his own. He wondered if the good reverend had gotten down with the nympho stepdaughter. That would be leverage. Apparently, this girl was getting down with anyone. Joe probably knew more than the average bear, but he had his own issues that he was trying to work through. He didn't think Joe was up for this. Nipsey didn't have a choice. He had worked with enough shady people to know they couldn't be trusted. At some point, his number would come up. At that point, he would lose everything.

Big Rock had already warned him that he wouldn't get any more chances from him. Nipsey owed more people in Chicago than just Big Rock. They wanted to make an example of Nipsey. They wanted everyone to know what happened when you didn't pay your debt. It was beyond the point of cash. It had reached the point of disrespect. Big Rock kept the vultures at bay. He wrote a check with the promise that if Nipsey didn't stay straight, they could have him. Given Nipsey's history, they took the deal. They figured it was only a matter of time before he screwed up again. This way, they had their money and, with a little patience, they could have Nipsey as well.

Then there was Dee. He couldn't, wouldn't under any circumstances fuck up her world again. He didn't know what the hell he had walked into, but it smelled like shit. He had to get to one of those churches. He would be damned if he got clean and sober just to be screwed by a crooked pastor.

He could have used Ilene's help. She saw things a bit more clearly than he did. He could always figure out the next step. She could figure out the next five steps and how people would react to each. She was good at that. Nipsey smiled.

She was good at a lot. He didn't know how he ended up that lucky. Even though she was only with them for a little while, it was worth it. Every minute with her was worth it. It was a crap shoot most days now. Sometimes he could remember her with joy in his heart. Other times, it was a crippling depression. Just knowing that he could feel that joy at times made it easier to get through the crippling depression.

He dealt a lot with what could be, the possibilities of life. That was what motivated him. There were times like now when the present was a horrendous experiment. However, he learned that he could live through the present. He had a daughter to think of and Dee meant everything and deserved even more. He wasn't raised to be a drunken, drugged-out bastard. He was going to show his daughter that there was more to him. He'd be damned if some punk bitch was going to get in the way of the last chance he would get.

CHAPTER 21

Dee looked down the hallway. Damn. Evelyn was coming straight for her with that look on her face. Dee hadn't seen that look in a long time. Normally, Evelyn would whisper to her friends or pretend that Dee didn't exist. Today, there was a confrontational glint in her eye and that was never good.

Things had started to settle down a bit at home. Nipsey was still trying to befriend her. He'd occasionally cook her breakfast. Since she had promised Auntie M she would give him a chance, she didn't feel right straight out skipping breakfast. So she suffered in silence. Even when he tried to engage her in conversation, she limited her responses to one- or two-word answers.

Auntie M filled in the silence with chatter. It was amazing how much Auntie M knew about the church families. Dee thought the church was way too large to really get to know anyone. However, Auntie M had two things going for her. She was one of the founding members so she knew all the original members and her best friend was the church secretary. Apparently gossip flowed freely from her mouth to Auntie M's ears. Auntie M generously shared the gossip with them. Thank goodness she did. Otherwise, Dee and Nipsey would be stuck.

Dinner was a different matter altogether. They only ate dinner together a couple of times a week. Dee was often busy at the spa or Nipsey was busy doing the church errands, which mostly centered on the properties the church owned and managed. With his track record or lack thereof, it wasn't like there were other people beating down his door to offer employment. He had the nerve to be hostile when his boss called him in and he had the occasional use of the church car. In Atlanta, you couldn't get around without some mode of transportation. The most he ever walked was a mile to pick up a car to go handle whatever business was required of him. The fact that he wasn't more appreciative rankled Dee. That's why she didn't deal with Nipsey at home.

The only positive to the situation was that Nipsey was becoming a regular handy man. She never remembered him so much as changing a light bulb. Now he would do what he knew and figure out what he didn't know. She would pass him in the evenings after she got off work, and he'd be at the kitchen table pouring over some home improvement book and taking notes. The list of things he could do was growing by the week, which was good because once his attitude got him fired from the church job he'd at least be marketable.

Dee's bedroom became her new sanctuary. She always claimed to be doing homework or studying and stayed in her room for hours. Auntie M refused to let her get a television. It wasn't as if this would be the first time Auntie M bought Dee a television. She even promised not to sell this one. Auntie M was adamant. She didn't believe in television in the bedroom. You can study in a bedroom or sleep in a bedroom. However, Dee had the run of the house for anything else.

Even the computer was stationed in the alcove by the kitchen. So any assignments needing the computer were completed at school or by staying late at the spa. Mrs. Love was gone by early evening. Dee kept her own jump drive and she used the office computer. She hadn't seen television in weeks, could be as long as a month by now. If it wasn't for the news on her cell phone, she'd be completely out of touch with what was happening in the world. Dee had even asked her aunt to upgrade her cell phone so that she could watch television shows; Auntie M was not buying it. So Dee was cut off from communications as a part of a self-imposed exile in her room.

Sometimes she would still look out and see Joe on his porch. She sort of missed talking to him. She still didn't really have any close friends here. She had her coworkers, but they weren't friends. Her female co-workers didn't fully agree with the attention she received from some of the male stylists. And the males that spoke to her usually also tried to ask her out. She didn't really get into the geriatric crowd like that. Her friends at school were cool, but she didn't really trust them with her deep dark secrets. So she had a lot of personal time with herself. She so needed a hobby.

And last night, Nipsey stopped by her room. He had access to everything. With all of that, what did he do? He came to her room. He made some half-hearted joke about the mountain coming to Mohammed and then he, her own father, asked her on a date. Not a creepy pedophile type thing, but a father/daughter reconnecting date. Funny thing is that they had never connected in the first place. So the "re" part of that was lost on Dee.

She said she was too busy between work and school. She really didn't have enough time for other activities. So what did he do? He suggested Sunday. The spa was closed. She could work on her homework before they left. *What the hell?* Now she was going to be trapped with Nipsey without Auntie M in the mix.

She wasn't in the best of moods. Between that and Evelyn and her cat-that-caught-the-canary look, Dee suspected her day was just about to get worse, much worse.

Evelyn sidled up to Dee. "So I've noticed your dad around the church. That is your father, right?"

Dee mentally sent up a prayer that this girl wasn't going to do something that was going to force Dee to knock her the fuck out. Then she sent up another quick prayer for patience. She guessed she should have prayed for peace; but with her mood, patience was probably more of a stretch. She hoped she didn't get pissed off past her ability to control her right hook.

"Yes, that's my dad."

"Hmm. That alcohol he's been consuming over the years must have helped preserve that fine specimen of a man."

"Really. Really. You're scoping out my dad. My dad. You know how old I am. You know he has to be double that."

"But he is well put together. He's sort of like The Rock." Evelyn checked the hallway and then leaned in closer to Dee. "You know he's probably old enough to be someone's father. However, if he showed up naked on my bed, I'd ride that until he was raw and screaming for mercy."

"I can definitely understand how someone fucking you would be screaming for mercy ... for their eyes. Damn, you have a twisted imagination for a preacher's kid."

"Well, see I wasn't always a preacher's kid; and according to everyone else, I'm a paragon of virtue." Her eyes narrowed. "Wouldn't you agree?"

"I agree that everyone believes that you are a paragon of virtue."

Evelyn leaned back her head and laughed. "Well put. I've got to be heading out. But I'd keep a close eye on that dad of yours. At least a closer eye than I've been keeping," she said as she flounced away.

Dee watched Evelyn. Something had changed. Something was wrong with that interaction. Evelyn was too … she was too happy? No. She was too … in control. It was like something had changed. It was like there were new rules and Dee didn't know them. Evelyn wasn't after Dee anymore. She didn't attack her. She didn't verbally abuse her. She didn't make her life difficult. It was if they had played a game and she had already won. That's it. Evelyn was gloating and Dee didn't know about what.

Dee continued to walk down the hallway wracking her brain about what had happened. Somehow Evelyn had leveled the playing field. *Could she have?* Dee shuddered. There was no way her dad would even think about Evelyn. She wasn't his type in so many ways. One, she was too young. He had always been uncomfortable with the attention Dee garnered. He called the men in the neighborhood that talked about her some choice names, of which pedophile was the cleanest. Two, he liked his women like her mother. Tall and gorgeous. He had dated tall and average, but he never dated short women. It wasn't in him. So that couldn't be it. Maybe Evelyn knew who he was messing around with and knew Dee wouldn't approve. That was a distinct possibility. Hell, Nipsey hadn't been celibate when her mother was alive, he sure as hell wouldn't be celibate now that she's …

Tears sprang to Dee's eyes. She rushed down the hall to the bathroom. There was no way she was making it to class on time, and she didn't care. This happened sometimes. She would be fine. She would just be chilling, enjoying her internal monologue, thinking about life. All of a sudden, she'd think about her mom and she would just want to sit down wherever she was and cry. Just like that. It would take all that was in her to keep it together. Sometimes she had to pretend she was having an allergy attack. The sorrow would be so sudden that she had no time to prepare for it. All of a sudden she would just break down.

She went into a stall in the bathroom and stayed there for about ten minutes until the tears stopped streaming down her face. It wasn't that she wasn't grateful for Auntie M, but she just really wished her mom was still alive. *Was that too much to ask? That her mom was alive and healthy. That she was still in Chicago. That Rocky was going to stop by any moment.* She had a life there. She existed here. She went to work. She went home. She didn't go anywhere. She didn't have anyone to talk to.

She couldn't go back to class. She knew how close to the edge she was. She knew that the least little thing would bring her back here. She decided to skip it. Literally. She walked right out of the front door and headed home. She just couldn't deal. Not today.

Dee saw Joe on his front porch this time as she arrived home. She went directly to his house. "Hey."

"I thought you weren't allowed to talk to me."

"I'm not."

"K. Aren't you supposed to be in school?"

"I couldn't. Not today. She's going to have a cow about that. So what if talking to you is off limits?" Dee sighed and sat on the steps. "What happened to your dad? How come you never mention him?"

"Shit. I don't know. He disappeared years ago. You know my mother, Ms. Minnie as she's called by the congregation." Joe held up his hand as if to testify. "Well, she used to say he just wasn't ready to be a father. He had me and then he would disappear for a few days in a row. My mother knew he was cheating, but she was a single parent with a newborn. What was she going to do? I do know that my mother found him having sex with someone in her bed. He was gone after that. I guess it's one thing to know, but something else for someone to sleep in the bed you're working to keep a roof over.

"My parents were pretty up there when I was born. So it's not like he was too young to handle having a child. Shit. By that age, everyone knows where babies come from. I was a surprise. Anytime a forty-year-old single woman has a baby by a forty-three-year-old single man, and neither one of them has any other children, it's a shocker." Joe laughed. "She thought she was going through the change early."

Dee smiled. "It must have been hard."

"I don't know. I guess it would have been harder if he was here constantly and I depended on him and he disappeared. I'm pissed, but I'm not shocked about it." Joe sat down beside Dee. "Thinking about your mom?"

"Yeah. I just don't know how I'm supposed to do this without her. I'm so lonely. I think it's actually worse with Nipsey being here. I mean he's all trying to be my friend and everything. It makes me miss her more. I didn't deal with Nipsey when she was alive. Not like this. I mean, I saw him and everything, but my parent was my mom. Nipsey was some guy who came around occasionally.

"Now I have Nipsey trying to be a father, which would be laughable if it didn't make me miss my mom more. She didn't have to try. She was my mother. And then Auntie M is looking at me with those huge eyes. Everything she feels is in those eyes. When she's happy, it's there. When she's pissed at me, it's there. When she wants me to try harder, it's there. And when she pities me, it's there. Her poor little orphan niece, right there in those eyes. It makes me want to scream and cry at the same time." Dee swiped at her face. "This is why I had to leave school. This is why I couldn't stay. I'm having a breakdown."

Joe held her as she began to cry in earnest. This was new for him. He was so used to playing games and having games played on him that he had truly forgotten real emotion. Now, he was sitting here with Dee in his arms and he wasn't even thinking about hitting that. Well, a little when she inhaled and those breasts pressed up against his chest. Mostly he just wanted her to be OK.

In the middle of her crying jag, he noticed her aunt pulling up. She did a double take and almost plowed her car into another one in the street. He took his hand and beckoned her over. At first she looked like she was ready to curse someone out; he was the likely candidate. Then seeing the shape Dee was in, she just sat down on one of the lower steps and touched her shoe.

Dee looked up. "I'm sorry. I know I'm not supposed to be here."

"You want to tell me why you're here at Joe's house crying during school hours," Auntie M said in a soft, sort of understanding voice as she played with her emerald ring.

"School was just ... I was there and ..."

Joe rubbed her arm. "She misses her mom."

Auntie M's eyes started to change to the poor-niece look. Joe shook his head.

"But what she could really use is someone to tell her ass that she can't just flood a player's shirt like this. It ain't a good look walking around with a wet spot in the middle of your chest. Looks like I'm lactating or some shit. Can't pick up a dime like that."

Dee hit him. "A dime isn't going to holla at you anyway. Not while you're living in the basement like some deranged serial killer." Dee wiped her eyes. "I'm sorry Auntie M. We can go home now."

Auntie M scrutinized Joe. "Can I trust you with my niece?"

Joe had a sad smile. "Unfortunately, the answer to that question is yes."

This time Auntie M hit him.

She patted Dee's leg. "Stay on the front porch. He is still a man and way too old. But maybe he's got a drop of good blood in him after all. Go ahead and finish your chat." She pushed herself up and headed back to her car parked that she had managed to steer to the edge of their driveway.

"Sorry about that. I normally don't have those kinds of breakdowns."

"Yeah well, I'm normally not that understanding. So whatever."

Dee perked up. "Oh, you're not going to believe this. Your little friend Evelyn."

Joe started to stiffen up.

"She has a thing for my dad. I think she's going to make a play for him. As if. She is so not his type. I mean I know she doesn't have many limits, but you'd think she'd stop trying to run through the congregation. How could that not get back to her mother? Or even Reverend Love? I mean, come on. Thank goodness that my dad has standards when it comes to women. Can't say that about everything he does."

Joe smiled a little. "Yeah, crazy."

"I know."

"How do you know she has a thing for him?" Joe asked in what he hoped was a nonchalant tone.

"She came to me in the hall and was all like, 'Your dad is all that, alcohol must have preserved him, blah blah blah. He's like The Rock. I'd do him, too.'"

Joe tried to look innocent as he asked, "That was all she said?"

Dee shrugged. "More or less. Those were the high points. Why?"

"Well, she could have, uh, just been commenting."

"No, you didn't see her look. It was an I've-got-a-secret look. She might even have pushed up on him already. I'm going to ask him when he gets home."

"For real? How do you ask your dad if your classmate has tried to sleep with him?"

Dee shrugged. "Well, I was just going to ask. Wait. If I ask, that may lead to a conversation. Or ... " Dee wiggled her eyebrows.

Joe shook his head. "I'm not asking your dad or Evelyn shit."

Dee sighed. Then she gave her best seductive smile while trailing a finger down his thigh. "Not even for me?"

Joe looked bored. "Not even for some high school chick who has the audacity to bat her eyelashes at me when we both know it's not giving me anything."

Dee's eyes twinkled. "Well, I figured since you've been there …"

Joe lifted his eyebrows. "You have no proof. All you know is that I'm a wealth of information and you benefitted from that. That's it."

"But I have my suspicions."

"Yeah, well suspicions aren't proof. Hell, sometimes proof isn't even proof."

"What the hell are you talking about?"

"Nothing. Let me know how that conversation goes."

"Right. I probably won't ask him. That would require me to say more than two words to him at a time. Evelyn is so not worth that much effort. I just thought it was a bit funny, a bit creepy, and more than a bit slutty that she would come and tell me that she wanted to do my dad. Who does that?"

Joe grunted. "Obviously, Evelyn. You better go. M let you hang, but that curtain moves every few minutes."

Dee looked over her shoulder and laughed. "Well, if nothing else came out of this, we're at least friends again—at least in public areas in full view of my aunt."

Joe leaned in, dropped his voice, and gave Dee a quick once over. "But just so we're clear. If you give me the go-ahead, and I mean the real go-ahead not that contrived shit that you just tried, I'll work that shit out until the neighbors know my name."

"They know it already. It's degenerate, right?"

Joe shrugged and leaned back. "Then I'll see you tonight on the back porch."

"Right! She'd love to peak out of her window and see me sucking down a beer on your back porch. That wouldn't go over at all. Her little ass would run you over with that Escalade before you even got two steps beyond your yard. But you'll see me around."

Joe gave her a half smile. "Run along, little girl."

"Whatever." Dee turned and walked across the grass to her house.

Joe leaned back on the porch. This was new. Evelyn truly hated Dee.

She usually was way more discreet. Now she was damn near putting her business on the street. And she definitely didn't want her business out on the street. She had so many skeletons that she upgraded from closets to storage units years ago. Only the devil knew how low that girl was. She probably fucked him, too.

She actually had two sixes tattooed on her inner thigh. He had asked her one time about the third, but she said she hadn't earned that one yet. She was at church. Every Sunday. Front row, looking up at her stepdaddy as he preached the word. She wouldn't let all that come crashing down. *Would she?*

He started running scenarios in his head. He assumed that Evelyn had been directed to trap Nipsey. However, what if that wasn't the case? What if she had done that on her own? There was only one way to find out, but if it wasn't approved then his involvement would be problematic. He had one goal. That was to get one big take and get the hell out of Oz. Things were precarious to begin with and now with Dee in the mix, they were even worse.

What the hell kind of game was Evelyn playing? The only reason this was going to stay under wraps was because Dee was hating on Nipsey worse than Evelyn was hating on her. He knew that Nipsey wouldn't tell his daughter about Evelyn. At least he strongly doubted it. With their relationship in shambles, it's doubtful that it would survive the news that he slept with a classmate, regardless of the reason or in this case the drug.

Joe looked back over at Dee's house. All the plans were set and now this. Shit. Just like life. He gave a self-deprecating laugh. What was the saying? "If you want to make God laugh, tell him about your plans." Joe laughed. *Ain't that the truth.*

CHAPTER 22

In the deepest crevices of Dee's mind, she was rolling her eyes. Constantly. *So this is what hell feels like.* She felt more at ease in the hood with the hard legs on her tail than she felt sitting across the table from her own father in a restaurant. It was actually a pretty nice sports bar in Atlantic Station. The real benefit of a sports bar was that there was always a television to help pass the time. The bad thing was you could only watch sports. Dee had never been much of a sports person, and yet here she was trying to get into a football game.

The broadcasters were talking about blitzes and routes. All of which was going completely over her head. All she knew about football was that a man was given the ball and he was supposed to head for the end zone. He made it. Yay! He didn't. Boo! And then they try again. Or they ran out of chances and the other team got to try.

There was another benefit of a sports bar. They were growing some fine brothers in Atlanta. The eye candy was definitely well represented. There were cute guys at her school of course, but they were on some bullshit. These brothers had jobs. They were paying bills. That's what she was talking about. However, she had heard there were a lot of rump rustlers in Atlanta, so it would stand to reason that some of these brothers wouldn't even look her way.

However, some of them were. Her dad was surely blocking her action. The most she had been able to do was shamelessly flirt with the waiter. Given where his eyes kept landing, he was definitely on the right team. Her father had to clear his throat twice and then threw her business in the street. It wasn't that man's business that she was still in high school. It wasn't like she was planning on going home with him or anything. She just liked the attention. But it did remind her that in between mental breakdowns, she needed to seriously figure out the dating situation.

She was so embarrassed by her breakdown in front of Joe. That was not sexy at all. She was supposed to be all hard and strong and what happens? She has such a breakdown that she has to leave school and cry on the shoulder of the one friend she had. He was only half a friend at best because she knew he would have no problem rocking the sheets with her. With him at least there were boundaries. He didn't cross them. That in itself was worth gold.

Another fine man walked by and Dee followed him with her eyes. Fuck a Joe, this was where it was.

Nipsey looked at his daughter and watched as her eyes followed the young man who passed the table. Her eyes had been following pretty much every young man that walked past. He was going to need to pick up a gat or a club. This was ridiculous. Yes, she looked like a grown woman, but she wasn't. Apparently, she didn't have any issues with older men.

Look at her relationship with Joe. Auntie M had told him about the incident when she was supposed to be at school. He had wanted to talk to her about it, but he didn't know how to approach the subject. Auntie M figured it was fine to just let it go. She just needed a few boundaries.

The last time he tried to give her boundaries, she literally laughed at him. It wasn't even a chuckle. It was a full-on, grab-your-gut, get-a-cramp, run-out-of-breath laugh. She was still laughing as she walked away. Auntie M said she'd talk to Dee, but this was his issue to deal with. He had to figure out a way to get into this. Dee listened to Auntie M. There wasn't any arguing or talking back or loud guffaws. Auntie M would ask Dee to do something and it was done.

He asked, and Dee either ignored him or laughed. She would ask if his arms had strangely broken in the middle of the night. Sometimes Auntie M intervened, but he had to get a handle on this. At least he was working now—working and not drinking. Since he was not drinking, he wasn't smoking anything legal, illegal, or any gray areas in between. Here he was at a sports bar where the mere tinkle of ice in a glass was a reminder that he could make all the discomfort go away.

The last time he drank in front of Dee, she pulled out her own beer. He couldn't even stop her because she had paid for the beer. There was no better way to make him feel like a dickless turd than to drink alcohol purchased by his sixteen-year-old daughter. He was tired. So no matter how bad it felt, he wasn't going to drink. Drinking alone was a bad decision. When he was drinking, he got into other things. *That was not happening. Well, not again anyway.*

No matter how evil she was, he was going to have a relationship with his daughter. Sometimes at night he would go to her room and watch her sleep. She was a miracle. The best of Ilene and him. So strong. So independent. He was proud of her. She was definitely stronger than he was. So he'd watch her just breathe. It was a heady experience to know he had a role in this young lady. Not a huge role, but still … One day Auntie M saw him in the room and came in and sat beside him. He whispered. "Does she talk to you?"

Auntie M had a sad smile. "She talks to me all the time. But not about anything that matters. Do you know she doesn't have one real friend here? I look at her cell phone bill when it comes in and most of the calls are to me, the house, and the spa. That has to be a really lonely existence."

Nipsey turned back to watching Dee. "How do you think she manages?"

"She just does. I don't know. When I saw her turning to Joe, at first I wanted to cut off his dick."

Nipsey's eyes bugged. "Auntie M!"

This time it was Auntie M giving the familiar eye roll. "I may be old, but I can still handle mine if the need arises." Auntie M raised her hand to the ceiling. "Have mercy. But as a church-going woman, I'd take him to the doctor afterward of course. The more I thought about Dee's situation, I realized, if not him, who? At least he's next door and I can try to keep an eye on him. We know he's evil, but if he can help her, bolster her, who am I to say no?"

Nipsey blew out a breath. "Yeah, but I'm not too comfortable with that either."

"But look at her. It can't be her against the world. That's not right either."

Nipsey nodded and they just continued to watch her sleep.

Now sitting across from her, he had exhausted all of his small talk. It wasn't as if he had an abundance of it anyway. She was pretending to watch football and not pretending to watch men.

"So, Dee, I heard you were doing well in school."

"I always do well in school."

"Oh. Well, what subjects do you like?"

"Any subjects that will allow me to graduate."

"Does that worry you? Graduating?"

"I just need to make sure I get to college and can take care of myself. You know I'm a kid, so depending on adults at my age is fine. But I don't want to be knocking on forty and need to move in with my elderly aunt. Not a good look."

It wasn't a good look, but clearly it is a good dig on Nipsey.

The waiter came with their food. Dee immediately dug in as if she hadn't eaten in about five years.

Nipsey figured she was trying to rush this meal along.

Earlier that evening when she had come down the stairs at the house, he had to do a double take. She did something she rarely did. She wore her hair down. He didn't know if she intentionally kept her hair in a ponytail. He didn't know if she realized how much she looked like her mother. It was everything, everything except the eyes. The eyes gave her away every time. Ilene had happy eyes. They were always laughing—sometimes a bit mischievous. Even if she was cursing you out, you knew fifteen minutes later she would find something to bring her joy back. She didn't let anyone steal her joy. After everything she went through, everything he put her through, she never looked at him like their daughter did.

Dee came down the stairs in over-the-knee, high-heel boots that were way too grown up for her. He asked if she thought she should change her shoes. Her eyes, which had been frosty, turned serial-murderer cold. "They were Mom's." She brushed past him and headed for the door.

Ilene's eyes lit up every room she entered. Dee's eyes chilled you straight to the bone and shattered every good intention. It had become easier to just let her go. He figured eventually she would run out of hate. Apparently, her hate was a bottomless pit and it wasn't going anywhere. So he brought her out to talk to her. He wanted to try for them to at least get on the same page. However, Dee still had little use for him.

"You know Dee, it is a disease."

Dee stopped and put her fork down. She inhaled deeply. "OK. I'll bite. What is a disease?"

"Alcoholism. It's a disease."

Dee narrowed her eyes even more. All Nipsey saw were two slits of hazel. He just hoped they would make it out of the restaurant without the police being called. *Damn this girl was evil.*

"Hmmph. Alcoholism and drug addiction are diseases. Yeah, I've heard that. But guess what? So is cancer. Mom didn't pick up a bottle to get cancer. She didn't go to the crack house to get a cancer hit. She didn't go to the store repeatedly to pick up a bit of that cancer. She didn't borrow money because she ran out of cancer and needed more cancer. *It* was a disease. *It* killed her. You're an *alcoholic*. You're a *drug addict*. You'll have to fight the temptation every day of your life. You have a choice to drink or not, to take a hit or not. You want me to feel sorry for you? Find a pine box and bury yourself six feet under and I'll think about it."

By this time Dee's voice had started to rise and people were beginning to stare.

Nipsey started to whisper. "You said you'd give this a chance."

Dee gave a fake smile. "I am. I showed up to this father/daughter fiasco. That took effort."

"I'd like for us to be able to talk."

Dee ran her hand through her hair. "We are talking. See you say something, I respond. That's called a conversation. Look it up." She picked up her fork again and started plowing through her food.

Nipsey barely touched his. This was how it was between them now. There was a time when she loved him. Even with his faults, she loved him. He was still her daddy. It wasn't even gradual. One day she just looked at him like he was shit. The look hadn't changed since.

"When did it change?"

Dee gave an exasperated. "What change?"

"Us. When did it change? When did I stop being your dad and became Nipsey?"

144   From Behind the Curtain

"I guess you wouldn't remember in your drunken, drug-induced haze." She put her fork down. "There was only one vacation that I ever remember my mother taking. It was to Vegas. You know she was so excited. I helped her pick out what to take. I helped her pack. She glowed. There is no other way to explain it. And when she came back without a husband … "

Dee looked Nipsey in the eye. "You broke her in a way that I had never seen before. She kind of blew it off and told me about the other things she had seen before she boarded a plane days early for her return flight. I remember that night so well. She cried. I mean if she was sobbing I would have understood, but she just lay on her back and tears streamed out her eyes. Dude. You were sober. There is a difference between being an alcoholic/addict and an asshole. You happened to corner the market on both."

Dee quit eating and stood. "Can you just pay the check? I'm ready to go."

Nipsey stopped her. "You don't owe me this, but can you give me five minutes? There is more to that story. Please."

Dee sat down.

Nipsey took a deep breath. Honesty was a tricky thing. Lying was so much easier. He could have crafted a story that could have wrenched the common woman's heart. He was good at it. Dee wasn't a common woman. She didn't have the time or the patience for his bullshit. He didn't want them to get worse than they already were.

The whole story did not put him in a good light. It gave him a reason, but not an alibi or absolution. Actually, she would probably hate him just a little bit more for being weak, for not doing the right thing.

Nipsey thought back to those days in Vegas. Dee was right. Ilene was glowing. She would walk down the street and perfect strangers would smile because she was smiling. She made friends with everyone. The hotel staff from the concierge to the front desk to the wait staff became her best friends. She had spun a web around everyone. She had that impact on people. Matter of fact, some people had asked for an autograph, sure that she was some film star. Ilene gave it happily. She was a cloud of perfection.

Nipsey wanted more than anything to marry her. He wanted to spend his life basking in her rays, but there was a problem. His ex-girlfriend was pregnant. He had just found out. He thought that he would marry Ilene and deal with the fallout later. She would be his. It would be difficult for her to leave. She took marriage seriously. Getting married is a whole hell of a lot easier than getting a divorce.

He had given the ex the name of the hotel they were staying at. He had to. She was pregnant with his baby. He had no choice. And she kept calling until she got a hold of Ilene. There was a temper carefully hidden in Ilene that no one ever saw. Hell, he'd only seen it that one time. She cursed that woman out from one side of the room to the other. Later, when Nipsey got a hold of his ex, she said that if Ilene didn't apologize he would never see his child. So Nipsey had to ask. And Dee was right. Ilene's eyes shattered right in front of him. She declined and started to pack. Nothing Nipsey said would change her mind. He watched the only good thing in his life walk out of the door.

His ex-girlfriend went into early labor two weeks later. The baby didn't make it. He went from a functioning alcoholic back to being an addict. He went into a spiral so fast, so deep. His ex was a trick. He didn't love her. She was just someone to hang with until Ilene got back on. But his son. He wanted his son. He loved his son already. He already had one miracle in Dee and he was so looking forward to the other. It wasn't meant to be, but he always wondered. Why? Why didn't he make it? Of all the children in the world, why was he called back to heaven before he took one step on earth? It was the question that drove him crazy. There was only one way to quiet his mind.

And the mother, Paula, didn't deserve to lose her child any more than Ilene deserved what he did to her. He had lost so much. So much. He tried to climb out of it, but it was too painful. He was flawed. He wasn't a man. Since he wasn't a man, he lost his love and his baby boy. He didn't deserve life.

Ilene did something extraordinary. She brought him back. She worked to get him straight and functioning in society. He couldn't imagine what strength it took for her to do that. After what he did to her, what he asked of her, she still did something so selfless that every day it astounded him. She was his rock. Always. He was never that strong. He might never get there.

After a while, he realized he would always be a disappointment to her. If they had gotten married, he would have changed her. Marriage to him would have turned that pure joy for life into something dark. So he would leave—often. He would just disappear to try to make it on his own, to give her the opportunity she deserved to make a life without him. It was never to hurt her, even though it did. It was to free her. She knew it in theory, but it still broke her heart every time. She loved him anyway—in her own way.

Ilene never really left him. Sure, she talked a good game; but since he always came back; she got into the habit of waiting.

Their relationship, whether he was there or not, always brought a strain to her voice and a cloud in her eyes. He would leave her and at the same time hang on to her for dear life. He couldn't function without her in his orbit.

He should have been strong enough to let her go completely. He should have been strong enough to walk away. He should have sacrificed himself for her. He wasn't her. He might never be. But she showed him what he needed to be. So now he was sober and trying. He would never be the pure joy that she was. Different personalities. Different experiences. But he could start with the truth.

He would be as honest as he could with Dee. He would start there. All he asked is that she wait and see. If she thought he earned some consideration, then she'd give it. That's it. That's all. He'd do all the work. Now he realized he had to be more in every way. He'd have to be better in every way. He would have to work every day. He would never be to Dee what Ilene was, but he could be a better father than she had ever known in the past. That was his commitment to her.

Dee looked at him. He could see her mind processing all of the information that he had just provided.

"Can we leave now?"

Nipsey hung his head. He had wanted more, but this was a war, not a battle.

Nipsey watched the restaurant as they were leaving. Nowadays he always looked around to see who was watching them. Sometimes he really had to eyeball a fucka before they looked away. As usual, his grown-up looking daughter was garnering all the wrong attention. The only thing helping him maintain his sanity was realizing that some of these guys, the ones with their ladies, were going to be in a world of hurt tonight. Some of those ladies looked pissed as hell.

He held the door open for Dee as she walked out. It was eerily quiet between them. This was a different kind of quiet. He was used to the why-the-hell-is-that-my dad quiet or the tension and animosity-filled quiet. This quiet was different. Her mind was processing, and he didn't know what side of the argument she was going to come out on. He hoped it would lead to a better understanding of him. But honestly, it wasn't like he told a story about how he saved a puppy in a tree or some shit like that. It wasn't a heroic act of kindness.

He had let her mother down, and Dee did not play with her mother at all. Fuck with her mother, and she was ready to cut a bitch. Even if the bitch was the only living parent she had left. In this episode of "The Fucked-up Life of Nipsey Bell," he had fucked over her mother (part of which she knew, a whole lot of which she didn't), he had screwed over a perfect stranger, he had lied to her, and had omitted the existence of a relative. Damn, he *had* done a lot of fucking up, but it was the truth. That was who he was. He wanted them all to be happy. He wanted it to work out for everyone; it hadn't worked out for anyone.

He would like to say he had turned a new leaf. He was working. He was working for the devil, but the cash was nice. He was stacking his money. One day he was going to have to quit this gig and find a real one. So he was going to have to be prepared for that. But if he was starting this new part of his life by being honest, he would have to admit at some point about all the crazy that was swirling around him. He'd have to admit that he slept with a high school girl and a classmate of Dee's. Even the thought of it made the bile rise in his mouth.

He guessed for all the shit he had pulled for all the years, he was due for something. He wasn't going to keep getting free chances. He was going to have to start earning some of those chances. Dee insisted that alcoholism wasn't a disease, but she had no idea how thirsty he could get. It didn't stop at alcohol. The drugs really brought him down. Mostly, he left his drinking for the evenings. But when drugs make their way into the mix, it was a wrap. Day, night, or anytime in between, he wanted a hit. That was one good thing about working with his hands. When it was really bad, he kept working until he was too delirious to think about a drink. Then he headed home.

In his meetings, he listened to other parents and their fear that their children might follow in their footsteps. He should have listened to his cousin Dotty. She told him to watch out. She said that alcoholism ran in their family. She had dealt with it and wanted to save him from what she went through. He didn't think that it would ever control his life like it did.

One thing he didn't have to worry about was Dee. She would never become an addict. Not because she was better than any other member of their family; she was stubborn in a different way. There was something in her that didn't want to be anything like him. While that was a painful thought, that alone would keep her sober.

He should have tried a different tack to explain what he went through and what he was still going through. She used to love those vampire movies. He should have described it like Blade and the thirst. Some people had the thirst and succumbed to it. Some people took medication to abate it. Some people found a way to cure themselves. It depended on the soul and strength of the individual. He knew, even sitting in his meetings, that all those there were probably not going to live clean and sober. It was a good idea, but the truth was, some would give up on the daily struggle. It happened before; it would happen again.

At this point, his only job was to make sure he wasn't one of those people that gave up. In spite of all Big Rock's threats, he knew he would never sic the dogs on Nipsey. That wasn't his style when it came to Nipsey. If he was going to end Nipsey, he would have done it when Ilene was still alive. Nipsey knew Big Rock had a thing for Ilene; it was hard not to know. The way he looked at her gave him away. He didn't have eyes like that for anyone else, not even the mothers of his own children.

One day in a drunken haze, Nipsey broke down to Big Rock everything that was going on. When he told Big Rock that Ilene had cancer, he asked if we were certain. Nipsey thought that was odd. Then Big Rock laughed and shook his head. Apparently, he had the impression that Ilene was HIV-positive. It wasn't surprising with all of the haters and the gossipers in the hood.

Big Rock started drilling him about doctors and treatment options. Nipsey didn't know most of it. All he knew was that she was going to die. That was enough. Nipsey fought even now to keep the tears out of his eyes. The last thing he wanted to show Dee was that he wasn't strong. If she saw his weakness, she might go back to striking at him like a snake—quick and deadly. He looked over, but Dee wasn't paying any attention to him. He could tell by the look on her face that the wheels were still turning around in her head.

Nipsey went back to his own thoughts. Big Rock was pissed off at Nipsey's lack of knowledge about Ilene's condition. Big Rock was concerned there was something else mixed in there. He looked at Nipsey and told him, "That woman of yours, she's ice cold. No other way to explain it." When Nipsey probed, Big Rock didn't give him anything else.

Something had obviously happened between Ilene and Big Rock, but Nipsey was too gone to care. It was always a possibility niggling in the back of his mind, though. He always wondered if Ilene and Big Rock ever hooked up. The thing about their neighborhood was people would gossip about everything—except Big Rock.

No one ever crossed Big Rock. No one ever told his business. It wasn't worth the trouble. There were enough people who had learned that lesson the hard way.

However, Nipsey would keep on the straight and narrow. Partially because Big Rock kept giving him reprieves, but it wasn't like he was a cat with nine lives. The other part was the girl sitting next to him. Truthfully, she was the biggest part. He couldn't say he loved her and was her father if he kept letting others bear the burden of raising her.

It wasn't about the money. It was about guidance and being a good role model—not getting duped into fucking teenage girls and not lying. He needed to be a person she could be proud of and one sip of any drink would only confirm what she already thought about him—he was a loser.

He wasn't letting his daughter go like that. She deserved a better dad and she was going to get one.

***

Nipsey had given Dee a lot to think about. She had a brother. For a brief period, she had a brother that she never knew about. Dee turned in the passenger seat and asked Nipsey. "Why didn't she ever tell me?"

"We talked about that Vegas trip only once. That was the one thing that was a non-negotiable with her. I tried to talk to her about it a couple of other times and she cut me out of her life cold turkey each time. She was not playing. She said, 'I knew you dated other women in between our thing. I didn't like it, but I knew. It wasn't a big secret. I even knew you were with Paula. You think the crew didn't rush to tell me that?

"I even knew Paula knew about me, because the same people that were whispering in my ear were whispering in hers. The baby. The baby hurt more than … I couldn't even think. I hurt so bad—and to be blindsided. You should have been the one to tell me. But no, you let your punk-ass baby's mother get her jollies off by telling me about the baby. What did you think was going to happen? We were going to get married, you would tell me and since we were married, I'd be like OK. Fuck you and the horse you rode in on.'"

Nipsey paused for a bit. When he started up again, his tone was different. It was softer, almost a whisper. "Your mom said she wished that Paula would have never gotten pregnant. She called it a 'closing the barn door after the horse had escaped' wish. She never thought ... she never wanted the baby to die. She said it made her face a lot of things that would never have been right anyway.

"She told me the pain didn't come from Paula; the pain came from the baby and the lie. After the baby died, the pain was even worse. So she carried that guilt with her; and she knew I was a bald-faced liar and manipulator; she carried that with her as well. The baby changed everything. She said there was no going back; forward wasn't looking too sharp either. Then she started crying and walked out. I didn't hear from her for a long time; but when I did, she had rules, and that was that."

Dee shook her head. "That still doesn't explain why she didn't talk to me about it."

"She didn't talk to anyone about it. She closed that chapter and shoved it in a corner. If he had lived, things would have been different. I think his death made the whole situation worse for everyone. We all had so much guilt."

"What was his name?"

"Ruben Lee Bell IV. He was named after me."

Dee stopped talking after that. It explained a few things, but it didn't make his behavior any better. It made it worse. It all went back to the lies. Lies by omission were still lies. He was prepared to marry her mother with a huge-ass lie and hope she'd forgive him afterward. He was such a selfish asshole. *Damn. How low can you be? And with someone that you cared about?* She'd hate to see what he did to the people that he couldn't stand. He's probably already stabbed a few and had them buried in a field somewhere. Shit, he was evil as hell.

After they returned home and Dee went upstairs, Nipsey sat out on the back porch and listened to the silence. He knew Joe was on his porch. He had heard the beer bottles clinking together. Joe didn't acknowledge him nor did Nipsey acknowledge Joe. He just wanted to be alone with his thoughts. Soon he heard the door open and close. He knew it was Auntie M. Ever since they got home, all Dee did was give him odd looks. She wouldn't dare shuffle closer to the steps and sit beside him.

"So how did it go?"

"Well, she didn't cut me. That's pretty much my marker for everything these days. If it isn't going to kill me, I can handle it."

"That's a hell of a low bar."

Nipsey shrugged. "Makes it easier to accomplish. I told her about Ruben."

Auntie M raised her eyebrows. "Wow. That's a lot for your first outing. How is she taking it?"

He blew out a breath. "She's still processing."

"Hmm."

"I don't think she understands, though."

"Hmm."

Nipsey said quietly. "Well, it's a start anyway."

For a while Auntie M and Nipsey sat and soaked in the silence of the night.

Nipsey broke the silence by saying, "I think I made a mistake in telling her. She brought up that Vegas trip."

Auntie M snorted and laughed. "The un-wedding? That was a bad plan from the beginning. You can't spring another child up on your future wife.

Are you nuts?"

"I was young."

"You were stupid."

"That, too."

"Maybe Dee will be the one that will get this relationship thing right."

Nipsey looked at her closely. "You got it right for a long time, Auntie M."

"Problem is I got it wrong for a lot longer."

"I always wondered what happened between you and …"

"What did happen? Everything and nothing. Back then I was looking on this big church search. I wanted a more personal church experience," she replied as she gazed into the trees before holding up her hand. "No smart remarks from you. You know when I first met Pastor Clifton, I didn't think he was that cute. I mean, he was good looking; he just wasn't really my type. I wasn't like bowled over by his looks. I was sitting in the God is Love Church before the service started. Now, you know our church was really small back then, so the few single ladies were all dolled up to the nines and he was speaking to the choir director.

"Let's put it this way. He was cute enough to keep me entertained through the service, but not cute enough to make me make a special trip to the church. Well, his spirit was so strong. The minute he opened his mouth, it seeped out of every pore. That little gap-toothed smile. One day he was trying to remember some passage out of the Bible and his eyes looked up and he slipped his tongue through the gap in his front tooth.

"It was then that he had my attention. He had my undivided attention. I joined the fundraising committee after that—and yeah, we were closer than friends. For a while there, I thought we could be together, but life happens and there are some things that you can't take back."

Nipsey looked puzzled. "What happened?"

Auntie M looked very sad. "Ahhh. That's a story for another day. You're young and all those drugs have preserved your looks. Eventually, you will need to start dating again." Auntie M punched Nipsey's arm. "Maybe you can pick up one of those young tenders at the church and show us how love is supposed to be done."

He shivered and grimaced. "Or maybe, I'll stay single and concentrate on my daughter. Goodness knows she doesn't need any more roller coasters in her life."

Auntie M stood up and clucked. "OK, chicken. I'll let you off the hook for now; but trust me, your time being single is coming to a close soon. Some of those women are relentless. Now that's going to be fun to watch." She chuckled a bit and headed inside.

Nipsey stayed out for a while longer. By the time he went inside, there was no noise from Joe's house.

Quiet. That's why he was enjoying this now. He looked up. Enjoying is not really the right word. It would be better to say he accepted the silence. He succumbed to it. Something in his soul said that it wasn't going to last forever.

***

Dee woke with a headache. The last thing she wanted to do was to go to school. Correction, the very last thing she wanted to do was to talk to Auntie M or Nipsey. So given the option, she guessed school would be OK. She stretched and sighed. She would prefer to just lay there with the covers over her head for the day. Auntie M would never abide that, so she just started shuffling toward the bathroom.

The warm spray started to wake her, but that just got her mind working. She sincerely hoped the stupid gene that was coursing through Nipsey's blood stayed the hell away from her. Really. He thought he was going to get another girl pregnant and marry her mother and tell her mother later. Then she lost the baby and what did he do? He preyed on the sympathies of her mother. He took her good heart and used her to get through the craziness he started.

It wasn't like he was in high school. He was a grown man. Adults are supposed to know better. He had knocked up a skank. He could have had her mother and instead he chose a skank. Dee couldn't say how many times she had turned this scenario over in her mind last night. She tried to look at it from every angle.

No matter how she tried, she came back to the same thing. Her father was an idiot. Growing up, her mother used to exclaim about how talented Nipsey was musically. Dee guessed she wanted to give Dee something to hold on to. After years of this particular snow job, Dee told her mother, "Look I can appreciate that Nipsey had talent a while back, but unless you can tell me what he's done that's amazing this year, I don't want to hear about it." Try as she might, Ilene didn't have anything within the last year to exclaim about, so she gave up. She would just say, "You know your dad loves you."

Dee turned around in the shower spray. Even that fact was debatable half of the time. Fathers took care of their daughters. It was that simple. Her mother served both roles. Nipsey was more like a sperm donor that hadn't quite cut the cord yet. But once again, Auntie M came from his side of the family. But Auntie M wasn't a direct line. Maybe that was the key. She was an aunt. Oh crap. That gave a higher probability that Dee might eventually show idiot symptoms from the idiot gene. Hopefully, it skipped a generation.

Dee made her way back to her bedroom and opened her door with a start. Auntie M was casually sitting on her bed. For real, she hadn't even had breakfast yet.

"You're moving a bit slow this morning."

"Yeah, rough night last night—full of revelations. Anymore nights like that and I might start to drink myself."

"Not funny, but that's life. It's not always pretty and tied up with a bow."

Dee snorted. "At this point I'd settle for average looking."

Auntie M managed a smirk at that one. "It was quite a bit to take in. Usually, when people open up like that, they do it to bring clarity to the situation. It helps you understand the situation better. Unfortunately, your understanding of that situation moved it from bad to worse. I can't condone or explain what Nipsey did. It was crazy, short-sighted, and selfish."

"Yeah. Listen I need to get ready for school. It's going to be a stretch to make it to first period as it is."

"But at least he told you the truth. He could have lied."

"Yeah. He could have."

"He doesn't balance all that well. He …"

Dee held up her hand. "There is absolutely nothing you can say about the situation to make it better. It was tore up from the floor up. No one won. There wasn't a silver lining. It was horrible. The situation was horrible. He handled it horribly. Everyone got hurt. There is nothing left to say."

"He's trying."

"He's an idiot."

Auntie M looked down. Dee could see everything she wanted to say move across her face. Auntie M settled with, "You know he loves you."

"Yeah, problem is that him loving me means nothing."

"Maybe you can't see it today, but one day, it will mean something to you."

"I still have to get dressed for school."

"Let me leave you to it then. Breakfast will be ready in two shakes."

"I'm not hungry this morning. Headache."

Auntie M nodded and closed the door. Dee sat down hard on the bed. She knew somehow she had hurt Auntie M. She didn't mean to do that; but really, this situation wasn't the easiest. Dee got up and walked to her closet. She pulled out a pair of jeans and a light sweater. She quickly pulled her hair back in a ponytail and secured it. No matter how she felt, she had to get out of the house. She didn't want any more run-ins with any more family members. Now Auntie M was going to have to drive her to school. She knew the weight of expectations would be rolling off of Auntie M in waves. Wave after wave of unspoken words, thoughts, wishes all the way to school.

Dee rushed down the stairs and announced she was ready. Nipsey came out of the kitchen.

"Have a good day at school."

Dee nodded, opened the door, and walked out. She waited until Auntie M pulled the Escalade out of the garage and she hopped in. As she expected, the tension in the car was suffocating. It made it hard to breathe, but it made it easier to go to school. There for the most part she could lose herself among the masses. She could until Evelyn spotted her. However, she had already heard the worst. Evelyn could have no effect on her today.

Nipsey heard Auntie M make her way back from dropping off Dee. He ambushed her the minute she walked in the door. She had put her purse and keys on the hall table. Usually she took time to glance at her reflection in the mirror, but with Nipsey on her the minute she walked through the door all she could do is sigh and turn to meet him.

"Well, what did she say? Is she OK?"

"I think she is still processing. "

"But what did she say?"

"She said that you were an idiot."

"She's not far off the mark there, but did she talk about it? Did she want to talk about it?"

From Behind the Curtain

"She was running a bit late and rushing to get ready for school. Timeliness is next to godliness."

"Did Dee say that?"

"No. Why?"

"For one, cleanliness is next to godliness. Secondly, that would mean she would have completely flipped her lid."

Auntie M smirked. She realized it was going to take quite a bit to pull this together. She wondered if it was going to take more than she had. Nipsey was no prize on the best of days. For Dee and him to get closer, she would have to forgive him for the entire past and start fresh. Even Auntie M wasn't quite sure what starting fresh was. She didn't know what to expect from Nipsey. He seemed on the right path, but even she had to admit that he had seemed on the right path before. He'd hit that fork in the road and headed full tilt the wrong way.

She totally understood Dee's reservations. As much as she nudged Dee, she knew this whole experiment had the potential of blowing up in a big way. Nipsey was going to work. He was learning a new trade, something he could make money with. He could eventually support himself and Dee. Not that she wanted either of them to leave, but he could do it. He could even do this during the day and pick up music again at night, if that is what he wanted. He had options. The problem was Nipsey always had options. He always chose door number two.

Nipsey looked into Auntie M's eyes and saw the emotions going across her face. "Auntie M. You don't know how hard this is."

"True, I don't know. But what you have to figure out is if it is worth it. Is giving your daughter a parent worth whatever it is you have to go through?"

"Of course."

"It wasn't in the past."

"Auntie M. I'm not up for this."

"Sweetie, you are going to have worse days than this. This is nothing. Your daughter is mad at you. You daughter has been mad at you for years. That's nothing new. Problem was Ilene ran interference. Now you get the full unadulterated version. This isn't even the worse bit of attitude you could be getting because I'm making her curb it a bit. As I said, it could be worse. What has changed for you?"

Nipsey took a deep breath and his eyes began to water. He took another deep breath and breathed deeply a couple of times. "Ilene isn't here. With her, I knew everything would work out somehow. With her, I knew we would somehow be all right. Without her, I'm not so sure. It's different."

"Sweetie, it's different for all of us. We all depended on Ilene to an extent. Ilene knew her best. Maybe you should ask yourself what Ilene would do in this situation."

"Ilene would rent *The Wiz* and find some way to relate it to the situation. That was their thing."

"Well, maybe you need your own thing, your own way to relate to your daughter. And I'd spread the bombshells out a bit. You need to win some points right now. Any new revelations coming from you will do more harm than good."

Nipsey nodded and headed back into the kitchen. When Auntie M was paying attention, she was damn near psychic. He didn't want her reading anything in his eyes. At this point he still couldn't spill the beans about Evelyn, even though he knew he needed to talk to someone about it. He looked across the yard. He could see Joe jogging his way down the steps and rushed out to meet him.

Joe looked at him warily.

"Let's walk."

"What now? I haven't done anything to or with your daughter.

Drop it already."

"It's not that."

Joe looked a bit more suspicious. "I'm not getting you anything stronger than Bayer aspirin. I don't care what kind of money you're stacking."

"Why is it everyone is always thinking I'm two seconds from using?"

"Can't speak for everyone. All I know is the hype mentality."

"Shit, if you're slanging, why wouldn't you sell to me? A sale is a sale right."

"Dude, I'm more scared of your people than you. Either one of them would cut my ass, no questions asked."

"Aren't you scared of Evelyn? She's the one having you going around doing her bidding."

Joe cut Nipsey a slanted look. He shrugged. "Evelyn is different. She's controlled by two things: power and her pussy. That's pretty much it for her. As long as she thinks she has control of the situation, then she's happy. Or if she doesn't have control, she's cumming too much to really care." Joe smiled. "She likes you, you know."

Nipsey grabbed Joe by his arms and swirled him around.

"What the fuck do you mean? What the fuck is going on?"

Joe stopped and looked at Nipsey's hand on his arm. "Not the best idea given your precarious position with everyone in your circle right now. The secret you're keeping will rock everyone, especially church-going Auntie M."

Nipsey dropped his hands and walked around in a circle. He started swinging at the air and let out a guttural yell. "Dude, this Neanderthal thing you have going is tired. Come on."

They continued walking down the block and around the corner. Joe led them down the side of a house and into the backyard. It was a Garden of Eden, full and lush with flowers. Plus, it had a couple of chairs.

Nipsey peered around. "Who lives here?"

"Don't worry. They're out of town. My mom is supposed to check on their house from time to time. She sends me. Go figure. Most people would go crazy if they knew I had access to their place. Mom knows that I'm very specific about my illegal activities. So have a seat. We won't be bothered here. What's the deal?"

"How did you do it? How did you handle all of this … this evil? I'm going crazy. I keep wanting to tell Auntie M, but I can't. I sure can't mention anything to Dee. I'm wound up so tight; I'm going to explode any minute. Do I want a drink? Sure. But I'm afraid to drink. Not because of what will happen with Dee or Auntie M. I'll wake up again next to some underaged groupie bitch. What the hell?"

Joe looked pained. "How the hell did I become your confidant? You don't even like me. I'm the one that wants to hit that sweet-ass daughter of yours."

Nipsey waved him off. "Well first of all, you know all the players. You know the most dangerous ones pretty well. Two, I've been watching you. My daughter has never seen the inside of your house, has she?"

Joe narrowed his eyes. "No."

"You know as well as I do that if you were serious, my little girl would have at least seen your living room if not your basement bachelor pad. Have you ever invited her in?"

"No. And why does everyone assume I sleep in the basement?"

"That's what I thought. My daughter has had men coming after her for years. You're not new. I watch her. I keep my eyes open you know. The ones that are really dangerous, she stays away from. She doesn't stay away from

From Behind the Curtain

you. You're not really trying to get at my daughter. It doesn't matter what you say."

"So I have your permission to tap that?"

Nipsey glared at him. "Too far. What am I going to do?"

Joe looked at Nipsey. Clearly, this man was losing his mind. There was no other way to put it. Everything wasn't firing on all cylinders. But Joe smiled. It wasn't a happy-to-know-you smile. It was more like an I-know-how-that-feels smile.

Joe leaned back against the cushions on the lawn furniture. He rarely actually went into the house anyway. There was really no reason. No one wanted the old shit that these people were trying to pass off as antiques. Old shit doesn't mean antiques. Sometimes it just meant you were too cheap to buy new shit. Even this plastic cushion with the orange, yellow, and brown flowers that spoke every time he shifted, was just old. He didn't know who in the world was calling need-to-be-retired lawn furniture 'collectibles.' He heard Nipsey shifting on the other chair, but still Joe looked ahead.

He knew Nipsey's frustration. He understood why Nipsey was coming to him, but at the same time, there were some people that Joe didn't fuck with, and to help Nipsey, he would have to fuck with the very wrong people. Joe looked at Nipsey.

He was leaning forward with his elbows on his knees and just looking down at the cement.

"You want a drink."

"No." Nipsey looked up. "I lost too much in the bottle. I can't lose anymore. I just can't."

Joe settled back again.

"You are merely a pawn in a bigger game, but you know that already."

"How do I get out the game?"

"Why are you asking another pawn? All I know is we're playing chess. I never played chess a day in my life. I'm just moving pieces around the board. Someone else has a bomb-ass offensive and defensive strategy. If I could get out, I would have a long time ago."

"OK. How about this? How did you get in?"

Joe smiled again. "That's easy. I wanted in on the game. I started out just wanting some extra money. I wanted to help my mom. My dad wasn't around. I was a man. A man takes care of his household. I didn't want no pizza bullshit. Taking motherfuckers' orders wasn't going to put a significant dent in my mother's situation. So I started slanging. It was just a little weed. I used to keep it in the basement. My mother's cousin was actually my best customer." Joe laughed.

He remembered how his mother was so happy that he was getting closer to the family. There was always someone coming over to spend a little time. She started to get suspicious when they were spending so little time. They would come over for fifteen minutes, maybe a half hour before cutting out. Joe wasn't flashy with his. It wasn't as if he was buying new gear. He was stacking his paper. He always stacked his paper.

The game shifted. His supply started drying up. Word was, there was a new player in town. He didn't know what he was supposed to do. He didn't trust all those big suppliers. He liked to keep his operation small, under the radar. He wasn't in it for the long term. No, his long-term goal was to get out of this and get to college. He knew if he wanted to change his mother's life, he was going to have to do it with a degree. The weed was just a step to the finish line. It was just a means to an end.

So he tried to talk to the new players, but they wanted major movers. So he went out of town for his. He had to get a bit more than he normally did, but he didn't have the pressure or the terms that the local people were trying to impose. He had just gotten his stash home when the police raided his house.

The look in his mother's eyes. She loved him, but she hadn't forgiven him yet.

He was not cut out for being a major player. It was readily apparent. So he got caught up. It was a first offense and he got time. He did his time. Now he just played at it. He had a few regular customers. Yeah, he'd take a puff or two in his yard. He had to keep up the illusion. One time whoever was running all this had contacted him. They wanted him dirty. They didn't care how dirty. They just wanted him dirty enough to weaken his position. So this is where they stood—circling the ring.

So he did what everyone wanted. He worked at the spa. He had special assignments. He came home. He ran errands for his mother, but pretty much kept it low key.

The problem was that Dee entered the picture. It was her presence that had everyone bugging. She was changing the game; she wasn't even in the game. The fact of her presence and people's reaction to it was enough.

It was enough to draw Nipsey into the game. Nipsey was going to have to be strong as hell not to be pulled under. It didn't help that Nipsey was a bit of a game changer himself. Evie had set her sights on him early. He was a bit old, but Evie didn't care. He was another notch in her bed post. She would get a lot of amusement out of knowing what she did. When amusement wasn't enough, she was going to throw Nipsey under the bus. She'd do it just to get back at Dee for being what Evie herself was not.

"You are going to have to tell Dee."

Nipsey looked up. "I can't tell Dee that. My Dee doesn't forgive. She never has. She holds her anger in a vise grip."

"I don't know what game is being played. I just know there is one. Secrets like the one you're keeping are going to kill you. You should have told her that first night. You should have gone home and told her and Auntie M. This shit is going to come back and bite you."

"Did you tell?"

"I didn't have to. The camera was a new addition. It was probably my fault. I called her bluff one day. Really. Why would I sleep with her? I was knocking off some prime pieces at the time. It's not that she's not cute. But she also knew the scandal alone would hurt her 'Pollyanna' image. Your setup was better than mine. She thought yours through and everything she missed with me she got with you. I'm sure there is even a part when she told you to stop. She wouldn't have left that out. Sorry, man. Tell them. ASAP."

"I can't. I need more time."

"Then keep the players happy until you do. You're going to need your family to survive this storm."

Joe stood up and started to walk away. He paused. "Tell me this. Why all of sudden are you looking to me? I'm the devil remember."

Nipsey shrugged. "You're the devil we know."

"I'd put a limit on these side conversations, too, if I was you. Nothing good is going to come out of asking questions with no answers."

"If you had the option, what would you do?"

"Move."

"Why don't you?"

"Because Mom would still be here. If I just up and left, she'd be alone. I don't know what exactly is bubbling up, but I do know that I don't want her to be caught in something because of my shit. She doesn't deserve that."

"You can take her with you."

"Tell you what. You go tell Auntie M to move and see what happens. That's *her* house. She ain't going nowhere on my word. Especially after all the other shit that went down. She's comfortable. She should be."

Joe went to the door and walked in the house leaving Nipsey in the yard. Nipsey pushed up from the backyard furniture and walked around to the

From Behind the Curtain

front and back to Auntie M's.

Auntie M was peeking out of the window when he returned. "I know you're grown, but I thought you'd at least tell me if you were running out. One minute you're in the kitchen, the next minute I'm hollering at the wind."

"Sorry Auntie M; just took a quick run."

M looked him up and down. "Nowhere to run around here."

"M, please. I'm still straight. Trust me."

Auntie M made a noncommittal noise. "What's on your agenda for today?"

"Actually, I'm just going to study a bit about electrical wiring. I don't have an actual job today, so I was going to get some studying in. What about you?"

"I really don't have anything planned. I might go to a yoga class."

"Why aren't you more active in the church? You seem to like to keep busy and anything that large would need a lot of volunteers. You used to work your tail off for the first Church of Love. Was it Pastor Clifton? Did it change after that? I know how much you loved him."

Auntie M stood up. "Nipsey. He was my pastor."

Nipsey laughed. "Yeah, but even high off my ass, I know he was more than just a pastor to you."

Auntie M blustered and blushed.

Nipsey took her hand. "It's all right. I saw the way your eyes lit up when he was around. Your smile was different. It was wider. You bloomed with him around."

"Listen, I need to run some errands."

But Nipsey didn't let go. "Do you miss him like I miss Ilene?"

Auntie M looked up to meet his eyes and then she moved in. Her tiny frame hugged his much taller one. When they pulled back, both of them had tears silently streaming down their faces. Nipsey knew. Auntie M knew. They had found a kindred spirit, someone who could understand their level of pain.

Auntie M started, "Sometimes it's harder to go to church. The new sign without his name. Sometimes every seat in the place pisses me off. It's a house of God and sometimes I'm so pissed off, it's everything I can do not to scream at the top of my lungs. How crazy is that?"

"I can barely look my own daughter in the eye because she looks like her mother, but then she opens her mouth and the similarity ends."

They both laughed.

"I mean really. Every time I see her I feel a slight pain in my chest. Every single time. Because for a second I think Ilene is back and just that quickly she's gone again. It hurts and I might wince. I don't know. What I do know is that time doesn't heal shit. Since the first day when I had to drag Dee away from her mother's body, I've been dying a bit inside. I know I have to be strong. I have to be strong for Dee. I think the thing that keeps me sober is fear that I'll dull the pain and eventually have to start over again.

"As bad as things are now, I know that I can get through every day. I know I can put one foot in front of the other and make it through the day. If I lost that, if I had to start over, I just don't know. That is what scares me the most. It's not losing myself to the bottle. It's not losing myself to drugs. It's what comes next. It's starting over again."

Auntie M started pacing. "We were good friends. Really good friends. We could talk and laugh for hours. It got to the point where every time something happened, he was the first person I wanted to tell. Just the thought of him brought a smile to my face. But he was the pastor. You know how many women were constantly throwing themselves at him? I didn't want to be another one in the bunch. Sometimes I would think what if? It got to the point where I analyzed every conversation, trying to figure out if there was anything

From Behind the Curtain

else there. We were friends. That's all I knew for certain. So it was irrelevant and so very relevant at the same time.

"I can't tell you the number of times that he sat across from me at that table laughing. But his voice is in my head constantly."

Auntie M sat down in a chair. "When I got the message, I broke down. I was a mess all through the funeral and for a long time afterward. Then all the gossip started—people making comments about our relationship. At first, I was a bit suspect. I will admit that, but after a while, it stopped. It was all above board. However, if he had given me even the slightest indication our relationship would have been different. If one of those hugs had lasted longer than normal, if one of those loud cheek pecks had become a lingering kiss. If one a pat on the back had become a soft rub, I would have gone for it. But it never did and it was my fault."

Nipsey shook his head. "That couldn't have been your fault Auntie M. It wasn't meant to be."

"It's not that I was lonely for male companionship. I had special friends over the years. They just didn't come close to Pastor Clifton. And so, I enjoyed them and I let them go. None of them lived in my mind. So there was no way they could live in my heart. That space was reserved. And when Pastor Clifton died ...

"People were gossiping so badly after his death that I couldn't let his reputation take another hit because I couldn't get myself together. So I woke up one Sunday, put on my best dress and hat, and high-stepped it to church. I've been high stepping, glad handing, and smiling at those folks ever since."

Auntie M stopped and looked at Nipsey. "But the thought of giving myself over to the new church puts such a bad taste in my mouth, it's about all I can do to make it there every Sunday. Another day would be too much to bear."

Nipsey looked down. "She was the best thing in my life. I certainly didn't treat her that way, but she was. The sad thing is I didn't tell her that either. I should have told her every day."

"He was the best friend, confidante, pastor that I could have asked for, but I know I didn't tell him that. I was scared. I thought he might read the truth in any comment that I made. Some days all I want is one of his hugs. Even if it ends with the friendly pats on the back. I want to be held by him."

"I saw the two of you together. It was magic. You should have told him. Both of you could have been waiting for the same signal from each other. As you said, he was your pastor. He might not have felt right pushing up on one of his parishioners, but both of you deserved that chance."

Auntie M shrugged. "Maybe if they had a confessional. That would have been a doozie all right. Can you imagine me sidling up? Forgive me, Father, for I have sinned. I've had impure thoughts about my pastor for months, years even. Now, how many Hail Marys will I need for that?"

Nipsey chuckled. "Auntie, he would have fallen out in the confessional."

"Yeah, but it might have been worth it. After all, since it was a confessional, the only person he could have told was God and trust me God already knew."

After they shared a laugh, Auntie M stood up. "You know, I think the hardest part about all of this is that he was truly my very best friend. He was the one that I wanted to share stuff with. He was the one that I would laugh with. He knew me better than anyone. And now he's gone. That bites."

Nipsey gave her a hug and watched as she left the kitchen, her normal energy dragged down by memories.

Auntie M walked to her bedroom to get ready for yoga. She really didn't feel like centering herself. She really felt like running a few miles to get all this energy out of her system. However, her knees didn't really stand up well to long runs anymore. That's why she had shifted to yoga, but it wasn't quite the same. Auntie M changed into her gym clothes and headed out the front door. She would do a brisk walk instead of a run. It wouldn't do what she really wanted it to do. It wouldn't tire her out to the point where she couldn't breathe or couldn't think. Maybe she needed to stop trying to block out her memories.

Goodness knows she had tried that for years, but they would roll back around at the most inopportune times. Sometimes she would just be sitting around minding her own business and someone would say something that would trigger a memory. Next thing you know, she'd be a mess. She understood Dee's breakdown in school. She understood hanging on to whomever you needed to hang on to just to get through the day. For Dee, for some ungodly reason, it was Joe.

The thought still made Auntie M shiver. Joe wasn't the worst person she'd ever met; he was just a bit lost. He was truly out of his element. If the drug conviction hadn't ruined his life, it would have been truly hilarious. Joe was not the selling drugs type. She guessed he figured if everyone else could do it, he could too. He always had that I'm-a-man syndrome. "I'm a man. I'm going to handle my business." He had that protective instinct in spades. The problem was he didn't have the cutthroat instinct.

Auntie M was sure his friendship with Stacy didn't help. Stacy was always so strong. Growing up with an ever-disappearing mother forced her to be. No one ever worried about Stacy starving to death. Stacy always found a way to handle her business. Joe wasn't prepared for what it meant to push the hard stuff.

Looking back, Auntie M contributed his change in direction to that hussy he used to date in high school. That girl was bad business from the beginning. She was cute and she knew it. Joe was good enough for her for a while. Then when something better came around, she switched in a hurry.

Auntie M continued to walk swinging her arms in rhythm to her stride, inhaling and exhaling and remembering. Even though it was easier to avoid it, she didn't want to. Today, she wanted to remember her dearest friend and the love of her life, Pastor Clifton.

Truth was, he was a pure soul. He was really guided by the word of God and the good book. Auntie M knew she was not—not all the time. Case in point, there were times when she had really impure thoughts about their dear pastor. He'd be standing on the pulpit passionately speaking the Word, and she would be sitting there fanning herself for reasons that had nothing to do with lack of air conditioning. His death was … It was the circumstances around it that were the most horrible. No one seemed to care that after everything he did, he died suspiciously of a drug overdose. Auntie M had asked some church members if they thought it was true. The odd thing is that no one thought it was true, yet no one was willing to go to the wall to fight for the truth or uncover the facts. She guessed they figured one of his death threats finally came to fruition. They didn't want anything to do with what happened to Pastor Clifton. They were scared.

Auntie M understood fear, but she also understood fairness and truth. It was unfair that Pastor Clifton's reputation had to take what it did. It was even worse that no one was willing to stand up for a man who had stood up for so many. But who was she to judge anyone? She was guilty of the same thing. She hadn't done anything to help him either. She never pushed anyone. She was the one who should have fought the hardest and she hadn't. Auntie M never quite trusted Pastor Love. She didn't have a particular reason. She just never got a great vibe from him. It was like he was always 'on,' like a camera crew was going to descend from the heavens in one swoop and catch him at any time.

Auntie M never did trust men like that. Those were the ones that usually had something to hide. She needed a bit more reality than that. Pastor Clifton's grace or his generosity came from his heart. He just did what he thought was right at the time. While, Pastor Love lived in his mind too much, she saw the wheels turning a bit too often to make her think he did things from his heart.

Granted, his leadership had expanded the church way beyond what she and Pastor Clifton thought it could be. *But what did that really mean? Did it mean that he was spiritually sound?* Auntie M sighed. She needed to think clearly without emotion about the situation, but she didn't know how she could keep emotion out of anything dealing with Pastor Clifton. Every thought was attached to an emotion. Every thought was a little stab of pain. She didn't think clearly about him when he was alive. She sure as hell didn't now that he was gone.

However, one thing Auntie M knew was that it was time to stop just surviving. Pastor Clifton died on the church premises and the most that the congregation managed to do was shake heads and cluck tongues.

Auntie M thought hard. She could go to the police; but after they determined it was an overdose, they didn't seem all too fired up to do anything else. They knew he was a church pastor without a history of drug use or abuse. Still, they didn't dig any deeper than they had to. One police officer even mentioned it wasn't like his death was on 'CSI.' She figured he meant that on television they actually solved crimes.

She'd need something solid to make them take action. She didn't know what that was yet. It was too late to try to find a needle with fingerprints or even pull any good prints from his office. It was a pastor's office; there were a ton of prints around at any given time. No one could build a case on that alone.

So how did she start? If she died, she'd leave less of a ripple than Pastor Clifton did. She was well aware of the stakes. She understood more than most that she was putting herself and her loved ones in danger. *But how could they live like this?* A good Christian would not let this injustice go untended.

A good Christian would pray on it. She had. A good Christian would take action. She had spent a lifetime being merely good. She never approached Pastor Clifton about what they could have had together. She had prayed, but prayer wasn't always enough. Sometimes you had to combine that with the gifts God gave one. She had to leverage what she had.

Joe could help her. Once she got past the fact that he wanted to date Dee, she took a closer look at who he was. Although he had made a number of bad decisions (and may still be making those decisions), at his core he was a good guy. Those lessons didn't go away forever. Sometimes they just hid themselves until the individual was able to deal with them.

She was sure at the very least he could help her get started. She'd have to work on that tomorrow. She picked up her pace a bit as she headed for home feeling the energy of having a plan in place. She always worked better with a plan.

CHAPTER 23

Joe sat in his basement sipping a Modelo. The phone was off. The fifty-inch flat screen on the opposite wall television was off. He didn't even bother with video games. He was sitting on his chocolate leather La-Z-Boy® couch. He kept this area meticulous so he didn't have to worry about heavy cleaning. The leather ottoman held a few college catalogues and the last three months of *Sports Illustrated* magazines.

How did he get in this position? Over the years, he had gotten used to people believing he wasn't worth shit. There were the people that whispered at him during church. Mothers gave him the evil eye. Daughters gave him the other eye. For years, years, the only person that really tolerated him was his mother. She would have probably washed her hands of him as well if she could have. She trusted him as far as she could see him. Meaning, she trusted him to be him.

His mother never had gotten over his father leaving. He had seen pictures of his mother before and she was smiling and happy. She had a nice hazelnut complexion and stood about five foot three. He rarely got to see that now. OK. He never got to see that now. Occasionally, she'd come across in a good mood, but mostly she looked like she wanted to cut somebody. Her lips were always smashed together in a perpetually pissed look. She walked around in jeans and gym shoes, except for church, there she wore a white shirt and black pants regardless of how fancy everyone else dressed.

She did her duty by him, but she wasn't a touchy, feely, huggy kind of mother. Hell, when he was thirteen, she sat him down at the table with a stack of condoms and a cucumber. She didn't give a fuck about embarrassment.

She told him, "You're embarrassed now. I see that. Who really cares? Cause if you bring some heifer bitch in my house talking about pregnancy, it'll be on in a way that you are not prepared to handle. Now put it on again. I know you're not cucumber big, but the concept's the same. Get to work."

He got to work. He figured it would be better to get it over with instead of complaining about it. She never questioned anything he did, but occasionally his condom stash would refill.

He went to her once in high school when a girl broke his heart. He knew she wouldn't hug him. He didn't expect a lot. He figured she'd at least raise her eyebrow and snort, or say something about the girl. No, she figured it was his fault.

"Listen, you should know these heifers don't care about you. Everyone is out for themselves. So you need to figure out what the hell she wants and provide it. You're trying to do the whole 'I love you' shit. That's for punks. See. Look at yourself. She got you punked, crying home to mommy." Then she looked confused. "It's amazing that I ended up with you. You're a boy with the sensitivity of a girl; interesting."

After he got popped the first time, she told him if she ever found any drugs in her house, the police would be the least of his worries. Joe wasn't stupid. At least, he was not as stupid as he was before. Joe didn't slang out of her house anymore. It wasn't so much his mother's threat. However, he saw a look in her eyes that, well, it was hard to explain. He had known for years that his mother had her limits. He figured that the only thing that saved him the first time was the fact that the police arrived before his mother found out about his stash.

He knew better than to keep it there after that. That would be the first place they'd look if he was popped again. He didn't want his mother to have to deal with the drama again. Once was enough. If he got caught up, he didn't plan for her to be anywhere near it. Not after the first time.

Here he was trying to take care of her. She was the one who had her home ransacked. She was the one who had to show up in court and hear about everything that had gone on in her own home. It wasn't just the drugs. There were also a few guns hidden here and there. He saw his mother age a bit every day. *Yeah. That's taking care of her.*

Funny thing was he never thought he'd get caught. Even when he did, he lied. Said the stuff wasn't his. Said his cousin left it. And they left him there, in that cell. All night they left him in that cell on that hard-ass cot with the rough-ass blanket. They wouldn't hold him. He didn't have priors. He wasn't a bad person. If they tried, his mother would bail him out. Of course, she would. She wouldn't let her baby boy stay in jail. It wasn't until morning that he realized he wasn't getting out. But he held onto the belief that his mother would bail him out—until she didn't. She looked him in his eye and told him in front of the court that if that's what he chose to do then he'd damn well be ready to do the time for it.

That's when he realized how deep in the game he actually was. Yeah, it was the jail and the jail time. Yeah, it was the easy drug money. But he really understood what it meant to be in the game when he looked into his mother's eyes. Her eyes shouted disgust, but there was also pain. She remained resolute as she walked out of the courtroom while they took him into custody.

There is nothing more life changing than seeing the complete and total disappointment in your mother's eyes and realizing you're the reason it's there. To see her lift her head, turn her back, and walk away and realize she's right to do it because you ain't shit.

Looking back, he should have flipped burgers or become a Wal-Mart greeter or something like that. He should have done anything. He could have taken on two jobs if he needed. Now he was the one being taken care of. He had to have a stable residence. So he had to stay at home with her. He didn't get in her way or anything. He didn't get all upset when she asked him to do anything.

Back then he told her she should have had other children so that he wouldn't have to do all the work. He told her if she wanted slaves, she should take in a few foster children. Now, he just did it. He didn't argue about it. He didn't fight about it. He just did it. But he was right; she should have had more children. She needed someone to be proud of. Clearly, that was not Joe.

Now he was caught up in a game that he didn't know or understand. He wanted to go outside for a cigarette, but he was afraid. Okay, he wasn't afraid, but he'd rather feen for nicotine than deal with his neighbors. They were trippin'. For real, they were treating him like he was the second coming or something. Everyone wanted something from him.

He could understand if it was weed or something like that. That shit made sense. The one that should be feenin' was trying like hell not to backslide. He wasn't asking for no shit. Dee didn't really deal in it anymore. She sold it at one time, but now she was acting all like that was a past life instead of a past year. Auntie M always used to look at him with contempt.

When Dee moved in, Auntie M looked like she had a shank ready in her clutch and was just looking for the opportunity to use it. She was trusting him with her niece. It seemed every time he walked out of the door, one of those crazy neighbors was crying on his shoulder or asking him for a favor. *What the hell?* He knew he was punking out by staying inside. The way things were going they'd start ringing his doorbell any minute.

His mom would let them in. All of them, of course, except for Dee. His mother wasn't senile enough and would never allow something like that to jump off under her roof. She used to be big on what did or did not happen under her roof. Now, she was manic about it. She never said anything. But he felt it. He felt the tension every time she was home. He felt the relief every time he left.

He also knew that when he left she would go through his shit. Couldn't blame her really. He did use to sell out of her basement. If she didn't hate dogs, he was sure she'd have a drug-sniffing something or the other in here to make sure he was straight. Now that he thought about it, she had probably heard about Nipsey by this time, too. So Dee and Nipsey would never get past the threshold. Auntie M would though. She was probably the most dangerous of all of them.

He was a bit confused on how this happened. How did he become the go-to guy? That damn Dee didn't help. She was built like a video vixen with a face to match. He was a male and wouldn't mind if she 'dropped it like it was hot' right here, but Nipsey had already called his bluff. He talked about it, but he never really moved on it. His game was hellatight. Somehow along the way he switched from being the played to the player. Smiling a bit, he remembered that was one good thing he got from jail—his boy Knuck (short for Knuckles).

Knuck was in for bribery, but he kept an eye out for him. Strangely, it started over books. Knuck's girl was always sending him books to read. As crazy is it sounded, books were another kind of currency. He never would have guessed it before going in. He thought you needed a steady supply of cigarettes. He wasn't getting those from his mom. But at least she kept money on his books.

So they didn't get bestsellers or recent releases. Knuck did. Knuck was the slowest reader on the face of the earth, and he wasn't giving up one book until he was done. But then, Knuck became the man. Knuck didn't have a lot of money on his books, but he had actual books. So they worked out a sort or trade. Joe got first dibs after Knuck was done, and Knuck got things from the commissary. It worked out well. Once Knuck heard the story about his ex, Knuck broke the game down to Joe.

Now Joe could get anyone that he wanted, even the dimes. He just had to figure out what they wanted and be that for them. He turned into the man they didn't have at home. If he wasn't paying attention to her, Joe did. If the man wasn't laying it down, Joe did. You'd be amazed at how many women settled for relationships without popping off. So if he couldn't get her there, Joe made sure he did. After a while, it was more about reputation than actual work. You had to understand the code in between the code—at least until you hit that. Then he had them falling in love and all that. He didn't have time for all that love stuff. He had a goal. He was still getting that degree. He didn't want to get tied up with some shit that was going to take his mind off that goal. Not even Dee, and he knew she was worth it.

Hell, it wasn't too late. She trusted him now. That made it easier. But there was something vulnerable about Dee. There was something still young about her. She had preserved something underneath all the bullshit spouting out of her mouth and that is the part he found it hard to take advantage of. That had been stripped from Joe. He didn't want to be the one to strip it from Dee.

It was that part that had him hesitating beyond the bold innuendos. Given her background and her father, you'd think she'd be a bit jaded by now, but he saw the hope that she still tried to hide. That was why he didn't fuck with her like that. When she cried on his shoulder, it stayed that. When he promised Auntie M, he meant it. She could trust him around Dee. Even though that went against what his body was telling him every time she walked toward him, he knew that Dee was off limits. There was some part of him that wanted to protect her.

Now it seemed that by protecting her, he had all of her other family members coming out of the woodwork. First, Nipsey ambushed him. Then Auntie M cornered him. That's why he was hiding out in his room. He didn't want to run the risk of running into one of them. He shouldn't be hiding from them, but he needed to think without one of them asking for his help, or even worse, asking him for updates that he didn't have.

Nipsey's issue wasn't that bad. The problem was, even Joe felt the temperature chill every time Dee and Nipsey were in the same room. Within two minutes, anyone within the vicinity knew she couldn't stand him. The fact that he slept with one of her classmates was going to make her flip her lid. The fact that it was Evie would make her throw up and then flip her lid.

Auntie M was a completely different issue. Auntie M was asking questions that would make people disappear. Auntie M wanted to figure out what happened to Pastor Clifton. Joe didn't know too much, but he knew which questions not to ask. Those were the very questions that Auntie M was asking. It was fortunate and unfortunate that she came to him. He at least told her not to ask those questions. The problem was, she had this glint of determination in her eye that told him that she had no intention of listening. *Wasn't that a bitch?*

No one ever poked at a case like that one. The police didn't even poke at it. Everyone knew he died of a drug overdose. Everyone knew Pastor Clifton wasn't on drugs. No one was asking why a man who was not on drugs was dead. Everyone knew. Someone had killed him. No one knew who. For a couple of months, people kept to themselves. They didn't know who to trust or talk to. Soon people came down off ten, but they don't even refer to Pastor Clifton. That's how locked down someone had the whole parish. The whole congregation was pretending like someone didn't murder their beloved pastor.

Joe was locked up when it happened, so he doesn't know all the business. He asked a couple of questions when he got back. One of his customers put a hand on his chest, looked him in the eye and said one thing, "Don't." Now if a crackhead was telling him not to start trouble, he knew something real had jumped off. They would usually try to deal information. If they weren't willing to talk for crack, you best let it go. So he didn't start any trouble. He had enough of his own trying to figure out how to get out of the game.

He had passed the advice to Auntie M. He held up his hand and said, "Don't."

Auntie M looked at him. "If I don't, who will?"

"Murder is serious business. They won't just go after you. They'll go after Dee and Nipsey, too."

"I thought about that. You think I hadn't thought about that? I would love to say my God will protect me, but he didn't protect Pastor Clifton. Still I know in my heart that this is what I'm supposed to do. But I need help."

"Unlike you, Auntie M, I'm not ready to die."

Auntie M actually laughed. "You took your life into your own hands when you brought those drugs into your momma's house. Now you're acting all particular." Then she touched his elbow. "Just think about it."

That's why he was here—in the basement, sitting on the couch, in front of a blank television screen, drinking a beer that he couldn't taste—because Auntie M told him to 'think about it.' And if he could do it; if he could find out what happened maybe his mother wouldn't still look at him as if she waiting for the police to arrive any minute to cart him off again. Just maybe, she would actually forgive him, instead of saying she did when they both knew it was a lie.

But what was the point of trying to prove something to his mother if he was going to die before she figured out what was happening? There was no other way around it. That murder was a bit fishy. Someone was powerful enough to make the police think twice. He didn't stand a chance—not against them.

But he needed a chance. He needed a chance to prove to his mother that something that she taught him had stuck. Some part of him was the man she once thought he was. Wasn't her piece of mind worth his life? Auntie M was right in a way. He had thrown his life away already. Hell, if he got caught on another drug charge he'd be under the jail anyway. So why not?

Even as he accepted what he was going to do, he ran his hand over his face. This still didn't sit well with him. *Who could Pastor Clifton have pissed off that bad that it would be easier to get him out of the way?* There were snitches still walking the street and Pastor Clifton was six feet under. He had a friend that they called TNN—Tim News Network. Any information that dude knew was leaving his mouth and going straight to the police.

From Behind the Curtain

It was a known fact.

That dude had an accident one day. He ended up in the emergency room without a leg. Tim said he didn't know what happened to it. He didn't know where he had been, who he had been with, how long he had been gone. *Post-traumatic stress disorder my ass.* Someone had gotten to him. This dude walked around today on crutches and happy as hell. He at least would tell you his name now, but you were not getting one more drop of info out of his mouth. That was TNN. He stuck his leg out and came back with a nub. At least he came back. So if the man who told everyone's business ended-up with a nub, one had to wonder how Pastor Clifton ended up dead.

Joe got it. He didn't need a cadaver dog to smell something rotting. He knew why Auntie M was looking. This shit was suspicious as hell. He understood that. It lacked even the littlest bit of common sense. But what Joe kept coming back to was, if TNN lost a leg, what made someone lose a life?

PHANTOM

Ahh. There she was again. One can only say she was indeed a blessing. She could look this way. She could smile this way. She could make eye contact this way. Hell, she could do a lot more than that—this way. She would learn. She'd be taught. This game was for the strong. She was passing all tests with flying colors.

This girl took up residence in the mind without invitation and lived rent free. Even now, looking at the congregation, you could see the attention she commanded by merely existing. These weren't proper thoughts for this sacred house of God. This house had secrets. Things went on here that would have Jesus spinning in his grave. No one saw. No one who would tell saw. No one who didn't participate saw. Others, well, the others had too much to lose. They wouldn't say anything.

Who knew if Dee could be trusted? At first glance, she was worth the risk. But first glances could be deceiving. No one got anywhere being deceived. No, there was no power in getting caught up. There was no respect in that. The craving for respect was strong. Pinning down the elusive Dee would help garner that respect. That wasn't enough. It wasn't nearly enough. Being seen with Dee would definitely bring respect, but one couldn't bank on that kind of respect. The kind of respect that was needed in this case, was the respect garnered by awe and fear.

It would come. When it was time to become public, people would see what it took to pull all of this together. It took nerve and concentration. It took the right moves at the right times.

Some of those moves had already been made. One merely had to look around to see the success of this church. One only had to pay attention to realize it was more than Auntie M and Pastor Clifton had planned it to be. Pastor Clifton.

Not upset he's gone, but not OK with how it happened. Pastor Clifton was merely collateral damage. It was disappointing for sure. Yes, they needed him out of the way. They didn't need him six feet under. They just needed to move to the left or right. It took a lot of energy to make people forget about that. It took a lot of energy and money. Now, there were favors owed. Debts would need to be repaid. It was necessary. But it was a less-than-stellar way to get this started. That move had been made. Others had been as well. You can't build an army without a few strong lieutenants or maybe it was sergeants. Who knew? The core group was quite solid. It was almost time to develop the next level.

Dee would have to be dealt with on a totally separate basis. Auntie M would never allow it. That actually made it all a bit more tantalizing. That would be a coup.

However, as the choir was swelling behind and church about to start, it was better to just look. Look and imagine what would be some day. Dee would come. They all would come. Look at them now. All of them there, standing, accepting lies as truth. If it was that easy with some that were hard core, it couldn't be that difficult for others. Somehow, some way, they all would see the vision and would come willingly into the flock. Once they joined the flock, it would be as it should. Dee would have a position of authority.

The swell soon led to the crescendo. The single note held by every choir member meant to uplift, to move, to demand attention. Yes. It was time to start.

CHAPTER 25

Dee and Auntie M walked into the house after the service to music playing loudly. And not just any music. It was *The Wiz* soundtrack. Dee stopped. It was more of the shock of it than anything else. She hadn't heard that soundtrack. Since … well, it had been a long time. She closed her eyes to the jolt of emotion that ran through her. There was pain. There was always pain. Even through the pain, she could feel the love. She smiled a little bit and opened her eyes.

She noticed that Auntie M looked worried. She touched her arm and nodded. It was hard, but it was all right. This was her life.

They walked farther into the house and saw Nipsey smiling from ear to ear. Dee narrowed her eyes in suspicion. *What the hell did he have to be so happy about?*

"You won't believe it. *The Wiz* is being shown at Piedmont Park, and we are going."

Dee looked at Nipsey. She couldn't answer. *The Wiz* wasn't his; it belonged to her mom and her, not to Nipsey. Here his ass was trying to bank on something he knew nothing about. He was either too high or too drunk for *The Wiz* when it mattered. *Now what? He was supposed to be an aficionado? Whatever.*

Auntie M grabbed her hand and squeezed. "Nipsey, that's a great idea for all of us to go. I haven't seen it in years."

Dee still couldn't speak. She knew that anything she said would be either mean or insincere. So she just nodded, removed her hand from Auntie M's, and went upstairs. They didn't understand. They couldn't understand. She didn't know if she was up to *The Wiz* yet. Then it happened. The wall she built was breached. Tears began to fall. She didn't know where they came from. That was a lie. She knew exactly where they came from. *Damn him. Damn him for making her remember. Damn him for making her feel.* God, she just missed her mother. She wished her mother was there with them. Everything would be all right if her mother was there. She wasn't. Dee was doing the best that she could. Sometimes even hanging with Auntie M felt like betrayal.

Her mother struggled to give her the bare necessities that seem to flow from Auntie M without any problem. Dee liked that fact that she didn't have to worry about the day to day like she did with her mother. Dee knew that she was betraying her mother's memory. That's why she didn't really concentrate on the things that connected her to her mother.

Now she realized that was a futile endeavor. At any point, some memory could turn her into a blubbering mess. Even when she sat around congratulating herself on how well she was doing, deep down she knew she wasn't doing well at all. She knew deep down she wanted to curl up next to her mother with her hand on her mother's heart.

Dee walked over to the closet. There was a box at the bottom that had stayed there since the move. It was her mother's shoes. All the shoes she had taken such great pride in. They were all in shoeboxes. Dee hadn't dared take many of them out. She had worn two pair. She had only worn them once. For all of her thoughts about how tough she was, the truth was she didn't know if she was strong enough to go through these effects.

Now she knew the truth. This was going to be hell, but she would do it anyway. She couldn't continue to be afraid of a box. *Really, who was afraid of a box?* It was cardboard. The shoes inside were leather. That was it—cardboard and leather.

She pulled the box out and took out the first pair. She rubbed her hand over the leather and gently put that box down. She found the shoes her mother had worn to her graduation, church, sandals, stilettos. The stilettos made Dee smile. Her mother was sure she was going to break her ankle one day. She said some shoes were worth a little discomfort. Dee thought she was crazy at the time, but looking at the shoes, she could see why her mother loved them. They were delicate and light. Dee tried them on. She was almost en pointe. She lifted her leg into the air to see them better. That was what was going on when her dad entered the room.

When he walked in, he knew. He knew what that music had done. It hadn't uplifted Dee. It made her remember. For that, he felt a little pain in his chest. He didn't know what to do. He never knew what to do. Each step he took seemed to hurt his daughter. He hung his head and took a deep breath.

The slight breath caught Dee's attention. She looked up.

"I'm sorry. I didn't realize. I thought you'd be happy about it. I will say, though, while those shoes are spectacular, I'm going to need you to put them back in the box. Those aren't shoes that any dad, even one as bad as me, would ever want to see on his daughter."

Dee had a sad smile. "She had great taste."

Nipsey walked all the way in the room. "Yes she did. You know, when you boxed up all these shoes, I never realized you had the same shoe size. I thought they were to remember."

"They are. I remember all these different moments that included each pair. It helps me remember her."

"Do you mind if I sit down?"

Sierra Kay

Dee drew a deep breath and shrugged. "No, go ahead."

"Listen, we don't have to go. I thought you'd enjoy it. I didn't know what to do. I, honestly, never know what to do when it comes to you."

Dee kept looking at the shoes as if they were the most important thing in her life.

She took another pair out of the box. She chose a pair of chunky black sandals. "This pair she wore one day on a date. She didn't date much. I remember being so pissed at her because she finally got a date, and she was going to ruin it with these shoes. She had so many other options in her closet. I thought she was doing it on purpose. No offense, but I wanted a new daddy."

"I would take offense, but I seem to remember you saying that consistently between the ages of five and ten. So that's really nothing new."

Dee smiled a bit. "My mother sat me down and explained to me that certain shoes in certain situations give certain messages. She explained that you don't wear stilettos on a first date. Ever. The man hasn't earned the right to see your A game. If he can handle a conversation with you and get to know the person instead of the face, then one day you give him the gift of your A game. Before then, you are just asking for a fling."

Nipsey took the shoe. "Knowing you, you were probably still pissed."

"Well, hell. I *really* wanted a new dad."

"Yeah. I can't blame you. Listen, I want to be that new dad for you. I want to be the one that you know and love and come to when you need to talk."

"The deal is I never want to be the one to drive you to drink. I know now how you got lost in the bottle, but who knows what else will tip that off."

"I'm not going to get lost again."

"That's just hope. I used to have that, too. Enough binges from you killed that hope. See these nude shoes. Mom wore them to Rocky's mom's anniversary party. Everyone there said she looked better than Rocky's mom at her own party. They didn't say that to Rocky's mom though. It was bad enough they said it behind her back. Rocky's mom looked great at the party, too. Mom made sure she stayed low key. Still didn't help."

Nipsey looked at his daughter pulling out memory after memory. He wanted them to have these memories. He was amazed at the strength of this child. At the end of the day, she was just that. She was a child. Yet, this child was facing memories that had to be devastating for her. She was doing it to free herself. She was doing it to remember her mother.

As he looked at her, he knew that any memories they shared now would be tainted by the fact that he was keeping such a huge story from her. Every day he got a little sheen of sweat on his brow as she walked in from school. Every day he waited to see if Evelyn had told his daughter about their tryst—if you could call it that. Every day he wondered how many days he had left until he lost his daughter forever.

The alternative may be too much. *How strong is she? Can she withstand the words? Would she even believe he was drugged considering his history? What about Auntie M?* His residency was conditional. The condition was Dee. *When he told them, if he told them, would he have to move out? Would he completely lose the little bit of family he had left?* Right now, he wasn't in the best position, but he sure as hell wasn't in the worst one.

He wanted to tell Dee now. He just wanted to blurt it out. The tears streaking down her face were an indication that she might be too fragile to hear it. Or maybe, he was too fragile to say it. He could write her a letter, but that seemed to be such a cop-out. Really, he couldn't tell his daughter about his sexcapades.

No he couldn't. He really couldn't, but he had to. He had to say something before it blew up. Today wasn't the day. Today was for shoes and memories.

"Let's not go. Let's rent another musical instead. Let's pop popcorn and rent *Dirty Dancing* or something. I'll let you choose."

Dee didn't say anything for a minute. She sat and looked at the shoes scattered around her bedroom. She'd love to think she was ready, but the thought of breaking completely down in public made her pump the breaks a little.

She turned to Nipsey, "Have you ever seen *Little Shop of Horrors*? It might not be applicable to every life situation, but at least you'll know how to behave if you run up against a man-eating plant hell bent on world domination."

Nipsey nodded. "Just tell me what day you would like to do it, and I'll make sure the movie and popcorn are ready." Nipsey looked down at his feet and then looked up again. He took a deep breath and, for possibly the first time, harsh lines etched themselves in his face. "I'm sorry I was such a horrible father."

"Well it could have been worse. You could have beaten us as well."

Nipsey looked shocked for a second and then laughed. "Shit. No I couldn't. You might see your mom as the little slight victim or some delicate flower. Had I raised a hand in either of your directions, it would have never come down. She would have either chopped it off or she would have knocked me out cold."

Dee threw her head back in a full belly laugh, joining Nipsey. "That I believe."

"Listen, Dee. I want to be the type of father that you don't want to replace every five minutes. For the record, I'll keep making mistakes. I'll keep fucking up because I have no clue what I'm doing. I just hope that we can come to some kind of agreement before I fuck our relationship up beyond repair."

Dee nodded. She couldn't make any promises. She didn't know what the future would bring. Her mother always said your word should mean something. Funny, that coming from a woman who loved a man whose word didn't mean anything. Maybe it was because of Nipsey that her mom knew the value of a promise.

Regardless, Dee couldn't give Nipsey her word. It was too soon. However, she may be able to give him some time. Time didn't cost anything. This time could be the change they all needed. Dee wondered how many times her mother thought the same thing. So she did the only thing she was prepared to do at the moment. She sat in a room with all those shoes, remembering.

Her father sat on her bed listening to every memory he had missed.

CHAPTER 26

Dee spent the rest of the evening in her room thinking about Nipsey. He was indeed a fuckup. She laid back and looked at the ceiling. She couldn't imagine a bigger ass. But to his credit, there had to be something Auntie M saw in him. There had to be something her mom had seen in him. Her mother didn't suffer fools lightly. Dee could never figure out if it was because Nipsey was a fool and she couldn't handle anyone else; or maybe, maybe there was something in Nipsey that drew good people to him.

Looking back, Nipsey should have been dead by now. If he didn't die from an overdose, surely he should have gotten capped for living on the streets. He owed people money. He jacked some pretty serious people for some shit during his hype days. Granted, it was all little shit and he was bad at it. One would think that, at the very least, he would have gotten a finger chopped off or a knee cap broken. Nipsey escaped all of that.

Nipsey had friends that helped. That was true. It wasn't that he was like a cat with nine lives. He hadn't used up the one yet. Maybe God looked out for children and fools. Nipsey could easily be described as a fool.

Dee got up and walked to the door. Reflecting in her room sometimes made her stomach grumble. At that point, food came to the top of the list. Dee shuffled down the stairs, but didn't make it all the way down before she heard, "That's a stupid idea."

"Shh. Your voice will carry."

Dee immediately stopped in her tracks. Auntie M and Nipsey were talking in the living room. She hadn't gotten to the point yet where they could see her. She stopped breathing, waiting for them to continue.

As Auntie M started talking again, Dee let out her breath very slowly. Trying not to pant from holding her breath, she listened closely.

"Dee doesn't need to know about this."

"But it deals with her, too. She'll be a target from this."

"There isn't a 'this.' I'm just having a few innocent questions asked and I'm not doing the asking. She will be fine."

"You know the stuff you see on television is a lie in more ways than one. The real bad guys operate for years, and no one knows who they are and where they come from. If they were in a database, they would have been caught years ago. Someone died. That's horrible. Someone killed him and no one paid for it. That's horrible too. You want to know what's worse? That person will keep killing until they are dead or caught. You're a nobody in this equation. They'll hit you the hardest. And right now, your Achilles heel is Dee. They'll either get Dee or you. Is that what you want?"

"You didn't mention you. They may come after you, too."

"It's a possibility, but I don't rank. Here no one knows me. They know that I used to use. I could be a scapegoat, but nothing more than that."

"Nipsey, understand. I'm not asking the questions."

"If he goes through with this, he's crazier than you. They will kill him."

"I can't be scared about this. I won't be."

Nipsey threw up his hands. "What other choice do you have than to be scared? They're killing people. You should be terrified."

Auntie M jumped out of her seat, and leaned over pointing in an angry whisper. "Do you think I don't know that? Do you know I feel his absence every day? Especially Sunday. Every Sunday I go down to that church knowing someone knows something. Knowing the wrong person is in the pulpit. Every Sunday without fail, I want to run out of there and come home. But I can't. Someone killed him, and everyone should know who."

Nipsey jumped up to meet her or more like tower over her. "It'll do more than kill you inside." Nipsey pulled Auntie M into a hug. "It will kill you outside, too."

"I have to. I owe him so much."

Auntie M didn't resist as Nipsey's pulled her into a tight hug. "You don't owe him your life. I'm sure if he was here he would tell you the same thing."

Sniffling through Nipsey shirt, Auntie M nodded. "He would. And I'd ignore him, too."

Auntie M pulled her head back and looked Nipsey in the eye. Even though he was never her biological son, he was her precious boy. He was the only one that would understand the next line. "Nipsey, I owe him love."

Nipsey hung his head. He knew about owing love. That's a debt that some people didn't deserve and would be indebted forever because of it. He owed Ilene love. That's why he never took another sip or did another line of anything now that he was clean. Yeah, part of it was rehab. It made him realize what it meant to have a support system. It also made him realize the gaping hole the lack of a support system caused, but the other part was something else. The other part was just love.

It was just that love was a gift. You should always give a gift of equal or greater value. The love he received from Ilene was huge. What he gave back to her wouldn't fill a thimble. So he owed her love. Since he owed, he didn't have the right to his life. He didn't have the right to make any decisions against what she would want.

He knew what Auntie M meant when she said she owed Pastor Clifton love. He got it in a way that no one else could possibly have. "Tell me about him. I never understood it really. You know, the times that I sobered up enough to care, I didn't really get it. Why didn't you get married? It wasn't as if he was a priest."

Auntie M pulled back and sat back down on the couch. She gave Nipsey leave to have a seat. She didn't know where to start. There wasn't a beginning. It was more like a gradual revelation. She smiled a bit. Yeah, each revelation had pissed her off. She didn't have a clue how Pastor Clifton had slipped under her defenses, but he made it. *Son of a bitch.*

"I don't know when it began. Or when I noticed what was going on. We were really friends at first. We used to hang out and laugh all the time. One day, I was talking to him on the phone and we said goodbye and in my head, I ended with 'Luv You.' Thank goodness that didn't pop out. I was mortified for a moment. Then I got to thinking. It was right. I did love him. So I was like, 'Shit.' How did that happen?

"It was little things every day. One time we went to a Mexican restaurant and they were playing a good salsa. I noticed that I was doing a little chair dancing. I stopped, but I noticed he was doing a little chair dance, too. Something inside of me just warmed at that thought.

"It was the day he called me before my birthday. I was just about to leave town the next day. He was like 'Check your mailbox.' In the middle of the junk mail and bills, there was a card from him. He wanted to make sure I got it before my birthday.

"It was the fact that he never ever allowed me to pay for a meal. I asked all the time, and he looked uncomfortable. He said, 'Umm, are we going to have to fight over this?'" Auntie M smiled at the memory.

"It was just seeing his phone number on the caller ID, and I was grinning from ear to ear. He made me giggle. Giggle. I am not a giggler. There became a point when it was actually an effort not to talk to him. I actually had to force myself not to talk to him every day. Every day something would happen, and I would feel a need to share with him and only him. I had it bad.

"When I was at my lowest, he never left me alone. He understood the concept that some days you just need a hug and someone to tell you it would be OK. Some days you just need that hug, that contact. He gave the best hugs. He would always give a little squeeze in the hug that made you feel so safe and secure.

"I was afraid. I was afraid that moving forward would ruin what we had, where we were. I never chased. I never knew how. I wasn't even a good flirt unless it didn't matter. He mattered. So I didn't chase. He didn't pursue. We just stayed where we were. Friends. I never had a friend like that."

Nipsey took one of Auntie M's hands in his as she continued her story.

"For the most part I was OK with the friendship part; it was just on occasion I would dream of him and want more than I had. There were others that filled the temporary void. You know the ones I did flirt with, the ones that didn't matter. They kept me occupied so I didn't become the oldest stalker in the world. Still, they weren't the ones that made me smile with just a hello. They weren't him.

"Who knows? Maybe it wouldn't have worked. Maybe it was all it was meant to be. I feel two loses, always. I feel the losses of my friend. I feel the loss of a dream.

"They both hurt and drug me down. I fought to get back up. I missed Ilene. I still do. I would do anything in my power to get her back. Please understand. However, I love having Dee here. I love having something to occupy my time and my love. You, too, of course. I've loved you forever. You are the son that I never had; and I thank God every day that Dee is in my life, partly because now I have someone to leave my paltry savings. I love you, but you're not even getting a $5 bill when they put me in the ground. Dee gives me purpose. I'm not quite sure about what I mean to her, but I hope at some point that she'll grow to love me.

"I get it. Right now, love equals pain. They are too closely intertwined for her. One day she will be able to think of something her mother did and smile or she'll be able to listen to *The Wiz* and dance through her own personal memories. That will come one day. Then I'm hoping she'll be able to accept me fully. Until then, I'll just keep throwing love her way and working on this project."

Nipsey rubbed at the creases settled into his forehead. "I hope Joe knows what he's doing."

"You and me both."

Dee made it back to her room with little noise. She couldn't believe it. Someone was going to start asking about Pastor Clifton. It made sense. Joe was the only person who Auntie M knew who knew the players. He was the linchpin in all this, but if Dee had learned anything over the years, she knew Nipsey was right. They had killed once. They would do it again. Most likely though, they would kill either Joe or Auntie M. *Who would stand up for them? Who would fight for them? No one else knew about what was going on.*

Dee needed to talk to Joe before it was too late. It would have to be tonight. The guard was clearly otherwise occupied. As soon as she saw him in the yard, she was going to walk over and check this out. Auntie M and Nipsey clearly wouldn't tell her a thing. She needed to go to the source and hope he was feeling generous.

"So are you going to do it?"

Joe had heard Dee come into the yard. He didn't turn around. He figured since he hadn't seen her out at night in a long time that it would be fine to come out. Shit didn't matter. It wasn't like he could avoid all of them forever.

"Do what? Light up?"

Dee leaned against the railing at the bottom of the step. "Help Auntie M."

"That my dear is a suicide mission. Think of it. We 'worship' with some of the biggest gossips the world has ever known." Joe turned and looked at Dee in the eye. "They haven't mentioned Pastor Clifton since he was buried. You don't even see a good headshake. You don't even hear an 'Ain't that a shame?' or 'We prayed for his tortured soul.' They pray for everyone's tortured soul. Not his. Why do you think that is?"

Dee shrugged.

"Whoever killed him wanted him not only dead, but dead and buried. Completely. It's a suicide mission. It was for Pastor Clifton. It'll be for anyone else."

"I'll help."

"You'll die."

"In my old neighborhood, Big Rock ran everything. Everything. Anyone that did something without Big Rock's knowledge didn't do it twice. He was the head guy. You just have to find the head guy here."

"Did everyone know that Big Rock was the man?"

"Well, yeah."

"No one here knows who the man is. Someone is going to a lot of trouble to make sure no one finds out."

"But you could find out?"

Joe turned his head and looked back up at the night sky with the moon offering a bit of relief from total darkness. "Probably. But will I live to tell anyone who that is? Probably not."

"I can help."

Joe threw up his hand. "How? Are you willing to sleep with some dude for the information? Did I miss something? Did you start hoeing yourself out when I wasn't looking?"

"You don't have to be a ho to get answers. Sometimes people will tell you stuff just because. Listen, we both know I'm cute. Got that much. I have a banging body, too. So what? My mother always said that was all window dressing. It was the luck of the genetic draw. It helps, no doubt, but I want to be a person she could be proud of."

Joe gave a scoff and a half smile. "A dead person? You want to be a dead person? She would be proud of a dead person? Who knew? Weird family."

Dee pressed her lips into a single line. Cursing him out wasn't going to get the desired result. She needed him as an advocate. She needed him to let her in. "It's important to Auntie M. She loved him."

"Yeah, I could see that. But she's willing to risk a lot of live, breathing people for one that's dead. I don't understand that. She's willing to risk you. Are you OK with that?"

"It's the right thing to do."

"But we both know you don't always have to do the right thing. So why now? Why is everyone so filled with the spirit all of a sudden?"

Dee stopped and thought. "Do you know this is the first time that I can remember having my own room? I have a space where I can close the door and just be. There is always food in the refrigerator. There is shopping for clothes on days other than special occasions. Do you know what it was like growing up? My mom, yeah, she did what she could. I can't fault what she gave me, but here there is a comfort that I never had before."

"You probably don't understand this, but I owe her love. That's a big debt to pay and I don't like owing people. So no, I don't have any intention of whoring myself out for information, but I will use all the tools in my arsenal to help you nail the bastard."

Joe looked. "And if you die?"

"Make sure I don't."

"I'm serious. What happens if you die?"

"It's your job to make sure I don't die in vain. You're going to have to handle that yourself."

"Don't put anything on me. If I need you, I'll ask. That's all I will promise."

"OK."

Joe looked Dee up and down. "She does it because she loves you. You don't owe her."

"Don't tell me who I do and don't owe. I know with every fiber of my being that my life is better because of Auntie M. Regardless of why she did it, she did it. She asks so little in return. If she wants to track down her lover's killer, I'm in."

"You don't know what this side of life is like."

"Yeah, I do. I don't talk about it, but I do. I know exactly who we're going to have to deal with to get this done. They will make the strongest man cry. I get it. But trust me, I have to. And know that it's not your job to protect me as we go through this. I came along on my own terms and I will continue on those terms."

"You are such a child. Don't you understand how wrong this can go?"

"Then why are you considering it? You could just walk away and tell Auntie M to hire a private detective. Why did you even listen?"

"Because I actually do owe. I owe more than you. This would probably just be the first thing in a long line of things that I owe."

"Who? Auntie M?"

Joe hitched his chin to indicate the house.

"I'm sure she's like Auntie M. She wouldn't expect you to do this."

Joe laughed. "Yes she would. You don't know her. Her love right now is very conditional. I need it to be where it was before. That will take some time. I'll call you if I need you."

"Wait, but—"

"We're doing it my way. I'll call you if I need you. When that happens, you will need to drop everything and get your ass wherever I say. Can you do that?"

"Yeah."

"Welcome to Dysfunction Junction. Let's just hope the train can really leave the station."

CHAPTER 27

Where does one start? Joe knew players, but he really didn't know players like that. It wasn't like he was deep in the game; he was more or less on the edge. His contact wouldn't tell him anything. This was information that made you call in a favor. The problem was he only had a couple of people that owed him anything. One was the cousin who used to buy from him, but he wasn't ready to call that one in yet. The family connection was pretty tricky. He didn't want his mother to find out what he was up to. When he got caught up the last time, his mother was on the wire to his aunt quicker than the police could leave the house.

Rumor had it that his aunt had beaten the shit out of his cousin. That was a grown-ass man of twenty-six. The family grapevine mentioned a cast iron skillet flying through the air. Cuz would be a bit tricky.

There was one other person that owed him a favor. He might as well start there.

He walked down the block and saw his friend coming toward him. He was on crutches, using them like a pro. Tim looked the same as he did in high school: tall like a basketball player and so thin you'd swear someone took him by the hands and feet and stretched him.

Tim's chocolate brown eyes lit up when he saw Joe. He hobbled a bit faster. They shook and hugged. "Dude, I haven't seen you since you were sent up. You're looking good. You need to get out of the game, though. That'll cost you. It'll cost you more than you lost the last time."

Joe held up his hands. "How did you … no one knows what I'm doing."

"Dude!" Tim laughed. "Someone always knows what you're doing."

"And you still know everything there is to know."

Tim shrugged. "So tell me about that hot neighbor of yours. That's why I should have made my way over to your house. Is she all that people are saying?"

"Really? All the women in Atlanta and you heard about my high school neighbor."

"Yeah, man. I heard she was worth the buzz. Can you confirm it?"

"Whatever, man."

"You hitting it yet? You can tell me." Tim laughed.

"She is in high school."

"Didn't stop you before." Tim tilted his head and lifted an eyebrow. "Did it?"

Joe clenched his jaw. Damn Evelyn and double damn Tim. Did the man have bugs in everyone's clothing? How the hell did he know so much?

Tim laughed again. "Don't worry. I only talk about your business to you. It never goes further. I know you're not hitting that. That would have hit the grapevine faster than lightening."

Joe slowly smiled. "You don't know what happens when the sun goes down."

Tim looked. "Yes, I do. And you're not hitting that."

"How do you know? How could you know all this?"

"I just do. That's all."

Joe took a deep breath. And so it began. "Pastor Clifton."

Tim looked at Joe. "Is dead."

"I know that, but I need more."

"He's buried. That's all you need. Everything about Pastor Clifton is buried." Tim turned away.

"He was your pastor, too. He baptized you. Remember the Boy Scout troop he started solely because you decided you wanted to be a Scout? He went camping and got poison ivy. Remember when you pawned your mother's engagement ring and then didn't have the money to get it back out? He gave you the money. He said that although he was in the business of saving souls, he wouldn't be able to stand to look at your human form if your mother found out what happened. He let you work it off at the church. Remember when your biological father came back around? He convinced you to talk to him. Who knew that man was loaded like that? Now you have a trust fund. Remember that. I'm not asking you to tell me. I just want to know who can, who would."

Tim looked Joe in the eye. "Funny you mentioned the trust fund. You know my dad offered to buy me a prosthetic leg. No problem. I could have one for every occasion. I had to turn him down. He offered to move me in with him. I told him in no uncertain terms that for my life I had to be an example to youth; I have to stay here, in this neighborhood. I have to hobble around on these damn crutches. I have to keep my mouth shut. Do I know who did this? We both know I do. So should you."

Tim stared off in the distance. Joe had brought up the one biggest issue with all that had happened. Pastor Clifton had been like a father to him. When his father was with his first family, his real family, Pastor Clifton listened like no one else did and cared like no one else could. He took a deep breath. He knew Pastor Clifton better than most. Pastor Clifton would forgive him his cowardice. Tim didn't know, though, if he could forgive himself.

It was easier because no one had asked any questions. It had happened and it was over. That was that. He didn't have to face his own cowardice. The police asked of course. They came by and did a cursory investigation. They didn't ask any deep, probing questions. Even in his day, he didn't give any information up to the police. It was a matter of principle. But to look at Joe and to lie was a different matter. Joe knew more than most what Pastor Clifton had meant to him.

Not only that, but he owed Joe. Joe hadn't explicitly called in the favor, but they both knew that he owed Joe. Tim told the wrong information to the wrong person once. They couldn't find Tim. They did find Joe though. Joe disappeared for twenty-four hours. When he came back, he looked as if he had been through a war. Joe never spoke about what had happened. Before that, Joe had been squeaky clean. After that, Joe started in the game.

Joe stopped for a second. "Your leg. Pastor Clifton. Same people?"

Tim looked at Joe. "Don't ask me that."

"I'm asking."

"Let's walk." Tim and Joe walked down the street talking about their shared childhood. They laughed, but the laughs weren't real. To anyone looking, they were just catching up. They knew each other well enough to feel each other's tension. They knew that they couldn't part without dealing with the issue that still lay between them, so they continued to walk and talk about everything that didn't matter. They reached Tim's condo.

"You should have bought a house."

"I feel better knowing there is a doorman. I know it's not really protection, but I get to sleep at night. That's worth something. You know I can't help you. I wish you the best of luck." Tim embraced him tightly. "You know how lucky you are. I hope to see you again soon."

They hugged and Tim went inside nodding to the doorman as he passed. Joe looked defeated and walked away. They both knew that when Tim said that he hoped to see Joe again soon that what he really meant is that he hoped he didn't end up six feet under.

Joe couldn't believe Tim didn't help him. *How could Tim not give him anything to go on? That was so selfish of him.* He never asked Tim what happened when he had lost his leg just as Tim had never asked him about the day he disappeared.

Luck. He needed more than luck for this. He needed a bleeding miracle. Of course, The Tigress. Why didn't he think of that? While Tim was TNN, The Tigress owner, Mo G, knew everything about everyone in Atlanta. The alcohol flowed freely. Mo G's, girls were the best in the city; and when they dropped it low, men lost their minds. The combination led to a lot of conversations that shouldn't happen.

Tim did get lucky once there. Stacy had gotten the private room for Tim and him as an eighteenth birthday present paid for by Mo G. The girls came out and each one was more impressive than the last. The G strings were off and the grinding was on. When one of them did a head stand between Tim's legs and slapped his cheek with her ass, Tim spontaneously came.

When it was all over, Stacy came in laughing. She looked at Joe. "I thought for sure it was going to be you. I even bet on it and you know how I hate to lose a bet."

Joe looked confused. "Why did you think I'd be the one to pop off?"

Stacy smiled. "That's easy. Tim has gotten some recently. You, dear, have not. I do still talk to my girls from school you know."

"What was the bet?"

"Mo G gets to pick my next act. Damn it. You couldn't just cum during the lap dance?"

"Wait. I thought he always got to choose your acts."

Sizzle laughed. "God was good to me. I got all this and brains, too. I don't know why everyone thinks my IQ dropped with the clothes. You know me better. Give me a bit more credit."

"I'm sorry. I just thought—"

"I was serious when I said this was my decision. All of this was my decision. Mo G actually does have a code that he lives by. There was no way he was going to pop my cherry. Come on. You of all people know how old I was when I started. My paperwork was airtight. So he let me dance. No one would touch me. If I didn't earn my tips on stage, I didn't get tips. There was no champagne room. There were no side parties. The other girls started to mother me. He looked out for me.

"You would think a man that was around tits and ass all day would have better control. Poor baby. Guilt gave me a house and a bank account. None of his exes got all that. My natural talent in certain areas keeps him coming back. It works for us."

For Joe's current mission, he didn't need Sizzle. He needed Mo G. He ran The Tigress with a strong hand; he didn't let any man do anything to his girls that they didn't want. Stacy's situation was a bit different. She belonged to Mo G. She saw too much. She knew too much. But she had food, clothing, and a roof over her head. She had property in her name. She had her own bank account; but she knew, this was her future.

Joe headed over to The Tigress to see Mo G. He'd see Joe because of Sizzle. Joe still didn't know if Mo G would tell him anything noteworthy. Joe was just Sizzle's friend, but lately he hadn't been a good one. He hadn't seen Sizzle since he got out.

When Joe turned into the parking lot of The Tigress, it was early and no one was out. He knew Mo G stayed on the same land. He turned to the back and noticed a road that led further back. About a mile in, he saw tall evergreen trees that hid a black electric gate. The gate was open so Joe drove through. As he reached the front door, the gate closed behind him.

When Joe knocked on the door of Mo G's residence, both the person who answered the door and Joe got a huge shock. Stacy was standing there. She screamed and launched herself at Joe. Joe caught her and swung her around before he set her down.

"What the fuck happened to you?"

Stacy laughed. "The usual." The next thing, Mo G was running into the foyer with his piece ready.

Joe held up his hands.

Now some people say Mo G isn't that imposing. If it wasn't for his money, then he wouldn't have anything. Some days that was true. Joe had seen Mo G on the street and not thought twice about it. Mo G was about five foot six, bald, and black. He looked fit, but he didn't look like he was going to muscle someone to the ground.

Mo G also never went anyplace alone. He always had one or two tall, beefy guys with him. So one figured he was a punk that needed a bodyguard. That was before he came barreling down a flight of stairs with his hand on the trigger. One look in his eyes and you knew that man would shoot the shit out of you without provocation. His eyes didn't flinch. They didn't blink. They were just flat—flat and ready. Joe held up his hands and took two steps back. He didn't know what his infraction was, but he sure as shit didn't want to die for it.

"Whoa. It's just me. Just Joe. I'm a friend of Stacy's."

Mo G turned to Stacy. "Baby, please. Don't scream unless you mean it. Never scream again unless you want someone capped." Mo G and Stacy shared a look.

She walked over to Mo G and kissed him on the cheek. "Lighten up.

From Behind the Curtain

This is our home. It's OK in our home."

Mo G walked over to Joe and held his hand out. Joe warily walked forward and shook Mo G's hand. Mo G stepped back and beckoned him in the house. "Come on in Joe. I'm sure you both have a lot of talking to do."

Joe looked a bit uncomfortably at Mo G. "Actually, I came to talk to you, Mo G."

Mo G stopped and looked over Joe. "Tell you what. You catch up with Stacy and then come see me. Matter of fact, I'll just join you. It'll save her from having to interrogate me later."

"This is business-related."

"If it wasn't you, you'd be right. Nothing with you is business-related to Stacy. You're her family." Those dark brown eyes flattened again. "I'm going to need you to act like that in the future. You've been gone too long."

Shit, Joe was sure that if he didn't do better by Stacy, he was going to wake up with a dead horse's head on the next pillow.

They went into an expansive loft-like room with skylights providing the bulk of the lighting. It was an open-concept living area that Joe would have guessed would have been more sleek and modern, but there was a very traditional aspect to it.

The dark wood ran the expanse of the floor. The living area was broken up by a throw on a dark brown leather couch with tan seating that faced the flat screen on the wall.

"Mo G, is that ninety inches?"

Mo G sank down on the couch. "About."

Joe eyed Mo. Mo's black Nike jogging suit was the most casual Joe had ever seen Mo G wear. He usually wore suits both at the club and while he was running errands.

The dining room had a huge wooden table with chairs next to the kitchen that had every gadget known to man. Beyond that seemed to be a family room area, and beyond that was an open door to the bedroom that Joe could barely see. He guessed it was as large as the rest of the house.

Joe turned back to Stacy. "This is off the chain."

Stacy laughed. "Yep. Come sit."

"Dude you need some security for this place for real. You can't be answering the door without knowing who is on the other side. That's insane."

Mo G spoke up. "Of course, I knew who it was before I let her go to the door, but she didn't know who it was. Trust me. Nothing happens on this property that I don't know about. Your license plate was run the minute you turned on the block. It was her scream that brought me running. Stacy has never been a screamer. Not like that." Mo G pulled Stacy down on the couch next to him.

Joe noticed that pretty much all remnants of Sizzle were gone. The hair just hung loosely around her shoulders. She was wearing jeans and not some slip of tight spandex. She looked happier than she did in all the years he knew her. It might have been the house, the ring sparkling on her finger, or the obvious baby bump.

"Now, you know wedding announcements do make their way into jail. Why am I the last to know that you got all domesticated?"

"I've always been domesticated. You all didn't give me enough credit in the day. I have to admit I was in a rough situation, and I had to make some decisions that weren't popular at the time. You know I always had the option to get a job somewhere and finish my GED at night. I didn't have to work here. I chose to work here. It worked for me.

"When I met Mo G, I knew why I was working. As I got to know him better, I decided what I wanted. I wanted this. I never really knew where I stood with him. Sure I got better gifts than the other girls at the club. Females talk, but for me it was love. I wasn't sure about Mo G. That weighed on me for a while. I would talk myself in circles trying to figure out his motivations.

"But come to find out, it was love for him—love and monogamy. Who knew he was capable of that? I thought I was going to be living with the black Hugh Heffner. I thought I was only trying to be the first girlfriend. This is more than I expected. So yes, we are married and he did knock me up. That was indeed a bonus." Stacy's eyes twinkled. "In a way you just don't understand."

Joe could believe now as he watched her cuddled under Mo G's arm stroking her belly.

"Did Pastor Clifton marry you?"

The minute Pastor Clifton's name came out of Joe's mouth, Mo G's attention shifted from Stacy to him.

"Yeah. We decided to get married about a month after you got sent up. Pastor Clifton almost passed out when I told him that we wanted to get married. You'd be amazed that he could still be surprised by something. He sat down and talked to Mo G. Apparently, Mo G passed his interrogation. Pastor Clifton still didn't like what Mo G did, but he said if it wasn't Mo G then it would be someone else. At least Mo G took care of us girls first.

"Mo G started coming to church with me. Now, Pastor Clifton still tried to convert Mo G every chance he got. All the way up until … " Stacy took a deep breath, tears started gathering in her eyes. "Trust me. I cry at least once a day for no reason. If you could excuse me for a few minutes. You wanted to talk to Mo G, anyway. I'll get it from him later. I just need … stay for dinner. Mo G, make him stay for dinner."

Joe watched as Stacy kissed Mo G and patted his hand before heading to the back room.

Mo G turned his expressionless face to Joe and looked him up and down. "Do you need a stripper?"

"No."

Sierra Kay

"Hmm. Do you know we don't mention Pastor Clifton around the house?"

Joe shook his head.

"It's hard on Stacy. I'm going to assume you are here for a different reason. I'm going to assume you didn't know that she was the one that found him. She wanted to tell him about the first baby. She walked into his office and was assaulted by the image of him slumped over his computer. She screamed and collapsed into a dead faint. When I came up there, she was lying on the floor of the office and he was slumped over his desk.

"I didn't know what happened. I thought I had lost her. Now you know why I came running when she screamed. She lost that first baby. It was not good. I'll always come running for her. Always!"

Joe nodded. He noticed that Mo G hadn't put the gun away. He had merely put it behind a cushion when he sat down. It was now back out and on his lap.

"What do you want?"

"I'm trying to find out who killed Pastor Clifton."

Mo G spurted out a loud laugh. "You are in no way prepared to handle that information. That's the type of intel that people die for. I'm not prepared to give it to you because like I said it's the kind of information people die for."

"He was like a father to Stacy."

"Yes, he was."

"Don't you want to bring his killer to justice? For Stacy?"

"Stacy isn't asking me to. You are. And Stacy had better not ask me after a discussion with you."

"You won't kill me."

Mo G laughed again. "Shit. I won't have to. That's how I know you aren't prepared for what you're asking. You don't know the players. And you sure as shit don't know the game. Yes, Pastor Clifton was important to Stacy. In a normal situation, his killer wouldn't have lasted twenty-four hours. This is not a normal situation. Drop it."

"But—"

"Don't think because you're Stacy's friend I'll tolerate repeating myself. I won't. Now you have two options. You can watch television with me until dinner is ready, and we can have a meal together. Stacy doesn't get many visitors. It'll be nice for her. Or you could get the fuck out of my house right now. Either way, we'll be alright."

Joe leaned forward. "Listen, have you ever had the sense that something was going to happen—something that you couldn't stop?"

Mo G assessed Joe. "You know I can't help you, but I will be curious to see how all of this plays out. What do you remember about the twenty-four hours you disappeared? Rumor has it—nothing."

Joe looked a little shocked, but still managed to look Mo G in the eyes. "That's right."

"You didn't do anything wrong and you came back with no nails. No nails on your fingers. No nails on your feet."

Joe assessed Mo G. "No one knows about the feet. That information wasn't released."

Mo G laughed. "Someone always knows and no it wasn't me who did it. Not my style. I stay in my lane. Keep all my fingers, legs, toes, and nails. Pastor Clifton asked the wrong question and he came up dead. What happens when you become the target?"

"Can you give me something to go on?"

"Who's really asking? This doesn't seem like a cause that you'd take up on your own. I mean look at you. You're a small-time drug dealer that got popped in his own basement. You go to church, but it's not like you're tithing your way to heaven. Why the interest? Why now?"

Joe thought about how much he could tell Mo G. He came back with not a lot. He knew that Mo G was on Stacy's side. Outside of that, it was a crap shoot.

"I just want to know."

"No, you're not that curious. That's not your style. The most initiative you ever took in life was the drug dealing. You don't even have enough energy to get all the way in or all the way out of that game. This isn't you. Your circle is smaller than it was when you started. Is it that cutie from next door? Dee? You'd do it for a piece like that."

Joe clenched his jaw. "It's not Dee."

"Hmm. No, but by the way your jaw clenched, you don't like me bringing her up. She means more to you than the average neighbor. See, this is why you're not good at this. You've already given me an edge. Couldn't help yourself. So it's not Dee. It's not her father. No one cares about what that fool has going on, but you both need to stay away from Evelyn. That skank is bad business. So not Dee, but if she's your Achilles heel and the most important person to her was also the most important person to Pastor Clifton, it has to be Auntie M."

Joe didn't say anything.

"See everything I know is in your face. It's in your every reaction. It's even in your lack of reaction. That's why I can't give you one damn piece of information. You're not putting me and mine in danger with your amateur hour. Are you crazy? So are you staying for dinner?"

Joe looked down and then tried again. "Think of what Pastor Clifton meant to Stacy."

Mo G stared at Joe like he was crazy. "Pastor Clifton is dead. Those things happen. The only thing you need to concern yourself with is what Stacy means to me, now. You would disappear—forever this time."

"Mo G, I don't know where else to go."

"I know. Trust me. That's the best position for you to be in."

Joe looked Mo G in the eye. Gun or not, he had to know. "Is it guilt?"

"What?"

"Did you marry her because you felt guilty because you were screwing her?"

"I never feel guilty about sex. Anyone who comes to my bed comes willingly, although that is none of your business."

Joe took a deep breath. "You can say the man that killed Pastor Clifton is none of my business. But Stacy. She deserved the best. Is that you? Can you be that for her with tits and ass in your face all day?"

"That's my business. This is my home."

Joe continued to stare at Mo G. Joe hadn't done a lot he was proud of since junior year in high school. It was high time he started taking care of his people. For all intents and purposes, Stacy was his people. He wasn't there when she needed him. He had been sent up, but now, now he could be there. He could be the friend that she needed.

Mo G cocked his head to the side and finally smiled. "Stacy is hard to explain. That girl is determined and pig-headed. Wow, is she pigheaded. Our relationship surprised me as much as anyone, especially the girls at the club." Mo G laughed. "The girls at the club almost revolted when Stacy and I got together. They were probably more protective of her than any fear of me or their jobs or anything. I thought for real they were going to put rat poison in my coffee. You know I wasn't known for sticking around. I enjoy myself. Why not? We were all grown.

"One day, we were celebrating someone's birthday, and I remember Stacy laughing at something. I apparently stopped in the middle of a sentence to look at her throw her head back and laugh. The girls still laugh about it to this day. It was then they knew that Stacy was different, and they didn't have to shank me in my sleep.

"Now are you going to be her brother or some joker that stops by every three years when he needs something? I love her, and she had the girls at the club, but I believe she needs something outside of this world, and if you can keep yourself out of jail, you might just be it."

"I'm not trying to go back to jail."

Mo G raised an eyebrow. "Shit, you weren't trying to go that first time. I will tell you this, though. Don't trust anyone. Not even me."

"I have to trust someone. I have to get to the next step. I need information."

Mo G got up and walked to the kitchen. He put his gun in a drawer of the black wood cabinets and started to take food out of the refrigerator. Joe followed him and sat on a stool by the marble counter with orange, brown, dark brown, and black swirls.

"You cook, too?"

Mo G laughed. "Hell, no. But I can heat stuff up like the best of them."

Joe leaned again. "How do I get the information I need?"

"You are a hopelessly lazy bastard. She'd done better hiring a private detective. That way she was sure to get her money's worth. You are damn near a waste of space. But that you're going to have to figure it out for yourself. This is all I will do for you." Mo G pulled a card out of his pocket. "Here. You are now a VIP at the club. That'll get you in. It'll get you free drinks. Now make sure you tip my girls. Don't be a total ass. Good luck."

Mo scrutinized Joe and continued, "So I know why you started sleeping with Evelyn. That first time must have been a shock, but why did you keep sleeping with her? That was just a waste. Dude, you were pulling then. I don't understand that. Shit, are you really that lazy?"

"Why the hell do you want to know about Evie? All the questions you can ask, and you ask about Evie. Didn't you just finish saying that she was a skank? Why waste your time?"

Mo G stopped prepping the food and smiled. "I have an insatiable curiosity and that skank makes me curious as hell. She's seriously hoeing and at such a young age. She's conniving as well. I just like to know what I'm working with. To figure that out, I have to get all the information I can about her. I'm not sure myself what her game is. That makes her dangerous, for everyone. So why Evie?"

"I'll trade you the info about Evie for what I need."

"Shit. That's not a swap. I can live without information about Evie, doesn't matter if you give that up or not. Have you asked her who killed Pastor Clifton?"

Joe paused and looked at Mo G trying to determine if he was going to get anywhere. Mo G had gone back to his task, turning on the oven and putting food in dishes to go in the oven. He didn't follow up or even look up. He just kept preparing dinner. Joe leaned against the counter.

"Evie. I don't understand her myself. She's been a trick for a while. I don't know why, though. Never did figure that part out. Look at Nipsey. Slept with her once. Now that fucker refuses to drink bottled water that still has the seal intact on the job. He'd die of thirst before he'd get caught up again. She's easy, but, no I didn't ask her about Pastor Clifton. It would shift the balance in this game that we play. Honestly, I would trust a hooker with a habit on the corner more than I would trust Evie."

"Ah, you're not totally hopeless. That's good to know. You know that's one female that I would never let dance in my club. It's not a look thing. It's a trust thing. She'd start trouble as sure as her ass is black. What about your

Sierra Kay

neighbor? From what I've seen in church, she's worth a bit of discussion. Are you sure it's worth it? Are you sure she's worth all this trouble?"

"It's not just about Dee."

"Bring her by the next time you come through. From what I hear, she'd be a welcome addition to the club."

Joe turned, eyes flashing, and looked at Mo G. He already had Stacy. There was no way he was going to get his claws into Dee. She was too young. Fuck it. "Listen—"

Mo G held up his hand laughing. "Dude, that is too easy. That is the easiest button in the world to push. There are little girls in pigtails with better poker faces. Let me at least do this for you. No one will be afraid of you. You haven't done anything to make them afraid. You won't scare them on reputation. But you can't ask the questions you ask and be this vulnerable. So listen. Practice.

"Don't believe anything someone says. Not one word. You take everything as if it's a threat. It shows on your face. It gives your enemies information on how to threaten you. That's not going to work. Don't believe. Don't buy into it. It's all a game. If someone comes up to say they are going to shoot Dee point blank in the head … see you reacted. Too easy. You can't react. Just take in the information. That's all you do until you can do more. That may be the difference between killing her and keeping her alive. Just listen. Don't react. Sing a song in your head if you must. Don't react."

Stacy came into the room. "Don't react to what?"

Mo G smiled. "I'm just teaching Joe here how to play poker."

Stacy smiled at Joe. "So tell me. I don't see Tim anymore. Is he still popping off in his pants?"

They all laughed and settled in for dinner.

CHAPTER 28

As strip clubs went, The Tigress was one of the best, from the glowstick pole in the center of the main stage to the variety of talent walking back and forth. When he gave his VIP card to the hostess, she handed him a stack. He asked if everyone got a stack to spend on the girls. She looked him up and down and responded, "Only those lucky enough to get a green VIP card."

Joe nodded and sat in the VIP section. He was really nervous for some reason. It had nothing to do with the fact that he almost ran into the stripper suspended from the ceiling by the straps that those circus performers use. If he hadn't ducked, he would have had pussy juice on his forehead. He had turned to see who had noticed. The hostess's eyes twinkled in acknowledgement. The episode clearly indicated he was a novice at this. But this was just tits and ass. The only difference is he couldn't touch. So that wasn't why he was nervous.

Maybe he finally got it in his head what this actually meant. He knew that Pastor Clifton was dead, but that happened when he was in jail. He didn't think about it much. Pastor Clifton was there when he got sent up and he wasn't when he got back. That was pretty much the end of the story for Joe. However, now he was in the lion's den or the Tigress's den to be more specific, and he was sweating bullets.

This was real. Mo G. had warned him this was real, but with each step he realized he could be dead tomorrow. He could ask a question today that would make someone kill him tomorrow. That was some real shit. It didn't get realer than that. So he was sitting there hesitating. He didn't know what he was supposed to do. However, he did know he didn't want to die because of it. *Right thing to do my ass.* People got shot all the time doing the right thing; people more important than him. Mo G was right. He didn't have a thing to leverage. There was no reason anyone would talk to him about this. Here he was wasting a good night in the VIP section. At least he could enjoy the show because he didn't think that he could ask the questions that he needed to ask.

That was the problem. Yeah, he had been to prison, but he hadn't really been to prison. He went to prison and someone told him that he was protected. That was that. He didn't mess with anyone and no one messed with him. He figured that one fight he had gotten into had spread the word. He found out later someone told them he was not to be touched. He didn't know who his protector was. He was told not to ask questions. He didn't. He just stayed out of everyone's way until it was time for him to get out of there. He didn't cause any trouble in the yard. When anyone got in his face, he turned and walked away.

His cellmate got a kick out of the whole thing. "You know normally if you turned your back on someone in here, you'd just get cut in your back. The fact that you're walking away whole means that you know someone serious."

Nothing Joe said would convince his cellmate that he didn't know anyone. His cellmate didn't care all that much. Joe's arrival meant more or less a vacation for the cellmate. Since no one messed with Joe, no one messed with the cellmate. He was never tested after the first night. He was just allowed to do his time and leave. No muss. No fuss.

He was now entering a world that even jaded people were steering away from. Mo G wasn't afraid of anyone. Mo G wouldn't have gotten as far as he had if he didn't have balls of steel. He wasn't even touching this one. Tim

... well he understood Tim. That wasn't that hard to figure out.

At least, Mo G helped him a little bit. Mo G allowed him to sit here and drink without asking anything other than a good tip for his girls. It was Joe that was second-guessing the brilliance of moving forward. All he had to do was tell Aunt M that this was above his pay grade. He'd tell her, and she would be OK with that. She had no choice. He didn't have to do this. He wasn't getting paid nor did he owe anyone. But then he thought of going home with his tail between his legs this early in the game. He stopped. He could at least ask a few more questions.

If he could get someone to talk, they would never tell who they talked to. His main problem was finding the right person without going through too many of the wrong people. His second issue was getting that one to talk.

Joe had waited a couple of days after dinner before going to the strip club. He wanted to make sure he was really going down this road before people started depending on him. He had seen Dee in the backyard. She had asked for an update. He didn't have one. The best he could say was that he was still looking into it.

Joe had thought about asking Tim to join him at The Tigress. It would be like old times again. At least it would be like the last time they were there. It might have been fun.

The problem was Tim had lost a leg talking about shit that wasn't his business. Joe didn't feel it would be right to ask Tim to sit in on this ... whatdoyoucallit. Well, he guessed it was a stakeout. Only, Joe figured, with a stakeout there should a partner somewhere for banter. For Joe's stakeout, he had beautiful girls serving him drinks, but that was about it. There wasn't a partner. He just stayed in the corner and sipped on his drinks. He had tossed the first one back, and then another drink appeared almost immediately. He figured he'd better slow down before he got too drunk to concentrate. He'd be the one trying to drop it on stage. That wouldn't accomplish anything.

He began observing the girls. It wasn't like he could just walk up to one and strike up a conversation. They were trained to work more, converse less. Plus, he didn't know who had the information. It wasn't like Mo G was going to tell him. Mo G made it clear where his priorities were.

He saw one girl after the next get on the pole with varying degrees of creativity. He was trying to figure out which one would provide him with the best information. He continued to look around and had just considered an older stripper that looked like she was going to have to have a retirement plan pretty damn soon. Joe hadn't figured out how to approach her yet.

Just then, someone covered his eyes. It was Stacy. This pregnant woman still looked comfortable as hell in the corner of The Tigress. The minute she sat down a drink was placed in front of her.

It wasn't juice or some fruity concoction. It looked more like sludge than anything else.

Joe looked at it skeptically. "What the hell is that?"

Stacy looked less than enthused. "That is chock full of vitamins and minerals and such to keep the baby healthy. Mo G found the recipe online. I have to drink that first before anything else. That's an order."

Joe broke out into a slow smile. "You tolerate that."

"I had no choice. He threatened everyone. The ones not moved by the threats were moved by the statistics that Mo G kept throwing at them. One lady that was already a mother felt bad for me and didn't serve me this shit first. Suddenly, her hours were cut. Let there be no mistake. This is Mo G's territory. Mo G says jump and almost everyone else says how high. I don't rank."

"Oh, please. You have Mo G wrapped around your finger. I'm sure you can get what you want."

Stacy laughed. "I used to think that too. That was a mistake, which I only made once. You remember in 'A Few Good Men,' 'We follow orders or people die.' Here it's more, we follow orders or people go broke. This," Stacy

224   From Behind the Curtain

motioned to include the expanse of the club, "is business. When he gives a command around here, people respond. I don't trump that. So if he tells his staff to give me this first, I'll drink this first. I suffer through this horrid drink. There really isn't an easier way to describe it besides horrid. And then I get back to drinks I actually like. I could complain, but then I'd just go thirsty. It's not going to change."

Joe laughed and shook his head. "You are so domesticated."

"Bite me."

Stacy put up her feet and got comfortable. "So what are you doing here, anyway?"

"Enjoying the view."

Stacy tilted her head to the side and assessed Joe. She stayed that way for a minute until Joe started to squirm.

"What?" he asked impatiently.

"This isn't your scene. We all know that. You look as comfortable as a snowman lighting a fireplace."

"I'm just thinking."

"You show up at the apartment a few days ago out of the blue and needed to speak to Mo G and today you're here. Mo G didn't tell me what you talked about. He damn near told me not to worry my pretty little head. It pissed me off, but I never get anything out of Mo G that he doesn't want to share. You, however, are really bad at lying."

"Why do people keep saying that?"

"Probably because it's true. You have an easy face to read, especially for me because I've known you for so long."

"Aren't you supposed to be asleep or something?"

"I would if I didn't have a baby doing flips in my stomach. Sometimes I just need to get up and walk around a bit. I went to the security office and saw you on the cameras so I decided to join you. You need information."

"How do you know?"

Stacy smiled. "Who did he tell you to ask?"

Joe took a deep breath. Mo G would kill him for involving Stacy. Really, though, she was involving herself. Either way, Mo G wouldn't take too kindly to this conversation. According to what Stacy had been saying, Mo G was going to learn about this interlude. Shit. He blew out a heavy breath. He was facing a number of no-win situations. He tried to stare Stacy down, but she held her own. So he willed her water to break instead. Again, no such luck. They stayed like that for what seemed like ten minutes, even though it had to have been one.

"He didn't tell me who to talk to. He told me I was the laziest person he knew and told me to do my own investigating."

Stacy laughed. "He likes you. You wouldn't be here if he didn't. He's trying to see what you are made of."

"So are you going to tell me who to talk to?"

Stacy stared at him for a while longer. He could see the wheels turning in her head. Then she surprised him. "No. No, I'm not. This is between you and Mo G. I'm interested to see how this is going to turn out. If he had wanted me to intervene, he would have told me that already. Since he didn't, I won't. I want—no I need—you to work out a relationship with him. Maybe one day we can be friends again. It'll be easier if you are friends with Mo G, too."

"You've turned into quite the evil bitch."

Stacy leaned her head back and began rubbing her belly.

"Oh shit, please tell me you're not going into labor."

Stacy kept her eyes closed. "The baby is just in an awkward position."

While Stacy was leaning back rubbing her belly, clearly making the staff nervous, Joe observed. He watched the older stripper. She seemed relieved to get off of the stage. She headed straight back to the dressing room. The next stripper they announced reminded him a lot of Stacy when she was on stage. She glowed as if she was meant to be there. The men in the place perked up when they heard her name. Some of them moved their dollars from their pockets. She was obviously popular. As she started to dance, Joe could see why. It wasn't just her flexibility or her dance moves. It was the obvious enjoyment she got from her job. It was the glow.

He looked around at some of the other girls. Some of them were smiling; most were trying to get their money on with the patrons. They were paying more attention to the men than the performance. A couple had clear envy in their eyes.

Stacy had glanced around quickly and assessed the situation. "They call her Golden. Mo said when he hired her she was worth her weight in gold. I don't know how he knew, but she is. She is an exhibitionist of the highest order. If it wasn't for the 'no shirt, no shoes' policy in most places, she'd probably never wear clothes."

"She reminds me of you."

Stacy raised her eyebrows. "How? You've never seen me dance."

"It's her comfort in her own skin. You always had that. Even when we were trying to convince you to try your hand flipping burgers, you just smiled and did what you wanted to do."

"True."

Nodding toward the stage, Joe asked. "Don't you worry at all about Mo G?"

Stacy laughed. "His old ass? No. He was tired of that train before I came along. I just had to convince him. Plus, we have something unique. At least I believe it will last forever. Time will tell. Today, he's given me no reason to believe it won't and so many reasons to believe it will. So I give him every benefit of every doubt. I know he told you about my first baby and Pastor Clifton. It was hard. Mo G was … mean he's … it's unexpected how special that man is. Any man, any day can walk away. His profession doesn't make it easier or harder to do that. Men cheat every day. Please. Half the men here would give their left nut to be with Golden, whether or not their woman finds out. But Mo comes home excited. Still. That means a lot."

Joe nodded. "So we were wrong to worry."

"No you were right to worry. I still need people that have my back regardless, but I'm good."

"Yeah, you seem better than me."

Stacy nodded. "That's not hard. You're fucking that high school girl. Seriously?"

"What the hell? How does everyone know about that?"

Stacy laughed. "Dude. Everyone doesn't know about that, but I damn near live at a strip club. We deal in information as much as ass. Mo G knows everything about everything. He tells me most. But he worries. So what am I not supposed to know about what you're doing?"

Joe looked at the ground. "If it was just me and you like the old days, it would be fine. Mo. He will kill me."

Stacy laughed. "Murder is a bit harsh. It's just he will protect me at all costs."

"He will kill me."

"Remember our pinkie swear?" When they were ten, they had sworn the truth in every situation.

"You're holding me to a pinkie swear. We were talking about who had a crush on who. We were talking about your mom and her men. We were talking about my mom and dad. We were talking about secrets that kids have. Those secrets didn't put anyone in danger."

"Remember when you were in jail? Who do you think protected you in there? Who do you think made sure you were never touched? And you never even came by to see me after you were out. You wouldn't be here now if you didn't need something big."

"What? How?"

"You always treated me as if I was an innocent. Even though you knew more than anyone what I was dealing with at the time. My mother's lifestyle never touched me directly, but being around it ensured that I knew more than I ever should. Someone owed her a favor. I collected."

"Did Mo G know?"

"Not at the beginning. It didn't come from here. It was my mother's contact. Eventually, I had to tell Mo G. Although the guy owed that debt, he confused owed with owned. Mo took care of it. So now that you owe me, you can tell me what's going on," Stacy said with an inquiring rise of her eyebrow.

There was nothing that Joe could do. This was Stacy. He had stayed away more because he was embarrassed than anything else. He was a dealer. He had a record. She had Mo G. She didn't need him. Now both she and Mo G told him he had let her down. And not only that, he had let her down after she tried to help him. Now he felt like the lowest heel. He turned to see who was nearby, then he leaned in. "I need to find out who killed Pastor Clifton."

Stacy's eyes chilled. "I asked Mo G once. He told me no. He wasn't going to risk me like that. Risk me. He wasn't going to risk me, but Pastor Clifton and my baby are dead. It wasn't a pleasant conversation, but nothing I said made a difference. Nothing I did." Stacy flipped her hair. "And trust me I know some of the best tricks in the business. I can have a man crying. Nothing. He's mum on it; and immovable, and he will kill you for involving me." Stacy leaned forward and grabbed a napkin. "Got a pen?"

He pulled out a pen. Stacy wrote a number down.

"Like you and Tim, my mother disappeared. This was before she left. She left for good within a week of her coming back. That twenty-four hours, she just disappeared. This isn't Mo G's choice. It's my choice. I can't sit by and see it continue to happen. Listen Mo G can't know about this. I'm the sole focus of everyone in the security office right now. So I'm going to hug you and get out of here. But call. It's time. It's past time. I owe Pastor Clinton so much. I can't… give me a hug."

Joe stood up and hugged Stacy. Then she playfully swatted him on the arm. "No smacking asses now." On her way over to the exit, the vision of Stacy was swallowed up by two security guards. She soon had them laughing as she turned, waved, and left. Stacy had always amazed him. She was stronger than he was on every level. Joe didn't know how to handle this new wrinkle. He had two women who wanted to help. However, they had no idea what the hell they were getting into.

They never lost twenty-four hours of their lives to a ghost. They were ready to slay dragons without knowing the repercussions. Stacy was ready to avenge Pastor Clifton, her mother, and her baby. At what cost? Dee was ready to jump into the fray, at what cost? Their lives hadn't been easy, but nothing had prepared them for what they were going up against. Joe looked at his hand. It had taken about a year for his fingernails and toenails to grow back. That was a long reminder, but he was whole again. Tim was walking around forever with one leg. He was still alive, but carried a constant reminder.

That ghost proved to be a resilient character. It kept appearing. Joe had originally thought it was Tim and him. He thought that he was only taken because of Tim. However, if that wasn't the case, if there was more going on, that was different. The problem was Mo G was too ingrained into the grapevine. He didn't know how in the world Stacy planned to meet him without Mo G finding out. This could blow up in their faces. However, if Mo G wanted to see what he was made of, having the audacity to involve Stacy would either prove to Mo G that Joe was determined or crazy. Either way, it was a move. But Mo G might be the least of their worries. If the ghost found out they were snooping, it would be over. Joe knew for sure the devil existed, and he took his pound of flesh at least twice now.

Joe wasn't seeing the dancers on the stage. The music changed and he didn't even shift. He was thinking about whether this project was worth doing. *What sense did it make for him to take two steps forward when everyone around him was taking two steps back? The easy way would be to leave it. However, how is it possible for him to have less courage than Stacy when she clearly has more to lose? How was it possible to not be the son his mother deserved?*

Sometimes you don't get the luxury of choosing your path. History taught that over and over again. So he exhaled and gathered his things. He left knowing that he was about to take a step into the abyss dragging at least one, if not two people with him, and all he had was hope that he'd find his way back.

CHAPTER 29

Stacy was lying down snug with Mo G's arm around her torso. She couldn't sleep. It wasn't the lying to Mo G. It was the fact that no matter how she ran the scenario, Mo G would find out about what she was doing with Joe. She'd prefer to have his blessing, but sure as shit that wasn't going to happen. She began to shift to get up.

Mo opened his eyes. "Babe, what do you need?"

Stacy smiled. She knew in her own way she was more pigheaded than Mo G. This was going to be a definite test. Mo would never agree and Stacy had to do it. Stacy touched her stomach. "We're good, Baby. I just couldn't sleep."

Mo G stretched and sat up. "How did your meeting with Joe go?"

Stacy remained quiet.

Mo leaned back against the headboard and continued to talk. "Of course, you knew we would have to talk about it sooner than later; middle of the night works for me, if it works for you."

Stacy bit her lip and still remained silent.

"There is no other way to put it. Your friend is in too fucking deep. He is going to die. He's going to ask the wrong person the wrong question and he will die."

"Listen, Mo."

"No, you listen. Death is final. I won't lose you over his amateur bullshit. I won't. If you go through with this, if you choose to go forward, you will be choosing Joe over me; it will be over. I love you more than my next breath, but you've already risked yourself for Joe once. You didn't even tell me about it until that fool started tripping. This is worse. Much worse. I won't go through that again." Mo G crawled out of bed and took Stacy's hands in his. "Stacy, just stay out of it. Please."

Stacy closed her eyes and remembered the fear in her mom's eyes when she came back. *How many more had there been?* In Stacy's circle, she could count three and her circle was miniscule. Three people had disappeared for twenty-four hours—long enough to be handled, but short enough not to involve police. She felt her baby move and knew without a doubt that she should stay out of it. Then one thought alone changed her mind. What if her baby disappeared for twenty-four hours and came back broken in some way? There were times that you had to do the right thing regardless of the consequences.

Stacy inhaled deeply. "Are you asking me to stay away from Joe?"

Mo smirked. "I'd love for you to stay away from Joe, if only for the next month or so."

"But are you asking me to?"

Mo knew there was a line being drawn. "Can we settle for limiting your exposure and mostly talking on the phone?"

The wheels in Stacy's mind began to turn. She had never denied Mo anything. She had never lied to him. Sometimes though, he was a bit overprotective, and she needed to sidestep his overprotective nature. This wasn't being overprotective. Stacy knew more than even Mo the risk that she was about to take. If she moved forward with Joe, she'd risk her love, her baby, herself—everything.

She knew that everything revolved around the church. It always had. Everyone that disappeared had some connection with the church. Even her mother would never miss church on Sunday. Back then, Stacy thought that meant her mother was praying for a respite from the alcohol and drugs. Every Sunday gave Stacy hope. What if that wasn't the reason for her mother's trips to church?

Stacy's mother had turned up at a couple of parent-teacher conferences strung out. She never showed up to church strung out. She was always put together for church. Wait, there was one time. She was getting jittery like she tended to do if she was without for too long. People were looking at her, but no one said anything. Eventually, she got up and walked to the lobby. When she came back, she had it together. Stacy had assumed that her mother had a quick line or pill or something in her purse. That was it.

When Stacy was dancing, she used to talk to men who would do anything except miss church on Sunday. She used to inquire about their religious devotion. However, they weren't devout. They just would never miss church. The girls in the club talked about it in hushed whispers. For Pastor Clifton to die, it meant that what was happening was so insidious that it wasn't even top down. It was filling the cracks and crevices and spreading like tree roots under concrete. Concrete seems solid, but if a tree needs that space to expand, the concrete will give. That expansion was happening at the God is Love Church.

Stacy knew she wasn't anywhere near as hard as concrete. The best thing to do would be to stay in this cocoon that she built for herself. She could tuck herself under Mo G and be perfectly happy. She could. She'd done it for years. Sometimes though, sometimes you had to take the risk.

Pastor Clifton took that risk. He faced the condemnation of the entire congregation. Joe and Tim were always on her side. However, the rest of the congregation would actually go to Pastor Clifton and tell him to ask her to leave. One sister wasn't even discreet about it. She brushed past Stacy and walked right up to Pastor Clifton. Bold as, well … pretty much bold as a stripper in church, she told Pastor Clifton what he needed to do about Stacy.

Pastor Clifton said something that Stacy would never forget. "Stacy, like us all, is a child of God. However, unlike everyone, she is like my own daughter. I would never kick a child of God out of this church. I sure as …." he stopped. With flashing eyes, he composed himself. "Let's just say Stacy will be staying. I suggest you pray on your devotion. Then we'll know both of you are in God's hands, Sister."

That was that. Stacy knew beyond a shadow of a doubt that Pastor Clifton would want her to hold on to her happiness and forget about him. He was one that never forgot or judged her, even when her own mother decided to forget about her.

Mo was still waiting. He shifted a bit bringing her attention back to him. She touched the side of his face. There was no such thing as a perfect relationship. She couldn't give him what he asked for. She just couldn't. Stacy brushed her knuckles against Mo's stubbly chin.

"Joe doesn't trump you. This isn't about Joe."

Mo reached up and grabbed Stacy's hand.

She kept talking. "Don't ask a promise of me that we both know I can't keep. Don't ask it. That way I won't have to lie."

Mo hung his head. "Stacy, this is bigger than me. I can't protect you on this one."

Stacy smiled that saddest smile. "But you will try, won't you?" Stacy rubbed her belly. "You will give everything you have to keep us safe, won't you? That's what one of us needed to do for Pastor Clifton. We thought he was bigger than life. We never even saw this coming. It's not Joe. It's Pastor Clifton. After the miscarriage, I was in no position to do anything. When I found out I was pregnant again, I was so scared. Whoever killed Pastor Clifton also took our first child. Do you ever think about that?"

"Every day, Stacy. Every day I think about that. There was nothing I could do."

It had been two years since Pastor Clifton died. Two years and there were still times when she wanted to curl up in a ball and cry. She missed him more than her own mother. *How crazy was that?* Pastor Clifton had that effect on people. She still remembered when Joe's mother started making him go to church. Stacy and Tim laughed hysterically. However, they were friends so Stacy and Tim tagged along. They scoffed at the uncomfortable folding chairs. They had so many inside jokes that all they had to do was look at each other and start giggling. Pastor Clifton got to the pulpit and they tried to pull it all together.

However, two minutes into his sermon, he said the word "duty," which to them always sounded like 'doodie' and it was all over. Joe's mother was frowning. They were laughing out loud. Pastor Clifton merely stopped his service. "Ahh. I almost forgot about duty vs. doodie. That was it, wasn't it?"

Only Joe had it together enough to nod his head.

The rest of the congregation looked like they were going to go back to the old days and grab some pitchforks. Pastor Clifton was different. He merely winked at them and promised to do better. You couldn't really laugh at a pastor that was that cool. So they got it together and the rest of the sermon went off without an issue.

Pastor Clifton was always able to make the most awkward situations right. It was his gift. Everyone was a part of the family the minute they walked through the door. It had to have been family that did him dirty. There was no other explanation.

Mo exhaled. "Tell me what you want Joe to know. I'll run interference."

"And that's why I love you. But it has to be me."

Mo shook his head. "Why?"

"I didn't do it when I was supposed to. No one did. Everyone went radio silent. I'm not proud of that. I should have forced the police to investigate. Really investigate. I didn't. That one's on me. This is my fight." Stacy took a deep breath. She was trying to stay calm, but it wasn't working very well. "Look, Mo, I need ..."

Mo held up his hand. "I heard you. I heard what you need. I need you alive. I need for nothing to happen to our second child. I need to protect you the best way I can. You're grown. I know I can't stop you, but with everything that's in me, your safety comes first. You need to know that now. I will lie to you, manipulate you, I'll do everything in my power to keep you safe. If you feel you have to do this, fine. Go do it. It will be with my rules, though. Fuck that. Shit, Stacy, don't you understand. They killed Pastor Clifton. Don't you know what that means? Don't you get it? You can die or the most important person to you will die. That's not me. That's our baby. Damn."

"But Mo."

Mo shook his head. "Give me two days. Then we'll talk." With that Mo walked into the closet. He exited a few minutes later wearing one of his suits.

Stacy started to ask, "Where ... ?

Mo held up his hand. "It's better if you don't ask."

He kissed her on the cheek and walked out of their bedroom. Stacy stared after him until she heard the front door close. After that, she sat down on their bed. She knew that Mo would have no problem taking care of himself. She knew he had connections that she could only dream of having. She also knew that she still felt guilty about dragging him into this. It was her problem. It was also Joe's and her mother's problem. They weren't Mo's responsibilities. She knew there was nothing she could say right now that would get Mo out of the way. Her only comfort was that if anyone would keep them all alive through this, it surely wasn't Joe or her. It was Mo.

Sierra Kay

CHAPTER 30

Mo walked into the basement. Concrete walls, concrete pillars, and industrial lights. The room smelled dank. Of course, it was a basement. There wasn't any air circulating down here. That didn't bother Mo. It was the lack of natural light, the lack of natural light and the feel of death. He didn't think anyone had ever died down there, but quite a few people spent torturous hours there. The things these walls knew.

"This better be important."

Mo stopped. He had to leave his bodyguards at The Tigress when he went there. They weren't allowed. There was no need to get any closer. He didn't need to see anyone's face. He just needed Stacy to be safe. He also knew there was evil in the world that no amount of prayer, holy water, or any other remedies could get rid of. That's the type of evil that you did your best to avoid or at best not fuck with. Now he was forced to go for a meeting.

"Joe is asking questions that are better left unanswered."

The shape at the other side of the room was silent. Then it said, "Joe?"

Mo nervously ran his hand down his thigh. He knew it was always better to have complete confidence going into any negotiation. They had known each other long enough to know that once he got something to lose, life got real. Quickly. Before, he had more room to maneuver. Fortunately, for the level of ruthlessness that was executed, there was a sort of code that was lived by. "Yeah. Listen I need Stacy to be protected."

He saw the head tilt inquisitively. "Why would Stacy be involved in this?"

Mo took a deep breath. "Joe reached out to Stacy."

"And?"

"Stacy doesn't know anything. I'm afraid she's going to start asking questions. I don't want her involved."

"So the great Mo G doesn't have control over his woman. Interesting."

"She told me you took her mother."

"What I do is none of your damn business. She was brought back, wasn't she?"

Mo pressed his lips together. "She wasn't the same."

"No one ever is. That's the point, isn't it? If no one ever adjusts their behavior, then what are we doing?"

Mo pressed his lips together. "I gave you the information you needed. Leave Stacy alone."

"Then you will have to help me. If Stacy breathes in the wrong direction, she starts on the same level as all the others. You control her or the clock starts ticking, and you know how I like the ticking."

"I've done enough." He heard a chuckle grow into a laugh.

"Are you successful? Are you? Isn't this how your involvement started? You wanted to be more, better. Remember the women that used to dance in your club? That one was five months pregnant, at least. You came to me. Remember. I didn't come looking for you. You looked for me. You wanted a piece of the action. You don't get out because your girlfriend might find out that your hands are as dirty as mine."

"I don't kill people."

"Really? Interesting. Too bad Stacy can't say the same thing."

"What? How? Stacy's never … " That laugh brought Mo up short and chilled him. "What did you do?"

"Not me. Stacy. Her mother was becoming unstable. That bitch was crazy high all the time. She was always where she wasn't supposed to be. The only thing she managed was church every Sunday. Her donations though kept coming up short. Stupid ass used the envelope the church mailed her and then shorted the church. We gave her time.

"Next thing you know, she's back running around the church during service looking to score a hit. She overheard something she shouldn't have, wouldn't have if she could have kept her hype ass still. At that point, it was too late. She copped a free taste in return for staying quiet; was forced to lace a few things in their house that night. We kept an ear on things to make sure. Once Stacy went to bed and we disposed of the body. Hypes are easy. It's in their nature to stray. It's not our fault that Stacy was the one that brought her mother coffee on that last night."

Mo fumed. "Stacy could have died."

"Yeah. Good thing she wasn't a coffee drinker, eh? Now, I'm going to have a little party here. I need you to make sure Nipsey shows up."

Mo's fists were clenched at his side. "Why, Nipsey?"

"He's the one I'm not controlling now. I only need Dee. That will bring Auntie M. Stacy can give the message to Joe. Joe can give it to Nipsey. If Stacy show's up, she's dead. If not, no problems. I'll resolve all of this and get us back where we were."

Mo's nose flared. "Where were we? Oh yeah. You're trying to take over the world."

"Really, Mo. You give me too much credit. Ambition like that will get you six feet under or locked in a six by six cell. I only want to maintain my corner of the world. That's all."

As Mo turned and started to leave, he threw back, "I'll do it."

"You know, Mo, if you want out, all you have to say is the word."

Mo stopped and smiled. "There's only one way out with you and we both know that. We both also know I have too much to lose now. So let's not pretend anything different."

"Well, Mo G, I just see your chest getting all swole over there over the fact that your baby mamma killed her mamma; or was it swole because she could have died in the process?" The voice watched him carefully. "Maybe a bit of both."

Mo clenched his teeth. "As with everything else, I'm sure I'll get over it."

The voice nodded. "I'm sure. Tick tock goes the clock."

The next day Joe met Stacy at the club. They touched cheeks and sat down.

"So, are we bugged?"

Stacy laughed. "Probably not, but I can't say for sure. This was the stipulation for me helping you. I had to do it here. At least he didn't try to put his foot down."

"What would you have done if he did?"

Stacy thought about it for a minute. "That would have been a turning point in our relationship. Don't ask me if it would have been a good turning point or a bad one."

"How do you know the stories you're about to tell me are true? You said before that you heard some things that you wanted to pass on."

Stacy lifted her eyebrows and looked at Joe. "Cause I'm an honest ho and all my hos is honest."

Joe snorted at the reference to Harlem Nights©. "Now are you gonna tell me someone shot off your pinkie toe."

"Naw, all my body parts are in the perfect position." Stacy skimmed her right hand down her body. "Do you doubt all of this?"

Joe looked at her. "Since when did you become a ho?"

Stacy laughed. "You got me. I'd like to consider myself more of a sexual scientist. I love to experiment. How do you think I rocked Mo?"

Joe shuddered. "Stop. Please stop."

"Fine, OK."

Stacy laughed. Then she got serious. "Listen, I have a message for you from Mo. He let me deliver it because it meant so much to me, but he didn't like it. That's why we had to meet here. This is the one place that he can control the security. No one will see us together outside of The Tigress. I won't be around for a while, a long while. Mo made me promise at least two months. He wants there to be space between the time all of this goes down and any connection to me."

Joe looked at her. "What changed his mind? I thought he'd kill me for involving you."

Stacy shrugged. "For the record, I think that option is still open. He isn't pleased that I'm involved and that's stating it lightly. I think he wishes that he could wring my neck or at the very least lock me in a room. The thing is, if you and I went off half-cocked, he wouldn't be able to control the outcome. He's doing his best now to minimize the damage to me. You will be all out there on your own."

"So? So who is it? Who killed Pastor Clifton?"

Stacy snorted. "I don't know. He won't tell me. I think he believes I will do my own retaliation. Matter of fact, we're leaving town today. Damn man. He made me promise before he would tell me anything."

"Where are you going?"

Stacy shrugged. "He won't tell me that either. He said I'd probably tell you."

"Hmm. Well?"

"Shut up. Fine. He's right on all counts, but anyway, here's the skinny." Stacy opened her purse. "On Tuesday, you are to go to this address. Follow these directions. He seriously suggested that you bring Nipsey with you. His exact words were, "You'd be an idiot if you didn't.""

"Why would I be an idiot? Why should I bring Nipsey of all people? Am I walking into a trap? What is it?"

Stacy held up her hand. "I asked him on the life of our unborn child if you would be OK. He said that it wasn't a trap and on the life of our unborn child, you should make it out OK. He said if I was in that situation, he'd trust me to go. I don't know what you're going to find, but Mo seems to think you'll find something. Tuesday is tomorrow."

Joe shook his head. "This feels too easy."

"Nothing about this is too easy. It's probably just a lead. It's not like someone will be there with a killer sign tattooed on his chest., but according to Mo, it's a major lead. I guess it would have to be if we're packing up shop. I'm sure he'll bring me back after the baby is born. Then you'll be Uncle Joe. You better start buying gifts."

Joe grabbed Stacy's hands and they leaned in and rested their foreheads on each other's. "If not for the baby, I'd stay. I owe whoever this is."

Joe shook his head. "Listen, I know Mo is your man, but as your friend, let me slay this particular dragon for you. Well, for us. I need this as much as anyone."

Stacy nodded and pulled back. Looking him in the eye, she said, "Dude, Tim came back without a leg. He's missing a leg. This is too big."

"It's a lead, Stacy," Joe replied. "When we were taken, we didn't go looking for it. It came for us. That alone makes this slightly better."

Stacy tried again. "Pastor Clifton is dead from whatever this is."

"Right. So I have to do this. Take a deep breath. Leave town. It's not a setup. Mo G said that much himself."

PHANTOM

Look at her—so peaceful. She doesn't even realize that her life was about to change—had changed. Changed the minute she stepped into M's house. Now she had purpose. She was going to get the greatest gift. Fuck M. This wasn't about her anymore.

Look at her. Sitting there with the telltale blue shirt from the spa. You'd think with all those matching uniforms, she'd blend in. She chose to tie it in the back. She chose to stand out. She chose to be noticed. She was audacious, this one. This one was what was needed to move forward.

Her sleep is peaceful, totally compliant. She has completely succumbed to the drugs she was given. The hair from her ponytail, though high on her head, flopped to the right side of her face. Her mouth was slightly open with light snoring sounds coming from it. It was unfortunate then she needed to be drugged to come—a shame really. It would have been easier if they could just speak over coffee. But, it wasn't that easy. There were other players now. Those players were bumbling too close and really just serving to piss people off. Did Maybelle really believe that they could bring this down?

No. Of course, Maybelle didn't. Better people than Joe had tried. He was merely an irritating fly in the ointment. Stacy. Stacy was a bit different. She was a sharp one. The fact that Mo G didn't have a tighter leash was again irritating. It wasn't a game changer though. They weren't game changer type people. They would be dealt with soon—probably tonight.

Dee was a game changer. There was enough in her file to show that she'd had enough strength to handle the empire. She didn't let being broke get in her way. She started slanging. She didn't let greed get in the way. When Joe asked her to slang in Atlanta, she turned him down. She didn't do it for money. She did it for a purpose. Those who were driven by purpose are the only ones that run the game instead of the game running them. Game changers had to be cold at times. Sometimes they had to be downright brutal. Dee possessed that steel core.

Now, her arms needed to be tied. Now, she needed to be placed in a dog cage to ensure she stayed put. She wouldn't take well to it, but it wasn't for long. Twenty-four hours is all that was ever needed to change someone's mind. Twenty-four hours. Well twenty-two now. It would have to begin soon.

M wouldn't tolerate this, even though she asked for it. Maybelle knew too much. She'd know the minute that Dee didn't come back home that the clock had started; it was time to begin.

CHAPTER 32

Dee woke up to find herself sitting in a rolling office chair in a dog pen. The overhead lights were on so she could get a good look at her surroundings, which consisted of concrete, folding chairs, and air. Her wrists were taped to the chair and her feet were tied at the ankle. She tried to rock her chair into the sides to see if she could knock it over, but noticed the pen was attached to the concrete.

Dee looked around. She seemed to be in a warehouse of some sort. It was empty except for some folding chairs that were set up in front of the pen. She screamed for help. She kept screaming, listening to her own desperate echoes. *What the hell? How did this happen? What the fuck was going on? This had to have something to do with Pastor Clifton's death. Fine, she knew Joe was investigating and Auntie M had put him up to it, but this wasn't her thing.* She hadn't even helped him yet. If she did something and this happened, then she would understand, but this was crazy.

Evelyn walked through the door at the other end of the warehouse.

Dee stopped screaming and watched Evelyn make her way to one of the chairs in front of the makeshift cage. Dee never took her eyes off of Evelyn.

Evelyn sat down in one of the folding chairs with a look of self-satisfied evil on her face. The stuff at school was one thing. This was kidnapping. *Was Evelyn a participant or a pawn?* Maybe someone was kidnapping all the teenage girls and Evelyn had a quick and hard case of Stockholm syndrome.

They sized each other up. Dee wasn't going to start first, and it appeared neither was Evelyn.

Dee didn't know what time it was, but she felt time just ticking away.

Evelyn raised her left eyebrow encouraging the unspoken question.

Dee gave up. They could stubbornly stare at each other for hours, or she could try to make sense of what was going on. Dee chose the latter. "OK, I'll bite. What's going on, Evelyn? Why are you here?"

Evelyn picked imaginary lint off of her top. "I'm just watching. Rumor had it that you were going to be the next pickup. It seems that some people around you have been very naughty." Evelyn's eyes narrowed to slits. "You have Joe running around asking questions that should remain unanswered. That's bad Dee, really bad. When Joe was with me, he didn't ask questions like that. He stayed in his place. It has to be your influence. "

"Evelyn. This is crazy. This is kidnapping. You don't want to be an accessory to this. You could go to jail."

Evelyn laughed. "This isn't kidnapping. This is an intervention. You've seen those on TV, right? An intervention is when everyone comes with their little letters and shows someone the error of their ways. That's all this is. You merely have gotten off track and you need to be put back on track. What are you going to tell people? That a high school girl, who doesn't drive, kidnapped you and brought you here? That a preacher's daughter who is in church every single Sunday wanted to do you harm? You? The drug dealer?"

Dee paused. "There is no proof of that. You're just repeating what you've heard. That's all you're doing."

"Yeah, well, it'll help my case a whole lot of hell more than it will help yours. Plus, it's not like no one knew you were doing that. Let's take your delectable father for instance."

Dee gritted her teeth. "He doesn't have anything to do with this! Leave Nipsey out of this."

Evelyn smirked. "Ahh, feeling protective of your father. That's so cute. However, I agree. We need to protect things of value; and Nipsey, hmm, he's very valuable." Evelyn's eyes caught a rapture and she shifted slightly to the left in her chair. "I mean, God, I swear that man rode me raw. He's that good. You should be proud."

"Ugggh. One thing Nipsey is not into young girls. That's not his style. Even if it was, you are not his style."

Evelyn got up and trailed her fingers across the front of the cage. "Hmm. You'd think, right?" Evie pushed a button that brought a screen down. She opened a box and brought out a DVD player. Next thing Dee was watching her dad, her father, fuck Evelyn. It wasn't lovemaking. It was raw and it was apparent that they both were loving it. Dee wanted to pretend that she was strong enough to watch her father flip Evie over and start again, but she wasn't. She started heaving. She turned away from the spectacle and threw up whatever hadn't digested until she was dry heaving.

"How could you, Evie? That was my father."

"Ahh, Dee. He's an adult. He can screw me into the door and it would still be legal." Evelyn smiled. "Poor Dee, do you need a Kleenex?"

"Evelyn, stay your ass away from me."

"Ahh, Dee don't be like that." Evelyn stood at the door of the cage. "Come to mommy?" Dee spit venom. "You're not my mother; won't be my stepmother. All you are is the biggest hoe on the block."

Evelyn sat back down and smirked. "Apparently your dad liked it well enough."

Dee hung her head and took a few deep breaths. She had to get her mind right. Now, Evelyn held all the cards, and she was relishing in the fact. She was pushing all the buttons and Dee was responding. It was just what Evelyn wanted. She had Dee where she wanted her. She held all the cards, and all Dee had to show was being tied to a chair with random chunks of puke in her ponytail. Dee closed her eyes. *God give me strength.*

Dee raised her head and looked at Evelyn. Evelyn cackled. Dee didn't even stir. Evelyn played the tape again. Although Dee's mind was screaming, now was not the time. She didn't even outwardly flinch. Evelyn kept talking to her. Dee didn't respond or move; she just stared at Evelyn.

Evelyn started to crack. "I know you hear me, bitch. Don't try to pretend that you don't hear what the fuck I'm saying, hoe."

Dee didn't move. To move was to allow Evelyn to win. Evelyn wasn't winning this. Physically, Evelyn could fuck her up at this juncture. So mentally, Dee refused to give an inch. She might not make it out of there alive. That didn't mean she had to succumb to Evileen's mental games. She had some pride. It was pride that kept her face straight. She forced herself not to clinch her teeth, not to ball her firsts, not to tap her feet, not to scream again, not to try to push down the cage. She forced herself to sit there, exist, and pray. She didn't know how long she'd been in this warehouse. She didn't know how long she'd be there. She did know that Auntie M would probably never find her. If her fate was tied to letting Evelyn mind-fuck her, she'd be a dead bitch walking.

Then a familiar voice spoke from the door. "Evelyn, pipe down. Your temper gets you in trouble every time. This was just as much as test for you as it was for her. Guess who passed?"

Evelyn fumed. Steam was damn near coming from the top of her head.

Then the voice spoke again. "Do you really want to go up against me? Are you really that bad? Sit your ass down and show some respect."

Although Dee had committed herself to staring down Evie, she had to know who had pulled Evelyn's card so quickly. No sooner than the words came out, Evie was attempting to control her temper and sitting down. Dee's eyes followed her all the way into the seat before turning.

She wished she would have kept her eyes on Evelyn or closed or never woke up at all because she was looking in the smiling face of Mrs. Robinson, Joe's mother. *What the fuck?*

Dee leaned all the way over and put her forehead on her thighs and tried to breathe.

Mrs. Robinson laughed. "I think you would have been less surprised to see the devil standing in front of you. If you faint though, I'll give Evelyn the key to the cage and let her have at you. I don't have much patience for weakness. Evie's temper is her downfall. It makes her vulnerable. Even with you tied at the wrist and ankles, you were able to get her goat. That's well—unfortunate—for Evelyn of course."

Dee struggled to get a hold of her emotions. She needed to get a clear head. She had never really met Mrs. Robinson. She'd seen her in passing a few times. She'd seen her at the church staring from behind the curtain. Joe pointed out her car at the spa a couple of times and she'd seen her on her porch. She always seemed to be staring at her. It made Dee a bit uncomfortable. However, she never spoke to her so Dee didn't worry about it. It was a hell of a leap from staring to kidnapping.

"You want to know why? I know you do. But I'm not telling you shit until you ask nicely. Unlike Evelyn over here, I have the patience to wait you out. I have nowhere else to be." Mrs. Robinson sat down, crossed her legs, and smiled.

Tension was rolling off of Evelyn like waves, but she sat still and quiet.

Dee's glance moved from Mrs. Robinson to Evelyn and back again. Dee had seen Mrs. Robinson's look before. Only the powerful had a look like that. Dee realized the fact that she was tied to this chair in a dog cage was the least of her worries. Her problem got monumentally bigger. Evelyn was young and crazy. She could be manipulated. Mrs. Robinson was a different animal all together. Dee realized she may never leave the cage alive. Tears began to roll down her cheeks.

Mrs. Robinson exhaled, laughed a little bit, and leaned forward. "It's easy. Just say please."

Evelyn started to stand, "I can make her—"

Mrs. Robinson held her hand. Evelyn sat back down in the chair.

"Evelyn here is a little anxious." Mrs. Robinson tilted her head and continued to stare at Dee. "But at least she's not pathetically crying in a cage."

Dee clenched her teeth.

"Interesting. There is a show of spunk in there somewhere. Good. I would hate to go through all this trouble and be wrong about you."

Dee looked to the left and then did her best to stare down Mrs. Robinson. "Will you please tell me what the hell I'm doing here?"

Another voice rang out from the door. "Yes, Minnie. Please tell me why the hell my niece is tied to a chair in a cage. Let her out. She has nothing to do with anything."

Dee's head whipped around.

Mrs. Robinson moved a lot slower.

Auntie M and Joe stood at the door.

Dee tried to stand up. "Auntie M!" Then she looked confused. "Get the police. We need the police."

"Yeah, Maybelle. Call the police."

Auntie M just stood there. "Untie her."

Minnie smiled and nodded. "Have a seat."

Auntie M nodded at Joe who sat down.

Auntie M took a deep breath. "My name is Maybelle, and I'm a runner. Is that enough? Is that what you wanted her to know? She knows. Untie her."

Minnie handed Maybelle a pair of scissors. "Do it yourself."

Dee shook her head. "I don't understand."

Minnie sat there with the smug look on her face as Auntie M untied her and brought her out of the cage to a seat. "What did you think was going to happen, Maybelle? You think that Joe was going to be the only one that knows the truth around here. Hell naw! If he knows, she knows."

Auntie M looked up trying to figure out how to start. "Well it started about twelve years ago. I was a hairdresser living in an apartment building next to Minnie. I was making decent money, saving for a house. I was never the type to focus on a man or a relationship. I just handled my business. Minnie had your dad—for all the good that did her. He was a boyfriend in name only. He didn't have a job. He didn't change a diaper. Dude was useless. I never understood why Minnie stayed with him. That's her story to tell. Minnie?"

Minnie shrugged. "He had his uses. That's how Joe got here. In my family, it was all about having a man. The women in my family had men coming and going. No one was ever without a date. Now, most of them had multiple kids with different last names. That's how I was raised. But men ain't shit, really."

"Mom?"

"Really. Jailbird. You're trying to be the poster child for a good man. Not only that, but you got pimped by more females than Dolomite had hos. You think I didn't know about that ho in school? You tricked around a bit, but Evie pulled you around by the ring in your nose. And this one," Minnie nodded at Dee, "will have you saying how high every time she says jump. Whatever.

"Point being, your daddy wasn't shit. Then he had the fucking nerve to cheat on me. As if I was just some random ho on the block. I am Minnie

Robinson. I'll be damned if anyone is going to make a fool of me. And they had the nerve to fuck in my bed. My bed! He couldn't even take the trick to a hotel.

"My theory is you live like a dog, you die like a dog."

Joe looked confused and shook his head. "No, Mom, dad left."

"Well, he tried. I just helped him on his way. It was an accident really. How was I supposed to know that the cast iron frying pan would cause death? I was going for pain. He was all right for a while, and then suddenly, he was gone. But I wasn't sorry about it. I called Maybelle because I needed help. For all her sweet, church-going, I'm-so-innocent act, men loved her from the boardroom to down on the block. Maybelle had them all panting. She made a call and some men came over and your dad was gone.

"His other trick put some feelers out, but Maybelle's people shut that down. No other inquiries were made. Shit, his ass didn't even make it to the back of a milk carton. If he hadn't screwed over so many people, I'm sure the search would have been a bit more intense."

Dee and Joe looked at each other. A murderer and a drug dealer. A murderer? A drug dealer? Mrs. Robinson and Auntie M. They were old. Auntie M and Mrs. Robinson were in their late 50s. They were old.

They were looking at Auntie M, but Auntie M was looking at that last empty chair. "All of them, huh, Minnie?"

"Maybelle, it's time. We can't go on like this. You know that. The game has changed."

Auntie M nodded. "We might as well wait then."

The group waited somberly. The silence was broken by Evelyn who started laughing. She laughed harder and harder. She couldn't believe it. "I knew your old asses were slanging, but killing motherfuckers, too?"

Out of nowhere, Mrs. Robinson hand snaked out and grabbed Evelyn by the throat and started to squeeze.

Evelyn struck out and hit her in the face repeatedly.

That only served to get her second hand in on the action.

Evelyn's eyes started bugging. All Mrs. Robinson said was, "I'm really getting tired of you and your smart-ass comments. The biggest and best lesson I can teach you is to shut the fuck up. Can you do that?"

Evelyn gurgled and did her best to nod, although she was being choked out.

Minnie lightened her hold, but continued to look at Evelyn in disgust. "Her lack of control will be the death of us all. You know I met her at church. There were these football players that took time to engage in a little, well, let's just say it was highly irregular to see that on church grounds." Minnie laughed. "Evie was there taking photos. They didn't even know they were being watched.

"I asked her about it. She told me that you never know when you would need a little leverage; girl after my own heart. We talked; every once and a while I'd have her run an errand. She doesn't feel remorse like so many unfortunate souls, but the anger. The anger. Well, let's just say we're working on that." Mrs. Robinson began to squeeze again and Evelyn began to choke.

By this time, they had another visitor. Nipsey was sprinting across the floor. Auntie M got up and blocked his path, shaking her head. She sat back down in her seat and merely commented, "The older she gets; the less patience she has."

Mrs. Robinson laughed. "Wasn't that sweet? Nipsey was going to save his girlfriend."

Nipsey looked around. He didn't think he walked in on a brothel, but apparently he was going to get straight screwed before he made it out. Everyone was sitting down. Dee was rubbing her wrists, pale as death. Joe looked like he would pass out at any moment. Mrs. Robinson of course looked pissed off. Auntie M was looking down. Evelyn looked terrified. He hadn't seen anyone on his way in. However, no one was making a move to leave.

Nipsey waved his hand. "Come on. We can get out of here before they come back."

Auntie M looked up. "Before who comes back?"

"The people that kidnapped Dee. We can get out of here and call the cops."

Auntie M shook her head. "Sit down, Nipsey. We're just here swapping stories."

Nipsey looked confused. "But the note said—"

Mrs. Robinson rolled her eyes. "Shit, I wrote the note. I know what the fuck it says."

Nipsey shook his head, "But—"

Then he heard Dee whisper, "Just ... just sit." Dee looked around the room. *Really? Her Auntie M was involved in all of this. How was that possible? Her aunt was a pint-sized dynamo for sure, but hiding dead bodies?*

Auntie M started. "I had a choice to make. I could have called the police. I could have. Maybe I should have. It's hard to say after all these years. Then, I wasn't looking into the eyes of the ass we have before us. Then, I was looking at a woman who had enough and was equal parts pissed and scared. She wasn't a murderer." Auntie M snorted. "At least not then."

Mrs. Robinson merely smiled.

Auntie M continued her story. "After I helped out Minnie, I owed a favor. There I was forty-three years old, and I became a mule. I'm carting drugs from one side of the city to another. I refused to spend one dime of the money they offered. I wasn't going to do it. I didn't need it. I had a job. Anything I couldn't afford, someone bought for me. I mixed it in with the

Church fundraising money. Pastor Clifton swore I was the best fundraiser ever. I guess he was right about that. After that, when we needed assistance, I never used local people. Local people deal in favors. My people deal in cash."

Mrs. Robinson let out an evil cackle. "She had all the men panting around her, writing checks. Good, bad, and everything in between. Do you know your precious Auntie M used to date a mercenary? She had everyone snowed. She's not better than any other whore on the street. She didn't want any of them, but they treated her like some sort of queen."

"Maybe if you were a bit softer and not throwing frying pans, you would have had an opportunity, too. The street knew what happened to his father. No one was fucking with you after that, but that fear was beneficial."

Mrs. Robinson surveyed the motley group of "family" in front of her. She was monumentally embarrassed to call Joe her son. She was an enforcer. Her son was a wimp. She was powerful. She knew what happened to soft motherfuckers. They died. Maybelle didn't even know the number of people she had put down. Maybelle didn't need to know.

Minnie turned to Maybelle, "You needed me."

"True. But then, you needed me too. You wouldn't have shit if it hadn't been for me. You and your damn son were project bound and you know it."

Minnie's eyes burned into Maybelle. Maybelle merely raised her eyebrow. Minnie seethed. "The house, the cars, hell, the neighborhoods. They gave you everything. You didn't even have to ask."

Maybelle leaned back in the chair and crossed her legs at the ankle. "I worked for mine. Not on my back of course. I wasn't loose. Men liked me. They wanted me. They thought money was the way to get me. So they gave it freely. And the only man I ever loved, all he ever offered was friendship, I was hooked. Minnie is always just pissed off. All the time. No man wants that."

Minnie snorted. "Since you know everything Maybelle, tell me what do men want? You're such the fucking expert."

"Nipsey, you asked me once why I didn't date Pastor Clifton. The truth is I couldn't. I'm a mule, running money and drugs for drug dealers and funding the church with the money. As close as Pastor Clifton and I were, that was one thing I could never tell him. How do you tell a man who had a goal to clean up our streets that most of the congregation was in the game in one way or another? I couldn't do it and so I couldn't be who I would have needed to be for him."

Dee shook her head. "Why didn't you just get out?"

Auntie M shrugged. "I thought about it a lot over the years, especially lately. You know to do what we did for the number of years that we did it means you have to keep a tight ass rein on a lot of people. If you loosen up for a moment, there is a situation that needs to be handled. I aided and abetted in a murder. After that, I worked for some of the most-wanted men in the city. While doing that, I was involved in kidnapping and torturing people. The only way to get out is to go to jail or climb my black ass into a body bag. Those were my only two options after my debt was paid.

"I never did get deep into the game. I made sure I wasn't selling. It was offered to me, but that's not what I wanted. Plus, I was able to leverage my exposure into a few pretty successful cash businesses. So it wasn't all bad."

Joe couldn't believe what he was hearing. His mother was the enforcer? Sure, she was a bit harsh, a bit rough around the edges, but she wasn't ... she'd never been this woman! He didn't recognize this woman in front of him. She looked evil. *She had her rough times sure. She was stern. OK. A bit removed, yes. But, she was a murderer? She had killed his father all those years ago! She had buried him. How could that be his mother? How could that be the woman who calmly took him to school every day? How could this be the woman who raised him?* For whatever reason, she killed his father; and now, she was talking about it as if it didn't matter. She was talking as if she didn't end someone's life. Twenty-four hours. He had his twenty-four hours. This was his mother.

"You were the one that kidnapped me? You were my mother and you kidnapped me?"

"Joe, don't be stupid. Of course not; it was supposed to be Tim. I've mostly used outside talent for years. I couldn't handle Tim the way I was supposed to. You should be happy it was me. When I found out they took you instead, I raised hell, but I couldn't let you go free. That would hurt my rep. That's why they only took your fingernails and toenails. And I had a surgeon do it. But it wasn't anything permanent. You got over it.

"That's also why Tim had to be a louder message. He hasn't made the same mistake about telling what he wasn't supposed to tell, nor has he made the mistake of being where he wasn't supposed to be. Has he? I know you went to him to ask for help tracking me down. He's still … what do you call him? 'Tim News Network'. Now he just works for me."

"You had people remove my fingernails and toenails? You called that? I'm your son!"

"Right, but people don't know that. I keep layers between me and the episodes. There are a few old church members that needed a message who know, but they aren't going to tell." Mrs. Robinson chuckled, "Trust me."

Joe looked. *This was his mother?* "If you were in the game, why did my supply dry up?"

With the look Minnie gave Maybelle, Joe understood why she was the enforcer. He had never seen hate like that before. It reassured him to know his mother was protective of him, but it was that moment, Joe understood exactly how ruthless his mother was.

He looked at the people gathered. Nipsey was still shell-shocked. His head swiveled back and forth to whoever was talking. Dee was looking strained trying to process what she had landed in. Evelyn looked smug, superior in her knowledge of what was happening and her role in it all. His mother said through gritted teeth, "I didn't have anything to do with your situation. That was Maybelle."

Maybelle shrugged. "That was simple. I couldn't have drugs being sold next door. Are you crazy? I dried up your supply and you go out of town. Are you serious? Your stupidity was going to bring us all down. Your mother wasn't trying to address it. Not the way it needed to be addressed. So I called the cops. Drugs next door wouldn't do. We don't need anyone investigating either of us for any reason. Minnie was pissed about that. Well, she was pissed at both of us actually. That's why she had to have your nails removed. She didn't take too kindly to how I cleaned up her mess."

Minnie got up, walked over to Joe, and slapped him in the head. "Sorry, I get pissed every time I think about that. Really? Drugs from the basement? How the hell did you expect that to end?"

Maybelle looked at Joe. "At least I kept you protected in jail."

Joe shook his head. "That wasn't you; that was Stacy."

Maybelle's eyes flattened. "You better believe what you're hearing young man. There are few people in this city with more juice than us. You were protected when you walked through the door. Stacy called in a favor for sure, but a favor wasn't needed. Whatever her contact told her is what he told her, but really, that was me.

"Even now, you think I don't know you should be in jail? You think I don't know what you're still doing? You think I don't know that your mother isn't saying anything to you? I know. I absolutely know."

"Why me? Why did you ask for me to investigate the death?"

Minnie's eyes glittered. "Yeah, Maybelle, why him?"

"You know, Minnie. I knew if I asked him, you'd either help or hinder. That would give me the answer that I needed from you."

"Ask me, Maybelle. I never lied to you. Ask me. "

Auntie M looked at Minnie with a hate that didn't look natural on her face. "Did you kill him?"

Minnie gave a half smile. "Of course."

Auntie M launched herself at Minnie and got in a good slap in before Minnie could react. Minnie was a street fighter. After a stunned second, she kicked Auntie M to get her off. She punched Auntie M in the stomach and Auntie M crouched over in pain.

Dee jumped up before Mrs. Robinson could do any more damage. She wasn't sure if she could hit an old lady, but if she threw another punch at Auntie M she guessed she would have to. Evelyn stepped in front of Dee. "Don't even think about it, princess. Let them handle it."

Dee looked at Evelyn incredulously. "She hit my aunt."

"Your Aunt is old as hell. It's about time she learned how to take a punch."

Nipsey stood up at that point. "Everyone sit down."

Dee and Evelyn spoke in unison, but their messages were different. "Stay out of it," Dee said.

"Thanks, Baby," Evelyn said.

Dee looked at Nipsey and Evelyn.

Minnie stood over Maybelle. "M we made a promise and you broke it for him. You let your heart get in the way of common sense."

"He wasn't going to tell."

"No, he wouldn't have told that you were a drug mule. Of course, he kept that to himself—until he found out about me, and how he got that fancy ass church of his. He was a man of God. How could you tell him?"

Maybelle threw up her hands. "How did you know that I told him anything?"

Minnie walked over to Maybelle and grabbed her hand. "I've spent the last twenty years dealing information. I saw this ring that suddenly appeared on your hand. I knew you didn't buy that yourself. You never bought yourself a lick of jewelry. When you left that office, he looked destroyed. You had been deflecting his advances for years. All it took was a shiny bauble and you broke. I saw the look on his face when you left his office. It was defeat. That wasn't because you both were continuing your dance. You changed the rules of the game.

"How could you kill Pastor Clifton? He was your pastor, too. You knew and worked beside him for twenty years. "

"Right. He was going to heaven anyway, pearly gates and all that bullshit. His ever after was solid. I did him a favor. I'm not a punk like you, Maybelle. I handle my business for real. You think I only killed two people in all these years. Please. Not everyone that disappeared just left. I killed a few just to make sure your hands stayed as dirty as mine—all high and mighty. You're knee-deep in the drug game, but God forbid you put a bullet in someone's head. That's why you need me. That's why you've needed me all these years.

"You're too weak to do what I do. You're fine being the man next to the motherfuckin' man, but you can't do it yourself. Punk ass."

Nipsey looked around. Now he got it. He got why Auntie M had made sure he made it back to Atlanta. He understood why Big Rock had made him go to rehab. He understood the threat Big Rock made. He understood the gravitas in Auntie M's voice when she said she needed him here. She'd never needed him before. Actually, she'd do a better job of raising Dee without him. It was this. She knew it was bubbling over. She probably had known for a while. She told him, "I can manage things when it's just me. With Dee here, it changes things."

Nipsey thought it changed her household dynamic, maybe even her budget. All of this was more than he bargained for, but if he was going to be of any use, he'd better get on his job.

"So should I assume that Evelyn was Minnie's idea?"

Minnie shook her head in disgust. "I don't deal in sex. Evelyn does that herself. I wasn't responsible for Evelyn and Joe. Sometimes, Evelyn is ... let's say she's difficult to contain."

Evelyn stood. "I'm right here you know." Evelyn walked over to Nipsey and reached out to touch his face.

He caught her hand and pushed it away.

Dee started dry heaving a bit.

Evelyn smiled. "Dee you just can't see it because he's your dad, but—"

"No, you're not going to pretend that I had a choice in that. You need to tell Dee the truth."

Dee rolled her eyes. "Nipsey, please. I saw the video."

Nipsey froze.

Evelyn taunted. "Yeah, Nipsey, she saw the video."

"Dee I was drugged. I swear."

Evelyn laughed. "He swears, Dee. Of course you can trust that."

Nipsey screamed, "Shut up you little evil bitch. You tricked me. I don't even know why. What did I do to deserve that?"

Evie's eyes continued to twinkle as she hitched her head, "You're *her* father. Watching her dry heave over the video was priceless. She'll never get the image of you humping me out of her head. Why wouldn't I fuck you? It'll drive her crazy forever. She needed that."

Dee got up and started to pace. Everyone watched her closely. Eventually, Joe stood up and went over to her. He touched her and she collapsed into his chest, crying. Joe led her to the chairs. Evelyn looked at this display of affection with envy, giving her skin a distinct green hue. Nipsey clenched his jaw, but Joe's hold on Dee wasn't sexual. Still. She should be turning to her father.

Joe looked at the mother he barely knew and the neighbor that was just as culpable in all this. "How is it you didn't get caught? Why are you two still free?"

Minnie and Maybelle looked at each other. Maybelle spoke. "We're good at what we do. I diversified the donations. Anyone that touched the game and went to church had a minimum that they had to donate. They got it back in a number of different ways—through the salon, an envelope in the glove box after a car wash. Simple."

Dee peeked up from Joe's shoulder. "The spa?"

Minnie and Maybelle both laughed. "You'd think, right? The spa is totally legit," Maybelle said. "I wouldn't let you work there if it wasn't. The last thing I needed was for you to stumble upon all this. You were never supposed to know."

Nipsey looked up. "But what about Reverend Love?"

Minnie shrugged. "What about him? He's a real reverend. He married Sister Love for the chance at this job. He's ambitious as hell, too ambitious. Can't trust him. Now, he's a ho to be sure, but that's about it. He tries to make sure he stays away from the women in the congregation. He has a look-but-don't-touch policy. Now, saying that, even I've seen how he looks at Dee. Once she's over eighteen, he probably would hit on her. Right now, his ambition wins out over his lust every time."

Dee looked surprised. "Then why was I kidnapped? I don't understand. What did I do to earn my twenty-four hours?"

With that the electricity between Minnie and Maybelle intensified. "You're payback for me getting Joe involved. That's all."

Minnie looked into Maybelle's eyes. "No, that's not all. Maybelle, you know we can't do this forever. You know we need to pass this on.

She'd be perfect."

Maybelle emphatically shook her head. "No, it stops with us."

Minnie looked harder. "Look at her. She's even better than you with the men. Joe will already walk through fire for her and he hasn't even kissed her. Are you kidding? If you'd just teach her, show her, she'd be better."

Maybelle shook her head again, then asked, "And what? Evelyn will be you? Are you kidding? They'd get popped for sure, either by the police or the others. Evelyn has no control. They aren't us."

Evelyn and Dee looked at each other. Each one itching to engage in the conversation, but seeing the ferocity in the exchange, they decided to let the conversation take its course.

Nipsey and Joe wanted to intercede, but they too realized; this was beyond them. So Maybelle and Minnie stood there squared off.

Minnie spoke again. "She can be better than us."

"Don't you get it? We did this for a reason. The reason doesn't exist anymore. They don't have a reason. They don't have a reason, a goal. Without focus, it'll get out of control too quickly."

Minnie smirked. "I didn't have a goal. I just enjoyed my role."

Maybelle pursed her lips. "I know."

Minnie moved forward. "Oh, do you really now?"

"Yeah, I do. Years ago, you killed Stacy's mom. Of course I knew. You're not the only one dealing in information. "

Joe pushed Dee off of him as the full realization of the woman who gave birth to him hit him. She was a killer, a murderer. She was evil. It was never just detachment. He had excused so many things over the years. But this? This was too much.

"Well, that is what happens. What did you think was going to happen with people that had their twenty-four hours and didn't get the message? What was the next step? Forty-eight hours? Seventy-two hours? What do you think was supposed to happen next? Do you think we were going to sing songs around a camp fire? She was an informant."

Maybelle screamed. "She didn't know enough to touch us!"

"Well, after I was done, we didn't have to worry about what she did or did not know."

Maybelle shook her head. "It's time for us to get out. The church is fine. We have more than enough money. Let's get out now. We're good."

Minnie laughed. "You always thought too small. We could have taken over the world by now, but it was always about you and your damn church."

"Keeping our scope small ensured we could keep our little corner of the world."

"Maybelle, guess what? I don't need you to build my empire anymore. I have someone better."

Maybelle struck first. However, this time, she didn't strike with a fist or a slap. She struck with a needle that no one had noticed. Minnie looked at her, then fainted. Both Evelyn and Joe jumped up.

Dee quickly took off her heel, wielded it in her hand and struck out, catching Evie in her arm. As Evelyn screamed and grabbed her arm to stop the bleeding, Auntie M stunned a distracted Joe with a Taser™. As he lay recovering on the ground, she made a call. Soon two men entered the room.

Nipsey's mouth was hanging open viewing the speed at which everything broke down. Dee, too, was looking a bit shell-shocked.

"She was right," Auntie M said. "I was never the enforcer. I was never the one that wanted anything to do with violence. What she didn't know was that while I preferred to stay clean, I'd always handle my business. She really thought that she was going to kill Pastor Clifton and kidnap Dee and I was going to let her live. She thought she was good enough to take me. She was right. All things being equal I didn't stand a chance. So, I made things a bit unequal."

Auntie M nodded at Minnie. "She needs to have an accident. Her body needs to be found." Auntie M hitched her head in the direction of Evelyn and Joe. "They get twenty-four hours. If you don't like what you hear or aren't sure, they get the same accident."

Auntie M looked at Nipsey and Dee. "Either you're with me or you stay here."

Dee scrambled to her aunt's side.

Nipsey looked at Evelyn. "She's so young."

"She drugged you and rode you like a wild pig. Don't look at the number age. She's worse now than Minnie was when we started. What do you think her future will look like? What do you think she'll do? Wait. It's all irrelevant. Where are you, Nipsey?"

"But—"

"Now know this. If you take one sip of alcohol, one puff of anything, or inhale or shoot up, you're done. I can't take the risk. You have to have all your wits about you at all times or you're useless to me."

Nipsey looked at his aunt. He knew as he looked at the fear in Joe and Evelyn's eyes that this was one of those defining moments. There wasn't any 'if' in Auntie M's statement. If he used again, he would die. It was simple as that. More than that, he looked at Dee. She was looking both terrified and a bit resolute.

Then Dee surprised him, by saying, "Auntie M, she's your best friend."

Auntie M's eyes darkened and flattened. She gave Dee the darkest smile Dee had ever seen. "Let's say that was true. Let's say Minnie and I were friends. She killed Pastor Clifton. She drugged you. She tied you up like a pig and put you in a dog cage. Really? That's friendship? There are places where friendship doesn't exist. For example, there is no friendship at a card table. And there's no friendship in the drug game. The most you can hope for is a good co-worker situation. If she lives, she will kill me next. That goes without saying. After me, there will be you. After you, she will kill Nipsey. She will keep coming for us. Now that death is eating at the table, it won't leave until it's full."

Dee looked back. "But—"

Auntie M exhaled as if she was trying to summon the patience of a hard-toiling ant. "Listen, you think I came to this decision tonight? Hell, no. This has been years in the making. When she fixated on you, Dee, I knew it was time to move. You were the game changer. Her plan was to replace my .... let's say my influence with you. Problem is you're not me. Not that you couldn't do it to the extent that I would ... I was old by the time I started this. I had lived. I didn't come here as an innocent. Even so, I still fell in love. It's a tricky business. You're not ready. All she saw was your beauty."

Looking at her aunt, Dee understood. Her aunt was probably beautiful, but there was steel there, too. There was a hardness that Dee hadn't seen before. Of course, that's true strength. You didn't have to flex to be strong. Now Auntie M was flexing. *The ghetto bitch. You have to put her down.*

Dee tried one more time, "But Joe—"

"Joe can live or die by his own hand. It's not my hand that will touch Joe."

Dee looked at Joe with worried eyes.

Joe shook his head. Dee turned back around and started walking for the door. Nipsey and Auntie M followed. As the door closed, they heard a scream. Dee didn't stop, turn, or pause. She merely kept walking until she got to the Escalade. She hopped in the back seat. Nipsey took the passenger seat and Auntie M took the driver's seat.

Tears began to stream down Dee's cheeks. Looking at Dee through the rearview mirror, Auntie M told her. "Evelyn won't make it. She's true evil without any controls. They'll get the truth out of her. Joe will be OK."

Dee pleaded, "You could just tell them to let him go."

Auntie M merely shook her head. "I can't. Survival has to be his choice."

Dee looked at her aunt. "But I owe him, Auntie M. I owe him."

Auntie M didn't look concerned. "I know. And that's why he'll survive."

Dee looked at her with something akin to hate in her eyes. "How could you possibly know that?"

Auntie M started the car and put it in drive, "That's easy. He'll live for you. Minnie was right about one thing. You're a game changer."

EPILOGUE

Dee walked through her backyard and over to the Robinson household. She was restless and just needed air. Auntie M's home was suffocating her. She sat down on the back steps. It had been a week since her twenty-four hours—a week in which she had to go to school; a week in which she had to go to work; a week in which she had to feign shock and horror at the death of fellow church members; a week in which all she wanted to do was roll up in her bed and cry.

The only good thing about the week was the bond she was starting to develop with Nipsey. He had been a rock. It's not as if they talked much. They were beyond talking. Everyone in the house was. Well, Nipsey and Auntie M talked. They talked and talked, but Dee could tell she just didn't get it. She never would. Nipsey, however, was making an effort.

Dee didn't even bother to try. Dee grew up in the hood. She knew what went on. However, her sweet aunt? She never expected that. She couldn't even fathom living with someone without a clue. Every time Auntie M tried to talk to her, Dee would just hold up her hand and leave the room. Now, when she used to try to do that to Nipsey, Auntie M would shut it down. There was no one to stop her from doing that to Auntie M. Nipsey wouldn't dare try. These days neither would Auntie M. It was funny. She thought she was living the life. She thought ... she didn't know what she thought.

She remembered when she first saw Joe sitting on this very porch, drinking beer, smoking weed, fake leering. Dee smiled. He was the only one that knew. He was in that room too. His world unraveled at the exact same time, in the exact same way. He would know what to say, even if it was nothing at all. She missed him. She started to cry. She really missed him. Sniffling a bit, she wiped her nose.

She jumped as the door opened behind her. *What the hell?* She thought ... She knew ... But how? She jumped up and ran into Joe's arms. "I thought you were gone."

Joe squeezed her back. "I did leave. I wanted to get so far away from here. The fire." Joe took a deep breath. "After the fire, there was nothing much left to bury. So I, I mean I have an urn. It doesn't seem like enough, you know.

"But all the people she killed, some just because she could. I can't." Joe shrugged and released her. He looked at her and smiled. He nudged her with his shoulder. "Those slippers look hot."

Dee smiled for the first time in a week. "You ass." She reached out and held his hand as she pulled him down beside her on the step and snuggled close to him. "Why did you come back?"

"What she did to Tim, to Stacy's mother, shit to me, to you ... I couldn't just leave. It took a whole day for me to realize that wasn't the answer. I needed to make sure everything was wrapped up tight. It didn't feel right to drop and run." Joe shrugged. "I couldn't help her. It was too late. Maybe it was always too late, but I felt I needed to see this through to whatever end. I needed to make sure my friends that I love—that she touched—are all right. Tim, Stacy ... you."

Dee looked up at him and frowned. She began to pull away. "Just a friend? Whatever. I bet if I was wearing my three-inch, red snake skins instead of these slippers, you'd be trying to get all up on it."

Joe looked at her, smiled, and pulled her back. "Ahh. I do believe red heels belong on either sides of my ears, never hitting the ground, but ... well, we need to be able to take care of each other. Right now, I just want to make sure that you're OK. You're not losing me 'cause I'm not trying to push up on you. We have the kind of secrets that you take to the grave. We'll be friends forever."

Dee tilted her head. "Speaking of secrets. What happened in that room?"

Joe shook his head and tears welled up in his eyes. "Don't."

Dee nodded. "Do you think anyone will ever know the truth?"

Joe shrugged. "The truth is that two women died in a car accident. One church secretary was driving the pastor's daughter home, lost control of the car, and drove off a cliff. The fire caused extensive burns, but a positive identification was made. There will be a memorial next Saturday at the Church of Love in both of their honors." Joe looked at Dee in the eye. "That's the only truth that matters."